CRYSTAL TRUTH

The Third Novel in the Projector War Saga

CRYSTAL TRUTH

The Third Novel in the Projector War Saga

K. A. Excell

CRYSTAL TRUTH

Copyright © 2021 Katerina Ann Excell

ISBN-13: 978-1-952856-06-8 (Paperback)
ISBN-13: 978-1-952856-07-5 (Hardcover)

LCCN: 2021900105

Front cover image by Jesh Art Studios.

First printing edition 2021.

Katerina Ann Excell
Hurricane, UT

www.KAExcell.com

For Amber, who is always excited to listen.

CHAPTER ONE

The Superior guarding the door to the server room fell dead on the sterile tile floor the instant after it saw me. It didn't have time to blink—certainly didn't have time to recognize that I was no ordinary intruder. If it'd had a moment to process what it had seen before I killed it, well, things may have gotten ugly.

My face was plastered all over this Superior base alongside the warning that Crystal Farina was to be stopped at all costs. An extra moment to process, to put two and two together and realize that I was Crystal Farina, and what had been an easy execution on my part may have become potentially disastrous.

Superiors had never been an easy foe, and the fact that I was on their home turf made it even more difficult. The fact that my psionic abilities had been crippled when the Agency removed my biocard last year would have made taking down a Superior impossible, except that the same fight that had resulted in the loss of my biocard had also healed my mind. Now, my teleprojection abilities were weak, but my processing time had been cut down to practically nothing. I was the fastest agent the Agency fielded—or I would have been, had the Agency still existed.

I stepped over the Superior's dead body and slapped my cellphone on the scanner to the right of the door. Dominick Steele's very illegal app did its job beautifully. The lock clicked free, and I set my shoulder against the door, my energy pistol in hand.

A moment later, I stood in the doorway of a dim room with screens that stretched from wall to wall. No one inside would have missed the opportunity to take a shot at me while I stood, backlit, between the sterile white light of the hallway and the shadow stung blue of the computer monitors displaying feeds from the seemingly endless array of cameras in the facility. No shots rang out. The room was empty. I holstered my energy pistol and padded silently inside. The door stayed open behind me because, although I would rather no Superiors passing by knew this room was occupied, there was no handle on the back side of the door. If it closed, I would be stuck. Superiors didn't want anyone who managed to get into this room ever leaving. If a Superior got stuck, they could either use their inhuman strength to break down the door, or stay there and die. The Institute would probably prefer the second, actually. Steel doors were expensive to replace, and Superiors were expendable.

I listened for another moment, wary of additional security measures. Just because the room was empty didn't mean it was undefended. But, perhaps the Institute was overdependent on the technology that had helped them stay ahead of the Organization so far. No alarms blared, and the door didn't have any sort of automatic closing mechanism. I holstered the energy pistol with a barely concealed frown. Tolden said there was some sort of algorithm running on the back end of whatever computer system the base was using to identify intruders, and that the app Steele made for me should take care of it. He'd also said that the same system ran security for this room. Apparently he'd been right, because I'd been in the facility for twenty-two minutes, passed too many cameras to count, and there had been no alarms. Well, that was about to change.

I crossed the room like a wraith, careful to keep my footsteps silent and smooth to avoid alerting any Superiors that lounged on the other side of the wall. Their hearing was acute, and they knew this room was supposed to be empty.

One wrong sound could undo everything I'd done since I entered the building—and make me very dead.

I tapped a few keys on the computer at the end of the room. It looked just like the others, but Steele's app had identified it as the control center. If I wanted to take the building down, this was the one I needed. It also contained the sum of all the intel stored here—which wasn't much. Three personnel files for Instructors; well, two Instructors and one pseudo-instructor labeled "Defective" who I'd met the first time I'd entered the Agency's Martial Base located underneath Martial Academy. I scanned over the files and stored them for later review. I would look over them once I wasn't in deadly danger.

A moment later, I checked the computer's data ports for the crystal I'd come to steal. The data ports were empty. A quick scan of the other computers in the room showed that none of them had the crystal either. It wasn't here.

My brain kicked into overdrive—the same way it did when I locked in the WATCH module before my encounter with Ms. King—and I did a search-and-compare between the images I'd collected of the building, and the blueprints. Nothing. This was the only room they'd fudged in the building schematics. There were high-security weapons vaults, training centers, a med-lab, and plenty of cell-like rooms to keep the Superiors from trying to kill each other during their down time, but nothing that would hold the data crystal I was looking for.

I stopped grinding my teeth and moved on. The information I'd come to steal wasn't here, but that didn't mean I couldn't leave an impact.

My smile was nasty.

I stabbed the enter button on the keyboard and watched as alarms in every hallway began to blare, directing Superior traffic into the narrow basement hallways I'd already rigged to blow.

"That's right, doggies, answer your alarms," I muttered, still mindful of Ms. King's lessons. Shouting in a situation like this—no matter how triumphant I felt—would get me killed. The fact that Ms. King had helped turn one of my friends into a bloodthirsty monster, and then killed another friend only hours later didn't change the fact that her lessons were the only thing between me and the hundreds of Superiors three floors down. It didn't matter who had taught the lessons I used. Ever since my ejection from the Agency and its subsequent dissolution, I needed every skill I had just to survive.

I redirected my thoughts away from self pity. No, it wasn't fair that the Agency had shattered my teleprojection ability then thrown me away like a used rag, but life wasn't fair.

I scanned the cameras one last time. If any of the Superiors had noted that most of the doors were locked and the hallways were lined with innocuous-looking explosives, then made the cognitive leap that I was the one who had infiltrated their base, they might start spreading out looking for me. Capturing me was starting to climb the Institute's To-Do list—and today would probably make sure that item made it to the top. Luckily, they were all headed the correct direction, and my escape path was as clear as it could be. Those who wouldn't get caught by the old-fashioned chemical explosive in the basement would be taken out when the base's self-destruct triggered.

I reviewed my mental map of the building as I strode through the halls. It wouldn't be a straight shot to my exit, but I was spoiling for a fight. Superiors weren't easy prey, even to me, but they weren't as fearsome as they used to be. The Agency might have crippled my teleprojection ability by ripping their biocard— the technology that had amplified my teleprojection abilities—out of my skull, but speed and a drive for vengeance more than made up for my suddenly minimal psionic ability. I pulled the semiautomatic Tolden had given me so many months ago out of its holster on my tactical suit and pressed a newly-installed button on the back of the gun. A nearly transparent four by two foot shield flickered to life approximately three inches away from the muzzle as one of my newest inventions—a shielding device—flared to life. When I held it away from my body, the shield would stop a bullet aimed at my head or torso. It blocked both incoming and outgoing objects, so I'd have to disable it again to shoot out, but that was why the button was where I could press it with my palm.

I broke into a jog and descended the stairs.

There! Even with a crippled telepathic ability, I could feel the aura of violence that surrounded the Superior waiting around the corner. Numbers whirled in my mind, calculating what telepathy could no longer tell me. This Superior wasn't here by chance. From his positioning, he knew exactly where I was. I couldn't tell if that was because of his boosted hearing, dog-like sense of smell, or if this one was just not quite as dumb as the other ones.

I tilted my head to the side just slightly as another thought struck me. My grin widened fractionally. Quite possibly, this superior was less intelligent than its compatriots. A smart superior would have run away if it knew I was coming.

I calculated where his gun would be aimed. Superiors were fast but, ever since Ms. King had somehow helped me remember my father's face, I was faster. I still wasn't sure why, but recovering that memory had healed my mind. Instead of waiting for the blue lines on my vision to analyze a situation, reading the information they gave me, and then acting on it, I could react instantly to almost any threat. My blue lines were still working behind my vision, but I didn't need to watch them any more. Analysis was effortless. What information I had once relied on my telepathic ability to give me, I synthesized from the Superior's stance. I could plot every muscle contraction five seconds in the future. I didn't need to know what it was thinking if I already knew where it was going.

I slid just under the Superior's gun, pulled my shield down, and sent two bullets into the monster's brain. Not even a Superior could shake off a wound like that. It crumpled into a heap before surprise could even register on its misshapen face.

There had been a time I would have regretted taking a life. I still would do anything to avoid killing a human, but Superiors were different. They'd killed two of my friends, abducted hundreds of innocent civilians and set in motion the chain of events that turned me from one of the most powerful teleprojectors in the world into a glorified empath. Since then, the Institute had killed countless agents in the Organization—which is what the Agency and the Company had become when they'd fused. I didn't work for the Organization, but I had friends there. I refused to let any more of my friends die because I acted too slowly. I owed Briggs and Tabitha Smith that much, at least.

Motion from the corner of my eye attracted my attention, and I threw myself sideways to evade the next blast of searing white energy as a new Superior rounded the corner with an energy rifle in hand. It jerked back behind the eggshell colored wall as I fired two quick shots. My bullets ate drywall, sending out little clouds of gypsum dust that spread through the air behind the Superior. I used the way the dust fell to pinpoint exactly where the Superior was behind the wall, breathing in and out, stirring the air.

My lip curled. Taking care of Superiors took time— which was currently in short supply. I growled a low, guttural sound and charged the Superior as it stepped back around the corner, firing shots that all went wide as it tried—and failed— to adjust its aim to my recklessness. I triggered my shield at the last moment, when the Superior was inside its activation range. Energy crackled, and both halves of the, now dead, Superior crumpled to the ground still sizzling from where the shield had sliced up its middle. That wasn't the intended use of my shielding unit, but cutting Superiors in two was certainly a perk. The shielding unit on my suit popped and then caught fire.

I snarled, shoved my semiautomatic back into the holster, and ripped the device off my belt before the fire could spread to any of my other gadgets. The stolen standard-issue black tactical suit I wore was flame-retardant, but that didn't mean I wanted to go around with my belt on fire. I pulled the energy pistol off my other hip and shot the unit once. The pulse ignited the battery in a single spectacular display of green and purple sparks that extinguished themselves almost as quickly as they'd lit. The unit was a pile of black goo staining the Institute's floor.

Superiors and shielding unit dealt with, I broke into a sprint. Twenty seconds until boom.

Ten seconds later, I was in the lobby, skirting Superiors who were starting to understand that there was something more dangerous than the line of chemical explosives in the basement. They tried to lunge at me—but I was already at the doors. I jerked off the thin layer of plastic covering the thermal tape I'd planted on the inside of the door earlier. It had been a risk to leave it there, but Superiors weren't known for their intelligence or observation skills. Now, the risk paid off. I slammed the doors closed on Superior claws—but bone was no barrier to the explosives I'd put together. The tape sparked. Superiors howled. The doors welded themselves shut. I turned and dashed away with the shadow of a smile on my face.

Superiors were paranoid, so they'd limited the building to only one exit on the ground floor. Now that it was gone, they were too far from the next exit. The Superiors didn't know it, though, nor did they care. Most of them raked their claws against the doors in a futile attempt to get to me— heedless of the danger, or their smoking claws. The inspired ones wheeled toward the stairwell to try and get to the second floor windows, where they could jump to the street and continue the chase. Neither plan would work.

Five seconds after the doors had sealed, I was barreling down the street. I grappled up to the top of the next building and out of the blast radius just half a second before the explosion shattered four stories of glass windows all the way down the street. The Superiors that had just made the second floor froze in a sudden, terrible revelation. Too late. The tinkling of glass was eclipsed by the successive blasts that leveled every wall in what had been the last Superior base in Indianapolis. The Superiors—all of them—ceased to exist.

I stared, ears ringing in the concussive silence, at the new smoking hole in the middle of Indianapolis. The Institute certainly didn't do things by halves. While indisputably effective, the waste was appalling. After only a few seconds in the camera room, I'd spotted a dozen technological advances. New full-body shielding technology that put my little unit to shame, medical gadgets that the Organization would pay billions to get their hands on—all now blasted into bits, and that smarted. If I could have stolen even a prototype, I could have reverse engineered some of the tech to give myself and the Organization an advantage in this fight. But, then, that was the reason the Institute's self-destruct was so thorough.

No one knew how they got the sheer amount of advanced technology they fielded, but it kept showing up in the most inconvenient places. Occasionally, I envisioned a secret lab of imprisoned neurodivergents working feverishly to provide the Institute with new weapons—but something about that image rang false. Wouldn't the Organization know if the Institute had a place like that?

I felt the last of the bloodthirsty Superior minds blink out. They were gone, and the city was safe from the Institute. The completion of this mission should have brought a feeling of satisfaction, but I couldn't help my frown as I turned and used the scaffolding that climbed the building to drop safely back down to the ground. This was one more battle won against the Institute that was kidnapping people off the street and turning them into bloodthirsty killing machines. That was good; a win for myself, the Organization, and humankind as a whole. The missing data crystal bothered me, though. The data couldn't have gone far between the time Tolden had learned about it and the time I'd infiltrated the base. No, bigger than the missing intel was the fact that the Institute didn't trust Superiors to move high-security information—which meant I was likely up against an Instructor.

Three hundred pounds of expertly trained muscle, poisoned claws, teeth meant for killing, inhuman senses, and psionic abilities that had put mine to shame back when I'd had my biocard—dealing with an Instructor was not my idea of a good time. Rather than shudder at the thought of going up against something like Ms. King again, I focused on redirecting my momentum as I dropped to the street, rolled, and recovered. A moment later, I straddled my motorcycle and donned the tactical helmet hanging off one handle, masquerading as a normal motorcycle helmet.

I probably should have worn it on the mission, I reflected as I settled the points on my electropulser glove into the grooves that would release the lock on the engine. Wearing the thing made me feel like a part of the Strike teams that were the only ones to get them as standard equipment. Still, the built-in comms system that let me receive and send Tolden's secure calls while I was weaving in and out of traffic was worth it, and so was the protection—both from potential road rash, and an electropulser blast to the back of the head.

Sirens were just starting to squeal in the distance when I pulled out of the alley. I kept my driving pseudo-legal until I cleared any potential police perimeter and then, frustrated with the cars that practically crawled along the street—really, the turnips might as well have just walked where they were going—I opened up the throttle. Using reactions honed by combat with Superiors to fight through Indianapolis rush hour traffic wasn't particularly fair, but I satisfied myself by ignoring any swear words hurled my way and reminding myself that any one of them could have been kidnapped by the Institute and turned into one of their dogs. The least that herd of turnips could do was pardon a little reckless driving as I tried to get home in time for a pizza-date with my boyfriend.

When I made the freeway, where driving didn't take up quite as much of my attention, I dialed Carter Tolden—the Agent In Charge of Tac 47. Up until a year ago, I'd been one of his agents. Now, I was more of an illicit asset. The Organization would react badly, perhaps even badly enough to imprison him, if they ever found out that he and the rest of the team occasionally helped me with these unsanctioned raids. Our team had some of the best minds in the Organization, though, so we were fairly safe so long as we all were circumspect.

Tolden picked up. "I just got reports of an explosion. Good going 32!"

"Thank you, sir," I replied. "Only one problem. The data wasn't there. It must have been moved."

There was a halting silence at the other end of the line as Tolden ran through the implications. "Well, that intel came from a good friend higher up on the ladder than I am. I don't think he would have let us down. That means—"

I jerked my head in a nod as Tolden reached the same conclusion I had. The only surprising thing was that the information had come from Joseph Medina, who was the friend higher on the Organization's ladder.

"Yeah. We've got an Instructor on our hands. Don't worry. If you can find the data, I'll handle the retrieval," I said.

Joseph Medina was a bit of an enigma. I couldn't be entirely sure what his job was now, but he used to be the Director of Intelligence at the Agency, before it had merged with the Company to create the Institute-fighting-machine that was the Organization. He had been the only other one to even suspect that Ms. King wasn't who she said she was, and he was the one who had encouraged me to ally with the Company when I needed help taking Ms. King down. His pet teleprojector had messed with my memories on his orders, and then he'd stood by and watched impassively as the Agency removed my biocard. To wrap it all up, he'd come to me a few weeks later to deliver the news that I was going to be on an Organization kill list.

I didn't particularly like the man, but he was the only one outside of Tac 47 who knew they were still working with me, although I couldn't fathom how he'd found out. He hadn't shut the operation down and locked my teammates up, so I was trying to withhold judgement for the moment. Occasionally, he found a block in the Organization that meant he couldn't act on a piece of intelligence, either because people higher than he was had forbidden it, or because he thought his people would end up dead if they tried it. When that happened, he called Tolden, who called me to deal with the problem. His intelligence had never been wrong; until now.

"Be careful, Farina," Tolden said. "Instructors are no joke."

I tried not to take the admonishment personally. Most of my psionic strength was gone, but I made up for it with enough sheer speed that I could take a Superior down in single combat. The last time an Organization operative had tried that, he'd taken two weeks in a medical pod to recover, and the medics still hadn't been sure he would pull through. Those same pods had helped me recover from gunshot wounds to the abdomen in a few hours. Still, extra analysis abilities that were almost as good as mind reading wouldn't defend me against a mental attack, and Instructors were powerful enough that they could debilitate me the same way I'd debilitated Ms. King before the Agency had taken my biocard. Now that my mental abilities were decimated, I had no way to keep them from worming their way through my fractured walls and taking control of my body. Perhaps my recent victories against the Institute were making me cocky. Superiors and Instructors were completely different creatures. "Yeah," I finally said. "See if you can find the Instructor for me?"

I heard typing in the background. "Give me an hour and I'll call you back."

His vocal cues—things my newly healed mind could now detect—pointed toward him being nearly done with the conversation, so I cleared my throat. "Any new information on my father's location yet?"

The typing stopped, and Tolden sighed. "Steele's running his information through the database, but it's slow going. He has to be careful. There have been a few walls, and he's almost thrown some red flags. We can't have the Organization coming down on us for this—it won't be a slap on the wrist. We still have no idea who this guy is, but the Organization's pretty touchy about him."

The Organization was that worried about a search on the face of an unknown telepath? It sounded like they knew who he was, at least. That was the biggest lead I'd gotten in a year, and I'd combed the entire Midwest looking for something. "Thanks for the info, sir. Let me know when he finds something new?"

"I'll try. Still, fair warning but Tac 47's on the rotation this week. If I don't pick up, I'm in the middle of running a mission."

I whistled, and allowed the topic change. This was a secured line, but it was probably a good idea not to discuss the search for my father if the Organization was so worried about it. Especially because Medina probably had some sort of way into our communications, and I had no idea how he would react to my using the team for a personal search. I shoved thoughts of Medina's prospective disapproval to the back of my mind and refocused on the conversation. "They finally took Tac 47 off the bench, after the royal screw up in Boston?" I could almost see Tolden's flush on the other side of the line.

"I told them not to hand us a newbie, but the Organization is intransigent. The kid they gave us had authority issues, and liked big bangs. Black was as careful as he could with the big weapons, but the kid still managed to blow himself up—and parade a dozen Superiors past Faneuil Hall. I don't need to tell you how the civilians reacted when they got a good look at those monsters. It was mass pandemonium. Mrs. Green had a conniption—and rightfully so. Civilians aren't equipped to understand the truth of what we're fighting, especially since they don't even know psionics exist. I think Robbins is still down in Boston doing damage control."

I nodded. He'd told me the story after they got back. I still couldn't understand what the Organization had been thinking. Sure, Tac 47 had handled newly minted agents before—after all, they'd taken me the day after I'd received my biocard—but always with Tolden's approval. He was good at figuring out who would work well together and who would not, and that was why he was the Agent in Charge. To just ignore his recommendation? They had to be crazy.

Tactical teams in a neurodivergent organization had a delicate balance. With the correct individuals working together, they could shake the foundations of the planet. With the wrong mix, they could self combust—and innocents could get caught in the crossfire.

"Well, I wish Robbins all the luck in the world," I said. Robbins was supposed to be a medical projector telepath, but his specialty was memory suppression. While we had a complicated history, I couldn't fault this particular use of his abilities. If turnips found out about psionics and our war with the Institute, things could get rapidly out of hand. The Institute would become the least of our problems as the world was consumed by a flood of panic and human experimentation as private companies and governments alike tried to find some reasonable explanation for people who could make things float with their mind, or project their thoughts into the minds of others. The Agency had been so concerned about the consequences of the psionic world going public that they'd ignored the Institute and tried to keep the Company from fighting them, too. Now, there were two factions in the Organization. The ones primarily concerned with undue publicity, and the ones primarily concerned with preventing the Institute from committing genocide with their Superiors—all in the name of *evolution* and *immortality*. I wasn't really sure which faction I fit into. I'd seen how the Institute stripped their victims of their humanity first-hand, but I could also see how more people like the Institute would exist if everyone started to experiment with neurodivergence.

I shook my head again to try and dismiss those dark thoughts. "Well, good luck out there, sir." I made an effort to keep my voice light. "And don't forget my research. Now, I've got a pizza date at my house in thirty minutes."

"You know, sometimes I don't know who's in charge here." Tolden muttered humorously.

"I am."

Tolden chuckled and hung up the line as I puttered my motorcycle into the garage and hung the sign "Dad's, Don't touch" on it. It was a little touch of…something. I could remember my father's face, now, and I imagined he would have loved motorcycles. They were fast, maneuverable, and easy to hide for a fast getaway. I didn't know much about my father, but I did know that he was good at running. A year of searching, and I had yet to find any physical traces. He did not want to be found.

CHAPTER TWO

A father who had more in common with a shadow than a man didn't really help my cover as Highschool Senior Talia Carmen, who still had both parents. In an attempt to get around that little hiccup, I kept Talia Carmen's imaginary parents out of sight as much as possible. My—well, Talia's—boyfriend, Nick, had only met them once, and I'd had to have Tolden's help with that one. Between a set of holographic projectors I made, Tolden's somehow believable electronic voices, and the imaginary cold I'd pretended into existence, we made it through that meeting with Nick none the wiser that I was actually living by myself. Since then, my imaginary parents had separated, and I had moved in with my imaginary father, who had gained a very time-intensive job so he didn't have to be around the house very often. Or at all.

I ascended the steps and arranged my "Dad's" bedroom as if it had been used recently. A couple pairs of oversized khaki pants went in his laundry basket, and I ruffled the bed sheets a bit. Other than that, my dad kept a very clean room.

I took a moment to strip my tac suit off and pull another shielding unit out of the fingerprint-locked safe to stash in my go-bag alongside my electropulser glove and energy pistol. Now satisfied that the bag was fully stocked with everything I'd need if I got a sudden call about a Superior attack, I put it back in the safe. My semiautomatic went in my sock drawer so it was a little more accessible, and then I carried my blood covered tac suit to the shower and turned on the scalding hot water so it could beat some of the stains out. The suit couldn't exactly go in the washing machine or to the dry-cleaners. Still, the black, wet-suit like material didn't show blood very well. As long as I got enough out that it didn't start to stink, it didn't matter.

When the tactical suit was reasonably clean, I stepped into the shower to rinse off. Saving the planet was a sweaty, nasty job, and I didn't think my civilian, turnip, boyfriend would understand.

I turned off the water and hung the tac suit up to dry. Probably. The material was exactly the kind of stuff that could hold water for a week, given the right conditions. It was practically a water tank. If I had time tonight, I would go over it with a hair-dryer, and then pray that it would be dry in the morning. While I had two extra tac suits here at Talia's apartment, I didn't like having one hanging out in the open. There was always a chance that someone would decide to snoop, and then find something they weren't supposed to. If a neurotypical found it, they might pass it off as a Halloween costume, but if someone from the Organization found it, they would start looking more closely at Tac 47, who had smuggled me the suits. Either way, it wasn't worth the risk.

I stepped out of the shower and dried my hair, which was now blissfully short to accommodate the tac-suit helmet. Taking care of shorter hair was easier, and it was harder to grab in a fight. Finally, I pulled on a pair of jeans and a *36 Screwdrivers* t-shirt befitting a regular seventeen year-old girl as the doorbell rang.

Most teens expecting their boyfriend would have just yelled 'come in' but I was still paranoid. I walked over to the door and opened it with a smile. Nick stood under the bug-plastered porch light beside the cracked flower pot with one hand shoved into his pocket while the other held a plastic sheet filled with sweet smelling star flowers. He was turned so that his body mostly blocked my view of the flowers, which may have worked on a neurotypical girlfriend, but I seized on the two purple petals sticking out from behind him and re-constructed the image. Still, his nonchalantly slumped shoulders, placed to hide the flowers, made his overly broad frame seem just a tad smaller, although that optical illusion was easy enough to quantify.

It was much harder to evaluate the emotion in his eyes. His mental shields were higher than most neurotypicals, although they also tended to vary throughout the day. Occasionally, I could get full thoughts from him. More often than that, I could sense broad emotions. Nick's variable shields had proved to be a useful training tool while I tried to come to terms with my own diminished abilities.

I scanned him out of habit as he shifted his weight to reveal the flowers. His surface thoughts were coated in a well-disguised anxiety, much like the thrill I felt before a particularly difficult mission. I wondered at that as I took in his giant grin. His shields shifted frequencies, his surface thoughts retreated. Once again, I faced an unreadable wall. I concealed a wince. Being locked out of someone's mind hurt on some primal level. I wasn't sure how much of it was because I was used to getting into almost any mind I wanted, and how much of it was actual pain, but the sensation was unpleasant regardless.

"Nick! You're early," I squealed in Talia Carmen's best high school cheerleader voice. I debated asking him about why he was nervous—hopefully he wasn't going to do something embarrassing like proposing to me. We'd been spending extra time together lately. Compared to an average neurotypical relationship, ours was moving a bit fast. I had thought about ending it a few times, but then I'd have to learn a new boyfriend's quirks, and Nick's company wasn't bad.

I concealed my worries behind a smile as I shifted my attention to the bundle of big purple star flowers Nick held out to me. "And you brought flowers! Best. Boyfriend. Ever!" I hugged him, then took the flowers back to the kitchen.

"I'm glad you like them." He shoved his other hand into his pockets and followed.

Despite my absolute assurance that he wasn't a threat—even if he'd wanted to hurt me, his broad frame and toned muscles wouldn't be able to so much as address my speed—I caught myself watching him through the mirrors I'd placed strategically on the walls.

I was officially paranoid. Still, it was with good reason. It wasn't every seventeen year-old girl that was on the kill list of the single largest neurodivergent agency in the world, or who had made herself, individually, one of the biggest enemies of a crazy, insanely powerful group of mad scientists and genetic cross breeds that could run as fast as a car.

"Are you kidding?" I continued the conversation without a problem as I walked and watched. That was one advantage of being whole. I could divide my attention in a way I never could have imagined before. "They're beautiful! I do have to say, though, I was expecting pizza."

"Er…about that…" Nick said, looking at the floor. "I have to work tonight and—before you say it—I know that's a lame excuse. The boss said that if I don't finish the repairs on the Fiero by tomorrow, I'll be out of a job. He said that was my reward for biting off more than I can chew."

I sighed. On the one hand, I was glad he wasn't about to propose to me. On the other, I'd been looking forward to a Superiorless evening when I could enjoy the fantasy that I was nothing but a teenager. Some places, like at school, it was exhausting to double-think myself into acting normal. Nick had always been so easy to be around, though. He understood when I needed my space, and respected that we both had a life outside of school. Part of the deal was that I didn't get in the way of his job, and he didn't get in the way of mine. Ironically enough, that exact quality meant that my cover personality of Talia Carmen wasn't the only one who liked him. Now, I'd started legitimately looking forward to spending time with him. I pushed away the unexpected slice of bitterness that accompanied my shrug. "It's OK. I get it. I'm just going to put these in some water. I left the vase in my room." I didn't augment the disappointment in my voice—but I didn't try to conceal it, either. I turned and walked past him.

"Wait, Talia!" Nick said. He reached toward me, then thought the better of it and let his hand fall back down to his side. "I don't have to work until seven. That leaves us almost fifteen minutes to sit and talk, or do whatever you want."

I sighed. At least he was trying. I wiped the frown off my face, although I didn't force a grin. "I guess that's better than nothing. I'll be right back with the vase."

Nick seemed to accept that, and when I returned, he was sitting on the couch with one lazy hand thrown over the edge and his legs crossed at an ankle. "So, your dad isn't here today, either?"

I shook my head. "He had a business trip to St. Louis. He'll be back in a few days, I think."

Nick shook his head. "Seems like you're home alone, a lot."

More than he knew. I shrugged. "He brings in the dough, but not much else. Still, my allowance is big enough to take care of anything that comes up. It's only a pain when he has to sign papers at school." I'd learned to forge quite a few different signatures since the Agency fired me. It was a handy skill.

Nick pursed his lips as I sat next to him on the couch. He put his arm around my back, and I leaned into his chest. "So, I guess he probably wouldn't care if you and I went to a concert this weekend? It's *36 Screwdrivers*."

A concert? Ugh. I made my face light up.

Personally, I had absolutely no musical preference, but Talia Carmen loved *36 Screwdrivers*. It was an element in my cover that had been working for almost a year now, so I figured it was a decent choice. Normal teenagers had a music preference, not a weapons preference. "Are you kidding me? I'd love to! And I'm absolutely sure he won't mind."

Nick smiled. "It's settled then, in six days, it'll be you, me, and *36 Screwdrivers*."

"Have I ever told you how great you are?" I asked as I leaned in for a kiss. He gave me a quick peck and stood up, anxiety spiking just over his inner shields.

"I'm glad you're excited. I hope it'll make up for tonight, 'cause I really have to go."

I stood up and followed him to the door. "See you at school!"

His grin revealed nothing of the anxiety brewing inside as he nodded and left.

I watched him climb inside his 1950s restored VW Bug and drive off as if a demon was after him.

When he was gone, I sighed and went back to the couch. Recently, even hanging out with Nick for a short time left me tired. It was getting harder and harder to act like Talia Carmen when all I wanted to do was shred my *36 Screwdrivers* t-shirt, take a long nap, and then bury myself in designing my next invention. There had been a time when I'd told Mom that I just wanted to go out on the playground with the other children, but I was afraid that I'd hurt them if I did. Now, I had control. If I hurt someone, it was intentional. And somehow, I had no more desire to pretend to be normal. What was so great about jumping and flailing about to patterned sounds inside a writhing mass of bodies where anyone could be a pick-pocket or worse? And the noise! My auditory processing was about fifty times better after my encounter with Ms. King, but the thought of differentiating the sounds of instruments from vocals, mashing feet, shouted conversation—it was enough to make me want to scream, and I wasn't even there yet. Sure, I had tools to handle the overload, but it *wasn't* my idea of fun.

Now, thanks to my infuriatingly neurotypical cover identity, I was going to be at a concert during time I could have been using to scout my next target. I shuddered. This was what came of wishing for a normal life.

CHAPTER THREE

My phone buzzed as I finally convinced myself to stop moping and go track down the bug that had shorted my shielding unit earlier. I checked the number. Tolden. I put the shielding module on the workbench and hurried back inside, phone in hand. Well, this was one good thing about Nick having work tonight. I didn't have to make excuses for ditching our date.

"Whatcha got for me, Tolden?"

"A party downtown. Our Instructor was just sighted by an Organization InDep agent. The invite is coming off your printer right now."

I drew my ear away from the phone to make sure I could actually hear the sound of printing paper. Sure enough, the printer was working.

"…so be careful." Tolden was just finishing his sentence.

"Sorry, didn't catch all of that."

Tolden grunted. "I said that there's at least one InDep agent at the party. Also, you're going to have to use that syphoning tech Cal slipped you a few months back. The InDep agent says the Instructor's got some sort of crystal figurine around his neck. We think that might be what you're looking for."

I walked into the office and pulled the piece of paper off the printer. "Oooh, it's a formal. Looks like I get to dust off my dress. And it's already started. Lovely."

I could hear the sound of fabric on fabric as Tolden shrugged. "That's not my fault. Blame InDep for not IDing him earlier. Still, you'd better get over there."

I put the paper on the desk by the office door and jogged into my bedroom. I pulled my secondary tac suit out of its drawer and donned it with practiced efficiency, pulling off extra tabs as I went. The hip holster, knife loops, belt—everything dropped to the floor around my legs as I turned the tactical suit into something that wouldn't imprint too badly under the dress. The under-arm holster went on the ground to complete the pile, and I scowled at myself in the mirror. I hated dresses. They made my weapons set-up so much more difficult and, even now, brought back memories of Zach's leering eyes.

My lips, full and pale under the single domed light of the bedroom, firmed into a bitter smile. If anything like that happened tonight, I would stab the guy and have done. I was finished playing nice in a world that just wanted to strip me of every friend I'd ever had and leave me on the street.

I strapped a really big knife to the inside of my thigh and attached what used to be a hip holster just below my knee. It would imprint a little bit, but I wasn't about to go against an Instructor relatively unarmed. While I knew they weren't invincible, I had a very healthy respect for their abilities. If it came to a knife battle, I was probably dead. Their claws were lighter than a knife, faster, and occasionally poisonous.

Finally, I pulled my red dress, matching leggings, and kitten heels out of the closet. I ran a practiced eye down the length, noting the beaded top and long, flowing skirt. It waved unnaturally in the still air as it tried to spread out all the motion through the entire dress. It was a gift from Cal, the head of the Agency's Research and Development department that had shown up on Talia Carmen's doorstep a few days after I'd moved in. The dress was bulletproof, and would slow a knife—and an Instructor's claws. If I was going to a formal event, this became my tactical suit. Technically, I wasn't supposed to wear an actual tactical suit underneath it, but stealth was secondary to my ability to defend myself tonight. There was no team waiting to back me up if things went badly. I had to be able to handle an Instructor all by myself, which meant I couldn't afford to shed any protective layers.

I pulled both the syphon-device and my energy pistol out of the safe, then grabbed the one peice of almost-jewelry I owned—a silver chain—from the closet. The syphon device was designed by Cal for situations for this, so it was encased in a diamond shaped block of amber, and looked stunning as a necklace. Really, Cal had a gift for pretty-looking inventions that put my soldered together contraptions to shame. I secured the clasp, then gave it a gentle tug to make sure the chain was sturdy enough.

I glanced at myself in the mirror—a mistake. I looked nothing like the Crystal Farina who had left the Agency. My hair was neatly cut at my chin, my eyebrows were shaped into high angled arches, and my eyes were the color of ice. Colored contacts weren't the only things that had changed, though. My cheeks were thinner, turning my face into something that was all angles. Constant smothered anxiety had curtailed my appetite. I still forced myself to eat, but I couldn't look at one of Mom's toasted cheese sandwiches without remembering that I'd left her without a word. I couldn't look at a tea cup without seeing her worried face.

I tore my gaze away from the mirror and focused on the two weapons in front of me. I hated to leave the semiautomatic Tolden had given me, but I only had room for one weapon. The energy pistol was more lethal to an Instructor now that I'd re-wired it to target their physiology, and its whine was more easily drowned out. I put the semiautomatic back in my sock drawer.

As a last minute thought, I pulled my med-kit out of the top of the closet and strapped it opposite the knife, below my thigh. I checked my phone to ensure the software Steele had written for me was active, slipped my boots on, shoved the pile of party-equipment in the saddle bags, and donned my helmet.

In record time, I was a block away from the party. I squirmed into the long, red dress, donned the heels, and raked a brush through my hair. I didn't have time to do any more makeup than simple, red, lipstick, but I wasn't actually there for the party, either. I just had to look nice enough to avoid drawing attention to myself. I looked at the leggings for a long time. They would match the dress better than the black tactical suit, but their real purpose was to dull my sensory issues enough to help me focus. Ever since my mind had healed, sensory overloads had started becoming a less frequent problem, and my tactical suit would serve the same purpose. I put the leggings back in the saddle bags, and checked over my appearance one last time. I looked nothing like the little doll the Agency stylist had made me into last year at the Agency's fundraiser. I'd seen the big bad world, and grown up. Now it was time to find that Instructor, take the intel, and get back out again. There was no synthetic school assignment to distract me from my true target tonight, and there was no traitorous teacher hanging over my head.

I squared my shoulders and made my way to the front of the building. I flashed a winning smile at the mountainous man checking invitations, even as I decided the most efficient way to take him down should he go for the gun proudly displayed in the tooled leather holster under his arm—or the less ostentatious hideaway in his pocket. It didn't imprint enough for most people to notice, but my mind picked it out with ease. He took the paper from my hand and pointed the way to the interior of the club without a word. I stored my analysis of him away where I could reach it if we ever came to blows, then dismissed him from my mind altogether.

The music inside was recorded, not like the live orchestra the Agency had brought in for their fundraiser, and the crowd was almost entirely neurotypical. I sorted through the orderly crowd of analysis, dismissing some things, and pursuing others as I looked for the telltale signs of Instructor cloaking. Like the Superiors, Instructors looked slightly inhuman. Ms. King hadn't mutated very far, and had been able to compensate for most of her physical oddities. Most Instructors hadn't been so lucky. They had longer, hairy, spindly limbs, and slightly rectangular green eyes. They generally kept their nails short so that the claws that retracted into their fingertips didn't rip their fingernails out when they deployed their claws. Their noses were longer, with larger nostrils to aid their dog-like sense of smell, and their ears were oversized and set farther forward on their heads. The resulting figure was just odd enough to set off alarm bells in even the most complacent turnip, so they used specialized technology to modify their predatory form to something more palatable to the masses.

It only took a few moments for my expertly trained eye to spot the Instructor. He was cloaked as a balding man with yellowed teeth. My eyes slid away from him as the Instructor's cloaking device worked to convince me that the bottoms of his teeth were flat instead of sharpened to razor points, but I'd dealt with people trying to manipulate my mind before, and I had safeguards now. That was my target. He gripped a champagne glass in his right hand as he talked to a woman that looked like a supermodel, dressed in a backless midnight black dress. I tried not to wrinkle my nose. My telepathic ability was just present enough to grasp the emotions behind the Instructor's unshielded surface thoughts. He was hungry, and the world was about to have one less supermodel.

His head perked up as I studied him, as if he was searching for me. I bit back a curse and changed directions. I had hoped the press of minds would keep him inside his own head, and prevent him from detecting me. It seemed I wasn't as right as I'd hoped. He didn't go directly towards me, though, so he hadn't pinpointed me before the crush of minds got in the way. He'd only caught a glimpse.

I sat down at the bar set up in the far, right corner of the room and ordered an italian soda. I'd had drinks before, but it had only taken a few times before I'd realized that my ultra-fast brain did not mean an ultra-fast metabolism that washed the alcohol out. I couldn't afford to confront the Instructor if I wasn't at my best. Ms. King hadn't been easy to deal with when I'd had an entire team at my back, and we hadn't had a prayer until my mind had healed. Now, I didn't even have a quarter of the psionic strength I'd used against Ms. King. I was still fast enough to take out a Superior, but Instructors were a different animal altogether. If he attacked me, my only chance of survival lay in the Instructor's demonstrated wish for secrecy. If he used all of his abilities, the turnips would see, the Institute would step out of the shadows, and the psionic world would become very public very quickly.

If only they hadn't taken my biocard—

I bit off my habitual cursing of the Agency and the Organization. I had bigger problems to worry about, such as how to get my syphon device close enough to the Instructor's crystal databank to hack it. I was sure the tech Cal had given me could do the job. This wasn't the first time Cal had donated one of her little devices to my cause, and the rest of them worked just fine. She had an uncanny grasp of encryption and technological communication that I could never hope to match.

My focus on the problem broke as I felt someone approach. "Hello, pretty miss…" The man's words were slightly slurred as he sauntered up to me, and I hid a grimace. I had enough problems without having to deal with drunk men.

I placed the italian soda back on the counter and looked the man in the eyes. "So not interested." I used what little of my projection strength I could muster, and made him feel like I wasn't a good target to pick up tonight.

"Is this man bothering you?" A new voice asked, as the drunk man turned around and left—buoyed by the suggestion I'd driven into his mind like a dull spike.

I looked at the balding man in front of me and noted the blurred teeth. It was the Instructor. Lovely. "Not anymore, thanks." I turned back to my drink and watched his faint reflection in the glass. Every line in my body screamed at him to go *away*.

He cocked his head. "Say, don't I know you from somewhere?"

I tried not to think of the base I'd blown up only two hours prior. He was probably in my head. This was not how this was supposed to go! I was supposed to identify him first, without him ever catching onto me. I caught my flustered thoughts and forced them back into line. "I'm sorry?" I raised a single eyebrow and took a sip of my drink.

"Yes, you seem familiar. I've seen you somewhere before." He sat down on the stool next to me. I felt the syphon device vibrate against my chest as it began its hack.

I swallowed a curse. Now I had to keep talking to him

until the thing was done, or I would have to clear it, reset it, and try again later. I looked him over very carefully, then arched my eyebrows in recognition. "It is possible we could have met, Mr..."

"Cane. Marion Cane. And you are?"

The device vibrated against my chest twice. It was half-way done.

"Maria Valine." I held out my hand—not because I wanted to touch him, but because it was the socially correct thing to do—and he shook it. I almost expected to feel his claws *accidentally* puncture my hand and fill my blood with poison, but he didn't. I released a pent up breath. After my thoughts earlier, he had to have recognized me. The Instructors were the ones that had put the bounty out on my head. Unless... could it be that my shields were getting stronger? That was the only reasonable explanation for why he wasn't inside my head. My projection and telepathic abilities certainly had healed over time. My telepathic range was almost that of a S6, and my projection strength had just passed PS2. But that wasn't nearly strong enough to keep an Instructor out. Walls that incomplete just begged for the Instructor to jump inside them. Why hadn't he?

"No, I must be mistaken," he said, and withdrew his hand. He glanced back toward the crowd. I stifled a sigh of relief. He didn't know who I was—in more ways than one. Still, there was the game to be played. If he walked away now, I would have to find him later—after he had a chance to think about it and match my face to the face of Crystal Farina, who the Institute wanted badly.

"What a pity, Mr. Cane. I am a fantastic card player." I put as much feminine appeal into that sentence as I could, fluttering my eyelashes. I'd never ranked high in espionage, or in flirtation—Ms. King and the other students in the Social History class had been quite clear about that. Now it was coming back to bite me.

He stiffened and shot a glance back over his shoulder. He was watching something in the crowd. I couldn't quite tell what. "I don't play." His words were clipped.

I was losing him! I scrambled to think of something more I could say to keep him from moving out of the device's range—

The device gave one more, long vibration. It was done with the intel breach. I relaxed my shoulders and turned back to my drink.

"That's too bad." I wished for him to go away—although I didn't dare project anything. My wish was granted, and when I turned back around, he was gone. I ran my fingers through my clipped black hair—wondering why he'd left so quickly. Ms. King said that getting rid of a mark after an exchange like that was supposed to be the most difficult part. The crowd was dense around where the Instructor had disappeared, and the bodies quickly erased his trail. I focused, though, and made out the pattern of shifting bodies. It was the small things—the way the crowd shifted to the pattern of shallow breaths and sweating palms on the dance floor. The Instructor ghosted out a side door and disappeared into the depths of the building.

I shook my head at the behavior. Something must have spooked him—and he hadn't shown any sign of figuring out who I was. After a moment of thought, I decided that he must have found that InDep agent Tolden had warned me about and left. I altered what I was searching for, and scanned the crowd for the telltale signs of an InDep agent monitoring an area—and froze.

Standing in the middle of the crowd, watching me from the corner of his eye and dancing next to a person I'd seen occasionally as I visited him in the machine shop, was Nick. He wore a suit like it had been made for him and, as I watched, turned to mention something to the man next to him, who radiated arrogance so thickly I could feel it from the other side of the room.

I sent my mind pushing through the crowds to reach Nick's. What was he doing here? He'd said he had work! My question was answered with crushing force as I brushed up against his mind. My eyes narrowed as hurt I hadn't known I could feel welled up inside me.

This was work for him. The machine shop was just a cover to keep an eye on the rebellious Agent 32, Crystal Farina. Nick was an operative for the Organization.

I extended my mind to brush the man next to him—undoubtedly his handler at InDep. The handler's face mirrored Nick's in its soft, almost boyish lines. Despite the suit the handler wore, his hair was a dirty brown mop that looked like it had been combed as an afterthought. That unintentional sloppiness combined with his aura of arrogance to create the insidious air counterintelligence sometimes relied on to keep their assets in check. The crowd shifted, and I met the handler's hazel eyes.

Hurt turned to hate in one blinding instant. Doug Houston stood next to Talia Carmen's boyfriend. Gone were the hard, layered muscles, and the square jaw of highschool—replaced by a softness that clashed with the predatory intelligence lurking in his eyes. His face bore only a forty-two-point-six percent resemblance to Houston's face, but not even the most talented plastic surgeon could change someone's mind, and Houston's was just as filthy as the day he'd shot me two years ago.

I ran through the implications in a moment. I'd locked Houston up with the help of Tac 47 during my first semester at Martial Academy. At the time, he'd been an independent telekinetic who was contracting with the Company. I had assumed that he'd stay imprisoned after the merger that combined the Company and the Agency. He'd killed Earl West, after all. That wasn't going to endear him to either side.

Now, I was starting to question my assumption. If he was still a lowly independent, then how had he broken out of prison? Maybe with D? But Medina hadn't mentioned anything to that effect when he'd mentioned the Instructor's escape. That meant he'd been released.

The Organization had changed his face so wildly that even my analysis tools couldn't identify him, then sent him to keep an eye on me. They knew I would spot his mind in an instant, even with the extra camouflage, so he posed as another guy from the machine shop Nick worked at. That kept him close enough to use Nick to keep tabs on me, and far enough away that I wouldn't notice him.

The pieces fell into place with startling clarity. Nick or Houston had identified the Instructor, and were following standard operating procedure by waiting around for the tactical team to get here and extract the Instructor. The Instructor must have noticed their attention, and the fact that Nick and Houston were also watching me, so it had come to see me for himself—perhaps to see what Nick and Houston would do, and perhaps to see if I could reveal who they were. When it figured out that Nick and Houston worked for the Organization, it beat a hasty retreat.

I forced my shoulders to relax, and my mouth to curl up in a smile. Surprised. I had to look surprised. Nick didn't need to know I'd gotten inside his mind, and Houston couldn't suspect a thing. If I wanted answers, I had to get Houston alone. That wouldn't happen if they knew I'd discovered who they worked for. I stood and let the crowd take me to them.

Nick and Houston were chatting amicably near the buffet table on the other side of the room. Houston spotted me out of the corner of his eye as I approached, and signaled Nick, who paled.

"Talia, what are you doing here?" he asked.

I arched an eyebrow. "We need to talk."

He swallowed hard. "Excuse me, sir. It seems my girlfriend wants to talk—"

I shook my head, trying and failing to conceal my fury. "I need to talk to your coworker."

Nick's eyebrows rose. "Tyler? Have you two even met?"

Houston's head shake was cut short by my dark chuckle. "It was a long time ago, but I never forget a face."

Houston shrugged. "If the girl wants to talk, let her talk. If I'm not back in half an hour, go in after me. You know how these things go."

I started the half-hour timer as I followed Houston out the door. Houston hadn't been joking in the slightest.

Nick's eyebrows skyrocketed. "Careful, Tyler. She can be a minx."

And he can be a murderer, I wanted to say, but I choked the words down. Nick and Houston suspected that I knew who they were, but they couldn't do anything until I confirmed their suspicions.

I jerked my head at the door, and followed him out to the street. When the door shut securely behind him, I took a deep breath.

I could tell his hand was in his pocket, and I could see

the imprint of the mini-energy pulser. I turned, grabbed his shirt, and pushed him against the wall. I let go, drew my energy pistol, and stepped back. I knew without even having to look that the weapon I held would tear through his system, burning out nerves and lighting muscles on fire if I pulled the trigger. He would have to spend time in the pods if he ever wanted to be functional again. I wondered, briefly, if the Organization would patch him up if I pulled the trigger. How highly did they value this murderer?

"How long have you been spying on me, Houston?" I asked. "Did you cultivate Nick, or is he with the Organization too?"

He pulled his hands out of his pockets slowly to make sure I knew they were empty. His lips curled into a sneer.

"When did you find out?" His voice was slimy, just like his mind. Beads of sweat had started on his forehead.

"Don't avoid the question," I snarled. "Just because I didn't shoot you last time doesn't mean that can't change real quick."

"Don't be stupid, Crystal. I've read your file. You don't kill, and you aren't out to hurt the Organization."

I snarled and smashed the side of my gun into his face. "I'd make an exception for you."

The emotions, the helplessness, the terror, all flooded through my mind in one blinding instant, only to be caught by the walls I'd erected in my mind. Houston wasn't in power here. I wasn't the wounded little girl he'd preyed on those years ago.

Houston spat blood, and looked back up at me with real fear in his eyes. "Fine. I was released shortly after the merge. The new face was just protection for me. I work InDep, but you probably already knew that. Nick and I worked together in the old Company days." He smirked again out of habit. The fear in his eyes didn't change. "Be careful, 32. After they find out about this, the Organization is going to want your head on a platter. We've been getting nervous about your increasing strength rating, and this most definitely lowered your danger rating. It was already bad enough."

I nodded. None of this was new. Tolden had been warning me about my strength and danger ratings for weeks. I'd camouflaged my resurgent telepathic abilities as best I could, but going off half-cocked here had probably just compromised all the work I'd done.

I looked Houston straight in the eye.

"This is the last pass I give you." I lowered the gun to my side. "Don't let me see either one of your faces ever again."

He nodded, still prepped for a fight. I didn't blame him, my file was complete with footage of what I'd done to Ms. King—or so Tolden said.

"Get out of here." My voice was tired as the shock of recognizing Houston started to be replaced by the full consequences of what I'd just done. Houston was a full Organization agent, and I'd just interfered with his mission. Worse, I'd assaulted him. I would have to move on quickly. Again. I hadn't ever wanted to actually set down roots, but I'd hoped to have more time here. For the first time since I'd had to leave Martial Academy, I'd had actual friends. I'd had Nick, who had always seemed so understanding. Well, now I knew why. He'd known my true identity the whole time.

Houston scurried back inside the building and I jammed my gun into its holster beneath the skirt of the dress. I pulled my heels off and jogged back to the motorcycle. I could tell immediately that someone had been messing with the grips. Whoever it was had been careful to replace everything almost exactly as I'd left it, but the saboteur didn't have my ability to compare images. I cast my mind around, encountering only one, shielded, individual, just out of sight. That was something I'd quickly become accustomed to after they'd taken my biocard. It seemed that everyone's rating was higher than mine was. I'd learned to make do, though, and my own rating had been growing. Despite his shields, I could tell the saboteur was above me. Likely watching from the top of the balcony on the building above. I craned my neck up to catch a glimpse. Sure enough, Nick was leaning against the railing with a phone to his ear. He glanced down at me a few times with worry on his face. I thought about shouting up to him that Houston was still alive. He'd have a split lip, but I wasn't a murderer like he was. I quashed that impulse as soon as it emerged. Further communication wouldn't help my case.

Nick evidently felt the same, because he put his back against the railing so I couldn't see his lips moving.

I wished I could hear his conversation, but didn't have to hear it to know what was taking place. He was on the phone—or, more probably the comms unit beneath the phone—with the Organization, making a report. They would have operatives on my location in a matter of minutes—perhaps less, if they could re-route the tactical team that had been on their way to deal with the Instructor. I pulled the zipper down and stepped out of the dress. After stuffing it in the bag, I adjusted each of the rings on my fingers so they would fit into their proper places and flipped a switch. The motorcycle roared to life, and I could feel Nick's shock.

A smile curled my lip as I placed the helmet on my head and roared out of the alleyway.

He'd no doubt sabotaged my ride, not knowing exactly how it worked. The motorcycle wasn't just a way to get around town in style, it was also built for combat. It had full systems redundancy, only one set was a whole lot smaller. It had taken a while—the technology wasn't simple—but I'd come up with a way to make the entire system run on one half of a square foot. The shielding for that had been even more difficult, but worth the three months of work it had taken. I'd never wanted to have to use it. I'd never wanted any of this. But Houston—

Well, he'd forced my hand.

CHAPTER FOUR

There was a chopper in the distance, closing fast. I kept going. Going home wasn't an option anymore. There was likely a tac team at Talia Carmen's place, already, which was just fine with me. I had duplicates of my technology at a second location registered to a Nanny named Emily Scott. Still, I wasn't about to rush over there, either. I'd taken some pains to make sure my life as Talia Carmen never intersected my life as Emily Scott. Not even Nick knew of this other girl, although I spent half of my life pretending to be her. That meant it would be safe—for a time. As long as I didn't lead the Organization there.

I pulled my bike around and gunned my engine into a parking garage that was stacked to the brim with fancy cars from the party. Up one level, two, three, four, five. I went around one last time. This was the tallest parking garage around. I revved my engine and charged towards the edge.

My helmet's comm device rang. I answered it as I flew through the air.

"Really not a good time," I growled.

The bike was too heavy for the jump I'd attempted. I was

dropping too fast. I flipped up a cover on the front of the bike and started to activate the small bit of antigrav tech I'd managed to build. Before I could finish pressing the button, the bike froze midair. My finger stopped, just a hairsbreadth from the button. The air around me had turned heavy and hot. My muscles strained against this new force, but I couldn't move. I clenched my teeth. It wasn't supposed to do that!

I saw the device—some sort of momentum arrester—mounted in the belly of a chopper still half a mile out. The chopper was coated in a matte black paint for stealth during night missions. The Organization Strike team had arrived. My breath caught as the momentum arrester suspending my bike in the air flashed. The field holding me and my bike motionless weakened just enough for me to break free. I jumped clear of the bike just moments before the pulse reached me, and my bike exploded into a billion tiny pieces. Nothing to salvage, and nothing for any turnips to reconstruct. If that pulse had hit me, I would have died instantly. The Organization wasn't playing around. I rolled onto the rooftop, already sweating in the Indianapolis humidity.

"Shut up and listen." The voice coming over the helmet speakers was auditorily cloaked. The display on my helmet showed Tolden's number. Cloaked and using Tolden's phone? It was Medina. "This is the last communique you will receive. If you cannot be subdued, these agents have orders to use deadly force. I wish this wasn't necessary, but you attacked an agent."

I could only partially focus on the words as I pulled myself out of the line of fire. Then I saw the rocket launcher produced from inside the chopper. "Do they have orders to blow up a building full of civis with me? 'Cause one of them just pulled out a portable missile." I fumbled with the extra shielding unit on my belt. It wouldn't stop a missile, but might protect me from some of the debris—if the initial blast didn't short-circuit it. I still hadn't worked out that kink from the earlier mission. I smothered a curse. I was equipped for an Instructor, not to take on the entire Organization. And killing these people for doing their jobs wasn't an option. They were just doing their job, like Tolden and the rest of Tac 47.

"I will see to this." The phone clicked, and I breathed a half-sigh of relief. That was the most shocked I'd ever heard Medina, which meant he was about to chew out the guy with the launcher. I grabbed the shielding unit off my belt, turned it around, and flipped a switch marked *last resort*. Buzzing started outside my head.

I ran off the edge of the building, caught the windowsill of the next building over, and pushed off again. The landing reverberated through my bones, sending needles of pain all the way up to my knees. Note to self: never do that again.

Tires screeched two streets over as an Organization ground team raced toward me, and knew I didn't have time. My shielding unit had just begun spewing energy in a way that wreaked havoc with any telepath trying to focus—the only way they would be able to aim at me accurately with anything other than a S.A.M. or sniper rifle. Basically, I'd turned my little tiny blip on a telepath's radar into a foaming mass of energy that would give them a headache if they got too close. They could still tell where I was, they just couldn't get close enough to do anything about it. Aiming at me without line-of-sight would be like hitting a needle in a haystack—which defended against most of the more deadly threats, but it wouldn't keep the ground team from running me down. Unless…

I pulled the battery out of the energy pulser and smashed the casing. Using some of the wires from the now-broken gun, I jury-rigged a way to transfer the power. It wouldn't hold for long, but just maybe long enough for me to get out of this mess. I would rather hand myself over than shoot anyone other than an Institute dog, anyway. I wouldn't be using the energy gun for anything else.

When the power boost kicked in, even I felt it grate on my mind, and I was inside the shield. It wouldn't take care of the telekinetics, but none of the telepaths in a ten mile radius would be functional for days.

The car screeched to a halt, but the helicopter kept coming. Thank goodness there was a telekinetic guiding the helicopter, and the telepath driving the car was well-trained enough to stop without swerving into anything. I hadn't thought about those consequences.

I pulled on my full speed and dashed down the street. The shielding unit went into the first dumpster I saw. I dodged into a little mom&pop bakery as the first telekinetic staggered out of the car, bleeding from her lip.

I flashed a smile at the people who owned the shop. They were two, low power, independant telekinetics that the Organization hadn't picked up yet. "Won't need shields today, I already incapacitated their telepaths."

The woman at the counter nodded and put a pleasant smile on her face. "Of course, Talia. I'll have Dan deal with the video footage. He is clumsy, you know."

I nodded in satisfaction and pushed past the curtain that separated the customer area from the back rooms. There was a trap door in the floor that had a tunnel leading six miles out, into the run-down part of town. For most people, that would mean a long, wearying walk. I crossed the gap in fifteen minutes flat and hoped to high heavens that the poor couple would be alright. They'd never done anything wrong, so the Organization probably wouldn't care even if they knew the two were gifted. Aiding me, though? Even if the only thing they'd done is destroy the video footage of where I'd gone, my pursuers might just imprison them out of frustration. I seriously doubted that. The Organization was harsher than the Agency ever had been, but there was a line between going after me, and going after the people who'd helped me. I had the couple with strict instructions when they'd set up the escape route to, if it came down to that, tell the Organization where I'd gone. After it was used once, the tunnel was pretty much useless anyway.

A message flashed across my helmet screen as I slammed the second trapdoor shut.

"Superior sighted at school. Careful." It was from Tolden, it had to be—even though there was no number listed.

I sighed as I broke back into a jog and took refuge under the trees. The Superior sighting put a hole in my plans. Why couldn't anything be simple? If the Superiors knew where I went to school, they wouldn't be above slaughtering every single one of those kids—or at least enough to make their point. Knowing the lengths the Superiors would go to in order to get their claws on me, I couldn't just let Talia Carmen vanish. The only way to prevent a tragedy at Talia Carmen's school was going back to give them a more viable target. Doing so would expose me to more heat from the Organization, but that didn't change my priorities. How could children learn if their every moment at school was overshadowed by fear? Schools were already unsafe enough. I refused to allow one to be targeted because I was afraid the Organization would get involved. Moving to my cover as Emily Scott would have to wait.

Even as those thoughts raced through my head, I scanned the area around me. The chopper was retreating into the distance—likely called back to base for their attempted use of the missiles. Tac helicopters for non war-zone strikes were unarmed for a reason. I couldn't roam outside my head without it wanting to explode from the shielding unit that still hadn't been turned off. No, I'd gotten away this time. It had been far too close, and I'd lost far too much equipment. My money stash was running low, even with Emily Scott's job. The components for tech like I built weren't exactly cheap.

I sighed again and turned back into the woods. I had a bunker buried around here somewhere. It was a little cliche—a bunker in the woods—but I couldn't pass up the opportunity to install a base that was unaffiliated with either of my cover identities. Indiana's woodlots scattered around as wind-breaks provided the seclusion I'd needed to install the bunker. It had been a while since I'd had to use it, and I didn't make a habit of going there. It was safer that way.

It took a moment to find the hatch that served as the first of two doors into the bunker. Twilight had given way to night while I trudged through the trees, but I didn't dare turn on a flashlight. My gift was still disabled because of the shielding unit, which meant I had no way to know if anyone else was in the vicinity. It was theoretically possible that an Organization telekinetic could have found my trail and was combing the woods for me. The last thing I wanted to do was give them a clue as to where I was.

I found the tree I was looking for outlined in silvery moonlight. There was a palm scanner in the base that would deactivate the bombs set strategically around the bunker for if someone tried to get through the bunker door. The odds that I would be incapacitated, my code stolen, and the location of the bunker revealed was slight, but the bombs made me feel just a tad bit better. Underestimating the Organization could be fatal.

Bombs disarmed, I dropped through the first hatch, secured it behind me, then entered my code into the next door. No boom. That was always preferable.

I shut the booby-trapped door behind me and looked around. It was rather disorganized. The last time I'd been here, I'd gotten a mission brief from Tolden that had left me hurrying to intercept an attempted kidnapping downtown. I took a moment to straighten each of the modules on the shelf, and hang up the three tac suits I kept here. I pulled the rolly-chair back to its spot at the desk and gathered up the scattered pieces of paper. Then, the majority of the mess remedied, I selected another shielding unit from the shelf.

My semi-automatic was still back at the apartment.

That realization hit me hard over the head, and a lance of pain slid through me. They would be watching my apartment, so going back would be suicide. Still, I'd been through a lot with that gun. Tolden had given it to me after I'd helped take Houston in, and again after my biocard was taken and I was kicked out of the Agency shortly before the merger. It was his way of telling me he was listening, even while my voice was stunted. And now it was in the hands of the Organization. Again.

I clenched and unclenched my fists. It was getting really hard to not hate the Organization for everything it had done. I'd been on the run for the better part of a year, dodging assassination attempts by the Superiors while trying to stay off the Organization's radar. I'd done impossible things to help them, and they were still trying to kill me! What had I done to deserve this?

I pulled the necklace off, jammed Cal's device into the reader that had come with it, and sent the information I'd stolen from the Instructor to Tolden's secure account that was routed through three different false identities. At the same time, I pulled a copy for myself and pushed it to my phone. This information had cost too much for me to simply give it to the Organization. Especially after Medina cut ties.

I opened the file. A screen appeared on my computer, but it fizzled out. I sighed. Either I'd pulled it without the data needed to run the thing, or it was encrypted. Probably encryption.

"You stupid file!" I slammed my fist on the desk. When it came to hardware, I was great, but software? I was going to need Steele's help for that, and Medina had been clear. I'd sacrificed way too much for this stupid, useless, hunk of data that I couldn't even read!

I slammed the lid of the laptop closed and spun around in the chair, huffing. I couldn't afford to let my frustration get the better of me here. I was being hunted. If I wanted to make it out of this alive, I needed a clear head, and throwing a temper tantrum about some random piece of intelligence wasn't going to help. I pinched the bridge of my nose and forced myself to take a few deep breaths. If I wanted to pursue this, my only hope would be to ask Tolden to send me a copy of the decrypted data. That would take time. He wouldn't be in communication with me until things cooled down; It was too dangerous for him to do so. No, I wouldn't be able to chase this story. The realization was bitter in my throat.

I shoved it away in favor of more immediate concerns. I had a Superior to divert in the morning, and it was already midnight.

I was still far too wired to go to sleep, though, so instead I thought back to the files I'd found in the Superior base before I'd blown it up. There were three: one for "Defective", who preferred to be called "D", although that preference was nowhere in the file, one for an instructor called Phrenolia, and one for an instructor called Psycho. I closed my eyes and tiled my head back, thinking. The file on D went over all the failed tests, and the rather extreme measures they'd gone through to try and make what they believed to be a latent psionic ability surface. Looking at the file, it was no wonder she'd seemed slightly deranged when I'd met her. The experiments that had been run on her were innumerable, and none of them looked good—including several lobotomies. And the person in charge of them all was listed as the second Instructor, Phrenolia.

I pulled the second file to find an Instructor with the standard green eyes staring at me. Her chin was sharp, but her nose was sharper, and her lips were curled into a feral grin. It said in the file that she was the most scientifically inclined of the Instructors, and had a preference for working with the third of the Instructors, Psycho. There was also a psychological assessment performed by someone who was labeled only as "Administrator", which concluded that she was no more unstable than her counterparts.

The third file was, perhaps, the most disturbing. It described an Instructor with a proclivity toward substance abuse and a set of psionic abilities that surpassed even the "progenitor"—whoever that was. From the file, it seemed like he was some sort of an elder sibling. There were numerous references to other Instructors, but no real information on his relationship to them. Only that he was tasked with keeping them from killing each other, and pointing them all in the same direction.

I snorted. I'd found the cat-herder, alright, and the file noted that he wasn't doing a particularly wonderful job of it—only a better job than any of his deranged counterparts could manage.

When I was done reading over the files, I sighed. There wasn't really much there. Vague clues about some sort of a progenitor for all the Instructors? Two crazy Instructors, and a horribly mistreated one? Really, they were just two more names than I'd had before. Disgusted with the lack of progress, I jabbed a button on my phone and one of the walls folded down to reveal a bed. I pulled my tac suit off and forced my body to sleep.

CHAPTER FIVE

Morning came, and I awoke with the same alertness as always. Within minutes, my tac suit was on and fully equipped with everything except my semiautomatic. The suit felt different without that familiar weight at my hip. I ignored the feeling and grabbed an extra shielding unit—just in case. I'd been going through them like hotcakes, so having an extra one could be useful.

I shoved an energy pistol in the empty holster and pulled my street clothes on over. I donned my motorcycle helmet and pulled a motorcycle from the secondary bunker. I kept three of the same, specially modified, motorcycles. One in the bunker, one in Talia's garage, and one in Emily's. It was more than expensive, but expensive was better than dead. The three motorcycles had cosmetic differences, of course. Talia's was green with a brown seat cover, Emily's was polished silver, and the one in the bunker was emo black all over.

I wheeled the bike through the trees, being careful of the tires. Odds were that a stray bramble wouldn't pierce the reinforced rubber wheels, but I wasn't about to underestimate Hoosier greenery. Nature had ways of getting back at people who forgot to pay her due respect. A flat tire would seriously derail the mission, and the Superiors wouldn't wait for me to fix my bike before they burst into the school to slaughter innocents.

Finally, I reached the road and mounted. Driving to Driver's Ed. That was ironic but, then, I'd been driving illegally since I was twelve. A little makeup, and no one had noticed—I was only two years younger than the other new drivers in Chicago. In Indiana, the rules were stricter. When I'd first designed the cover identity, I hadn't worried about getting a license—partially due to sheer cost and the time involved—but when people had started giving Talia sideways glances when they learned she couldn't drive, I'd caved. Perhaps it was a misplaced conviction that I could live a mostly normal life as Talia Carmen that had caused me to enroll as the oldest person in the Driver's Education course, or perhaps it really had been to maintain my cover. Regardless of the reason, I was now glad to be in the class. It would provide the perfect way to divert the Superiors circling the school.

I gunned the motorcycle down the street, careful of cops but not much else. Getting pulled over would be awkward and—more importantly—would make me late. I had to make sure I was the first one in the car. I shuddered to think what would happen if a poor, helpless high schooler was at the wheel when Superiors started coming out of the works.

Ben Davis High was only a few blocks from Talia's apartment, and that translated to thirty-six miles away from my bunker. I crossed the distance in ten minutes and arrived a block away from her school—in a convenience store parking lot—with plenty of time to spare. I checked the charge on my weapons and shielding unit, then bought a muffin at the store using a tiny part of the wad of cash I had for times when the Organization was uncomfortably angry with me; they weren't above tracking my cards. I ate it as I walked quickly into the school parking lot. As I'd hoped, I was the first one there.

In the silence between my arrival and when the teacher, Mr. Grangy, pulled up in his dented red pickup truck, I scanned the area. That Superiors would be there was a given. No, I was more worried about the lack of Organization presence. Unless their intelligence department had suddenly become incompetent, they would be watching every location where I could possibly show up for the next two weeks. I scanned the sky, but no Strike helicopters appeared. I monitored the street, but there were no black-suited men or women watching from the illusory safety of surveillance vehicles. The school was deserted. Maybe I should have used a card to buy the muffin, and let them trace it back to me. That, at least, would have pointed them in the correct direction.

But, then, perhaps the Organization's absence wasn't nearly as strange as I'd originally thought. Numbers cycling in the back of my mind noted how many operatives I'd taken out yesterday with my use of the shielding unit, and wondered if the Organization was currently understaffed. The damage to their people wouldn't be permanent, but none of the telepaths that had gotten caught in the crossfire would be going back into the field for another few days—if only because it was difficult to think through a headache that severe. If that was the case, the Organization would only be watching places they thought I was likely to reappear, and they knew that only an idiot would return to her blown cover identity's high school for one last Driver's Ed class.

It was a shame. There was a part of me that had wanted to flag down the Organization operatives assigned to watch me, point them at the Superiors, and let them deal with it. Was it the wisest course of action? It would probably get me shot, actually, but it would have caused a certain amount of satisfaction as I watched the Organization do its job for once.

No, it was safer for everyone involved that the Organization wasn't watching me right now.

Five minutes later on the dot, the instructor got out of his truck to greet me and the other two kids who had wandered up to me as their parents dropped them off. They tried to start up a conversation. I stayed silent—although I tried to keep the stay-away-from-me, I-will-put-you-in-mortal-danger vibe to a minimum. When I learned that the third student had called in sick today, I relaxed just a bit. The fewer people I endangered in my desperate quest, the better.

"Mr. Grangy." I greeted the teacher with a nod even as I noted the roar of a motorcycle engine gunning its way down the street. If Tabitha had been here, I would have asked her to use the way the sounds echoed off the buildings around us to pinpoint the Superiors location, but I didn't have that skill set, and Tabitha was dead. I clenched my jaw against the familiar cut of pain. The Institute would pay for killing my friend. Better, I would make it so they couldn't do that to anyone else ever again. I would tear the Institute apart, Instructor by Instructor.

I fixed the teacher with a manufactured grin. "Would it be possible for me to drive first?"

I could almost feel the Superiors perking up at my words as I heard yet another motorcycle near the school. They weren't being subtle today, were they?

A glint in the window drew my attention as a piece of glass I wasn't supposed to be able to see shifted somewhere in the parking lot. Their shielding was good, but it could be better. That one flash of light helped me localize the aura of violence that surrounded the gathering Superiors. It was hard to distinguish individuals in that mass of blood and hatred I felt, but I could count at least three. While three Superiors weren't an insurmountable obstacle when I was fully armed and unhindered by the necessity of keeping turnips safe, taking them out while driving a car full of high schoolers was going to be a problem. Actually, the students probably wouldn't interfere. I turned my calculating gaze on Mr. Grangy, who still hadn't answered my question, and grit my teeth. I would have to find a way to keep him out of my way. First, though, we needed to get going before the school day started and more innocent people could get caught in the crossfire.

"Mr. Grangy?"

He looked at me through beady eyes. "The last time you drove first was…"

"Two weeks ago," I said, struggling to keep my tone neutral. He was a turnip, and didn't see the three killing machines in the parking lot behind us. Losing my cool wouldn't help my case.

"I see." He looked down at his clipboard and scribbled a few things as I stood there, weight distributed, already fighting adrenaline. "Well, I don't see why not." He didn't move to *get in the car*.

I turned back to the Superiors gathered in the parking lot and reached into their minds with what little projection strength I had. Forming words was still beyond me, but I managed to project a sense of challenge as I slapped a camera on the back of the car then settled myself securely in the driver's seat. Mr. Grangy, as slow on the uptake as always, stared at us for a moment while I watched the other two kids get in the back seat of the car. When they were safe inside, I pulled out my phone, tapped a few buttons to narrow the first shielding unit's field, and tossed the shielding unit under the passenger side dashboard so it stuck on the bottom of the teacher's brake pedal. I tapped the screen a few more times to pull up the feed from the camera I'd placed on the back of the car, then peeled the back of the phone case off and stuck it to the dashboard.

I scanned the mirrors to make sure I had a full view of the car, and stopped as I saw Mr. Grangy's wrinkled forehead.

"Miss Carmen, what are you doing to my car?" He had opened his door to get in, and was resting his forearms on the top of the car as he stared at the phone I'd just glued to the vinyl of the dashboard. I looked at the phone and stifled my impatience. The method I'd used to secure the phone was fast, dirty, and hard to remove, but it would stay where I put it, even if I rolled the vehicle.

"It's just a precaution," I said. I accompanied my words with a thread of compulsion for him to get in the car. He obeyed with anger-tinged confusion, and then started into his speech about checking mirrors, inspecting the car, and the dangers of using a phone while driving. I tuned him out, and focused on getting the rest of the car's electronics integrated with my operational equipment. I tapped the tablet embedded in the front dash of the car, just to the right of where I'd stuck my phone, until it displayed a map. My phone buzzed, transferring some of Steele's software to the tablet. The map turned into a duplicate of my phone's camera feed. If I lost one, the other would continue to display. Redundancy was the difference between life and death in combat. I tapped my phone screen, then the car's tablet—just to make sure the interface was operating smoothly—then locked the door, pulled the car into reverse, and backed out of the slot.

"Miss Carmen!"

I gave Mr. Grangy a flat look. He was pointing at my phone that was still stuck to the dash. "You know you aren't allowed to use your phone. I've asked you three times to put it away—"

I tuned him out again.

"Yes. I'll put it away in a moment." I fed him another spoonful of compulsion to keep him quiet. Sweat was beading on my forehead from the effort of using my tattered gift. I wasn't going to be able to keep him under control for much longer.

As we exited the parking lot, the Superiors dropped their shielding to reveal three fully equipped Superiors on motorcycles in all their bloodthirsty glory. None of them wore the crystal shields they'd been equipped with the first few times I'd met them—probably because they knew I couldn't do much even if I could get inside their minds. Lack of shielding meant that there was nothing to keep their promise of pain and death from coating my mind in a thick black fog. I grit my teeth. Not today.

"Talia Carmen, this is your second hour, right?" Mr. Grangy asked, back to his usual script. There was a bit of mist behind his eyes, showing that my compulsion still held. For the moment.

"You may want to buckle up," I replied.

He raised his eyebrows and reached for his seatbelt—but he wasn't happy. Oh well. He was going to be a whole lot less happy by the time we were done.

I pulled out of the parking lot and looked at my teacher out of the corner of my eye. "I was wondering if I could work on passing on a two-lane road? You know, the ones where you have to charge oncoming traffic to get around the slowpokes? The last time you took us out to the fields, and I had to pass that semi-truck, I was absolutely terrified." Not really. Not much scared me any more. I just really wanted to get those Superiors into the middle of nowhere, and the cornfields were the best place to do that.

Mr. Grangy stiffened in resistance. I pulled the car onto the road and turned right. I let my right hand drop off the wheel and moved my left to the 12 o'clock position. It was easier to drive quickly and accurately with my hand there—

regardless of what the manual said. I could see Mr. Grangy's lips tighten, but he didn't say anything. The compulsion was thinning. I glanced at the rear camera feed and saw two motorcycles behind me. "Everyone's buckled up, right?" I asked as the motorcycles swerved into position behind us. I looked at the two highschoolers in the mirror. They nodded. I sounded more like a teacher than the guy sitting next to me.

The traffic in Indianapolis was thick, and the motorcycles pursuing us were far more maneuverable than we were. The trade-off was that the city had lots of escape routes I could take advantage of if I got cornered somewhere I didn't like. If I used them, though, the Superiors would take their frustration out on the populace.

I made sure to stay in plain sight of the Superiors gunning toward us as I led them out of the city. They were being patient for now—displaying intelligence I hadn't seen in a Superior before—and working together as they tried to herd me toward the major speedways. I shook them off and headed for the corn fields. As the city fell into the rearview, I started to breathe easier. I pressed the gas pedal to the floor, grateful that the road ahead was clear. Another round of adrenaline spurted into my system, and I could feel my mental processes speeding up. I could feel my blue lines working at maximum efficiency just below the lining of my mind, calculating distance, speed, momentum, acceleration, and jerk. My face was curled into a savage grin as the full exhilaration of battle at full speeds dumped endorphins into my brain. Mr. Grangy was still yammering about letting someone else drive. Slowing down. Not looking at my phone. Putting both hands on the wheel. Finally fed up and completely free of my compulsion, Mr. Grangy slammed on his brake pedal, but it didn't do any good. My—now extremely short ranged—shielding unit was wreaking havoc with the extra pedal. They never should have changed the student driver cars to electronic communication with something as essential as the teacher's pedal.

The guns installed between the headlights of the motorcycles behind us started spitting lead. I could just hear the *tat, tat, tat* of bullets slamming into asphalt as I jerked the wheel to the side. The student driving car wasn't quite as responsive as I'd hoped. I nearly clipped the bumper of the minivan in front of us in an attempt to evade the bullets aimed at my tires. My reckless driving got us out of the way in time, but it didn't help the minivan. The bang was unmistakable as a stray bullet tore into the minivan's back left tire. The lead motorcycle didn't get clear in time, and the two vehicles collided in a shower of metal.

Sirens sounded behind me as I whizzed past a cop car. Mr. Grangy squeaked out something about pulling over when he realized we weren't stopping at the scene of the accident. The cops didn't go back to the accident either. They'd seen enough to peg me as the culprit, and they were going to try to run me to the ground.

I stifled a curse. If neurotypical law enforcement wasn't set up to handle regular psionic criminals, it certainly couldn't handle Superiors. The Organization monitored police bands. Maybe they would hear about the chase and come help—but it was a futile hope. Unless one of the officers identified the fact that the creatures riding the motorcycles looked inhuman, then described them over the radio, the Organization didn't have enough resources to respond right now.

I had to keep the officers from engaging the Superiors, or my actions were going to cost them their lives.

Luckily, the Superiors didn't even spare the cops any disdain. When the flashing lights started riding uncomfortably close up on the Superior's exhaust pipe, the bike let loose a spray of black goo, and the cops dropped back to a safer distance. I prayed that they would stay there.

My teacher lunged toward the wheel, so I put the palm of my hand into the side of his face. Hard. "Stay where you are unless you want to get us all killed." I could have been ordering breakfast, for all the inflection I put into my voice.

There was a whimper from the back seat as one of the kids realized that we were in real danger. I couldn't spare any attention to discern whether he understood the threat behind us, or if he was just reacting to the violence he'd just witnessed. I wanted to reassure him, but there was no time.

I pulled my car around the corner, cutting it a little close. The car wasn't really massive enough for the stunts I was trying to pull. What I really needed was an Agency vehicle with a lower center of gravity, jet boosters, and guns of my own. Complaining wasn't going to help anyone, though, and I let the thought go. I'd already completed my first goal of getting the Superiors away from the school. Now I needed to get the civilians I'd dragged into this mess with me, out in one piece. I let the car drift to the edge of the road, and then tightened the turn. The wheels started to slip underneath me, and I corrected it. Just a little bit more…there!

The car edged back into its proper lane just in time to avoid a speeding farm truck. The Superior behind me didn't get clear in time. The truck swerved to try and avoid it, but was too late. Both vehicles tumbled off the road in an explosion of bent metal and sparks.

"You stop this car right now Miss Carmen!" My instructor's voice was a full two octaves higher, but he didn't try to grab the wheel again. I raked an eye down his form, then dismissed him completely as a threat. He was folded in on himself, already shaking. This was not someone who knew how to harness his adrenaline in a combat situation. Fear had paralyzed him.

I glanced in the back seat to see terrified tears in the eyes of both students back there as they clung to whatever they could find in a desperate attempt to convince themselves that they could make it out of this safely. Before I could find words to reassure them, I noticed the two police cars visible on the camera feed on my phone.

The road ahead was clear, which was fortunate for any civilians in my path, and not quite as fortunate for my tactics. Motorcycles were easy to scrape off on larger civilian vehicles. They were delicate, and would do minimal damage to the larger vehicles and the poor civilians inside. Now, I was going to have to switch tactics.

Evidently, the last remaining Superior was also growing tired of the chase. He pulled his bike along beside us and leveled his energy pistol at my face. I pursed my lips. This student driver car didn't have the juice to outrun the Superior, and energy pulses could wreak havoc with the car's computers. Best case, the camera screen in the car would blow. Worst case, the engine would overload, and we'd all go up in a fireball.

"Brace yourself!" I shouted, and slammed on the brakes. I jerked the wheel around to send the front of the car careening into the Superior's back tire. My calculations were impeccable. The bike spun out. Not even a Superior could keep his seat in that sudden vortex of G-forces. He flew off, smashed into the asphalt, and bounced twice before he landed in a corn field outside my view. His bike tumbled along the highway, scattering smashed and torn components around like deadly legos thrown by a child's temper tantrum. It was going to be scrap metal by the time it came to rest. The rider, had he been human, should have died on first impact. As it was, I wasn't willing to call it. The important part was that he wasn't chasing me anymore.

The kids in the back seat had wide eyes as they watched the carnage unfolding behind us. I clenched my teeth. They'd need some real therapy, or some time with a high level tele-projector like Robbins, to get over this. For one terrible moment, I wished I had never let them get into the car with me. Then I shook it off. I couldn't let the guilt sink its claws into me yet. The mission wasn't through.

I checked the backup camera for signs of more Superiors, but could see nothing except the approaching police cars. The first set of cops must have called for backup. More were undoubtedly on their way. If I didn't get out of this fast, I'd end up in government custody—where the Organization would be able to find and execute me at their leisure. It was time to get clear and lay low. I'd already expended my measure of luck for the day.

The fields on the left side of the road were a good place for Superior reinforcements to hide—if they'd managed to get there first—but that was statistically unlikely. Still, when dealing with Superiors it was best to not take chances. I'd been on this road long enough to let them get advanced teams in place at likely places for me to stop. I let another half-mile of road go by. The police were starting to get antsy, and soon there would be air support to add to this chase. The last thing I needed was a turnip helicopter in the mix—especially not when, police chopper or not, any Superiors who could get on it would be there. They didn't have Medina's same inhibitions when it came to missiles, and I'd been enough of a pain that they might settle for turning me into a blazing crater in the road.

I pulled over to the side of the road and scanned for an escape route. The small lake to my right would provide a perfect place to wait out the cops—and the Organization, once they finally got their people moving. I pulled a syringe of liquid from the tactical suit and squirted it at the base of my phone case. It started to eat away at the vinyl-coated dashboard, but it also succeeded in freeing my phone. I donned the tactical helmet and grabbed the handle of the car door, scanning for anomalies. A glint drew my attention. The sun was reflecting off of something on the far side of the road. It moved, and the reflection of the sun came with it. More Superior cloaking.

I checked my weaponry. Did they just have Superior scouts in every cornfield in Indiana? I must be a higher priority target than I'd thought, for them to go to this level of trouble. And it was no wonder after I'd spent the last year blowing up Superior bases and intercepting their kidnapping missions.

"Get out of the car," the human cop shouted. His partner was behind him and slightly closer to the center of the road. Both pointed their firearms in my direction.

If bullets started flying, the turnips would get caught in the crossfire. I hit the car locks, then tapped a button on my phone and secured it on my belt. The doors of the car—all but mine—started to smoke as they welded themselves shut, trapping the turnips inside where they would be safe. I stepped out of the car, kicked the door closed behind me, and watched it start to smoke like all the others.

I braced for the gunshot I knew was coming. It would be hard to move fast enough to avoid the bullet, but it was the only choice I had right now. Continuing to run would only make things messier, and the three turnips in the car hadn't signed up for this. I could calculate the intended trajectory and get out of the way—or at least make the shot less lethal— if I needed to.

The cloaking on the Superior's suit flickered as it charged its weapon. I saw the projected path the energy discharge would follow and hissed. It wasn't aimed at me. In one smooth movement, I stepped to the side of the police guns, drew my own, and shot the Superior. I pivoted to see both officers fall to the ground and bit back a curse. Where had the second shot come from? There was another Superior, and I'd missed it. I spotted an anomalous reflection behind a rock. The cloaking flickered as it tried, and failed, to cope with the excess motion of the Superior reloading its rifle. Well, it was a good thing Zeta-Superiors were the least intelligent breed the Instructors had trained. It was too overconfident of its hiding place and shielding technology. I discharged my weapon once more, checked to confirm that both Superiors were dead, and that there were no more, then surveyed the damage they'd left behind.

I kneeled at the side of one of the dying officers. The Superiors had used energy powered poison capsules on both officers. Their skin grew paler with every new heartbeat as the poison spread. Now, they lay, sweating and breathing hard, twitching. In a few seconds, their breathing would grow more labored, then fade until they looked comatose. In a few minutes, they would waste away. I'd seen it before, in other victims I hadn't been able to save. Tolden had snuck me the antidote once the Organization had synthesized it. I had one dose in every medkit I carried. The problem was that half a dose was only enough to dilute the poison. It would give the two officers an extra fifteen minutes of agonizing life, and then they would be just as dead as if I hadn't intervened. Even with the half dose of antidote, they had twenty minutes left to live. If I did nothing, that shrank to ten minutes, give or take.

I stood above them, indecisive. Even if an ambulance got here in time, they would die before they reached a hospital. Even if an Organization response team was in the area, they would have to find them, figure out what was wrong, and then treat them. I had an extra dose at my bunker, and at Emily Scott's house, but neither were close enough. The officers would be dead before I got back.

The clock ticked down in my mind. I closed my eyes, hands fisted. I was the one who decided to start this wild goose chase. I was the one who put these officers in the line of fire. I would not be responsible for their deaths.

There was only one choice that would leave everyone alive at the end.

I injected half the antidote into each officer with swift, efficient motions. Then I reached for my phone. Information appeared on the screen. I scanned it with the helmet. Since the merger, the Organization had local tactical nets set up all over the world. I grit my teeth and entered the final code Tolden had given me.

The line connected with a click. There was a chopper in the background, covered by occasional chatter.

I grinned, in spite of myself. Two years ago, I never would have been able to make out these sounds. Of course, two years ago, I wouldn't have been in this situation to begin with. "Hello boys. 32 here. We don't usually do business, but you need to listen up—"

"—32?" The chatter cut completely. My old agent number certainly had gotten their attention. Maybe this wasn't such a good idea.

"How did you access this channel?"

Well, I was in too deep, now. "I've got two human turnip law enforcement officers down by the lake. They've got maybe five minutes before the half-dose of antidote I've given them wears off. Also there's got a car full of civis that won't understand what they just saw. If Robbins has finished fixing the mess in Boston, you might think about getting him down here."

The Agent In Charge ordered the helicopter around.

"Why'd you call us?" a new voice asked as the AIC continued giving orders.

I sighed. It should have been obvious, but the Organization was more focused on finishing old vendettas than on working together. Of all the Agency's traits they could have taken out of the merger, this was probably the worst. "'The enemy of my enemy is my friend'. Right? We're both trying to stop the Institute, therefore we're friends. Even if you all spend an unhealthy amount of time trying to kill me."

I killed my connection to the tactical net and tapped my phone a few more times—grateful now, more than ever, for Steele's illicit help putting the software I needed together.

"Stored air engaged." The sound came over my helmet speakers as the air vents in my suit closed. The seals hissed, and suddenly the entire suit was pressurized. A timer appeared on the HUD of how much more air was left. I tucked my phone into the upper waterproof pocket, then dove into the water. Moments later, I was on the other side, hiding in the greenery. I checked my location to ensure I couldn't be seen from the air, then settled in to watch. If those two policemen died because of me, I would never forgive myself.

Three minutes after I broke into their tactical net, the Organization's chopper hovered over the car. I watched as one of the agents administered the antidote while another cut through the car doors to let the civilians out. He ducked his head inside, and came back out holding my shielding unit in his glove. I winced. That was a rookie mistake. If they managed to reverse engineer it, one of my biggest aces would be gone. Not only that, but they would be able to disable me the same way I'd disabled them yesterday. I hit a button on my phone, then watched as the shielding unit self-destructed. Immediately, I could feel the agents' surface thoughts retreat behind their walls. They knew I was here.

As much as I would have liked to stay until they'd stabilized the policemen, it was time to go. I snuck off into the overgrowth and started a nice, leisurely jog as I tried to fill my mind with inane thoughts. The more my mind looked like an ordinary turnip's the less attention they would pay me.

Dog food. I had to buy dog food for my imaginary dog, who I would then feed the moment I got to my ordinary house. And roses! My imaginary anniversary with my imaginary husband was coming up. I began formulating an entire shopping list.

CHAPTER SIX

By the time I made it to Emily Scott's house, I was completely and thoroughly done with thinking normal thoughts, but it couldn't be helped. I looked at the clock and groaned. It was time for work. I took a long, deep breath. If I could survive Zach, Houston, and Ms. King, I could pull myself together for long enough to go to Emily Scott's job. I closed my eyes and focused my gift. If there were any psionics in the area, I was going to be in trouble. Still, if any of them had followed me here, it was best to know about it now before I brought my fight with the Organization to my employer's house. I scanned the streets close to Emily's apartment, then slowly expanded my search until sweat dripped down my chin and I was panting. Nothing. I'd made it away clean.

I found a towel to mop my face, moving with muscles that felt like lead. I hadn't been this exhausted since Neal Black had started my one-on-one martial arts sessions. The difference was that, then, I had friends to pick me off the mat and help me keep going. I could go home to Mom on Sundays and rest. Now I was utterly alone.

I looked at the mirror in the wall and blinked at the woman staring back at me. How had it come to this? I was on the run, chased by people to whom I'd done absolutely nothing. Monsters hunted my every move, and enemies stood on every corner. I hadn't seen Mom in a year. My friends were either dead, or unable to help me because they worked for some of the people trying to kill me. My father was stubbornly refusing to come forward—I was starting to wonder if he was even still alive. What could he possibly gain from continuing to hide in the shadows? He'd left to keep Mom safe, but hiding from Mom wasn't the same as hiding from me.

I jerked away from the mirror before I tried to smash it in a sudden surge of rage. How long could I be expected to dodge the Organization and the Institute? How long could I keep this up before I slipped?

I closed my eyes, and suddenly the two Superiors were in front of me with their energy propelled poison capsules. If they hadn't aimed at the police officers, that much poison would have dropped me like a rock. No one would have come to save me, and I didn't have enough antidote to heal myself. I would be dead.

I missed Mom, and Tolden, and Steele, and Hunt, and Tabitha, and Briggs, and Mr. West—even Black. I missed Martial Academy. All I wanted to do was lay down and cry, or maybe punch something into submission, until my fists hurt more than my heart. Instead of doing either of those things, I took a deep breath and deliberately placed the wall between my emotions and the rest of me.

Tension drained out of my shoulders, I lifted my chin, and started to get ready for work. I stripped the tactical suit off, hung it in the shower, then put a fresh one on. Usually Emily didn't wear a tactical suit, but I wasn't about to take chances. There was a difference between being Emily and being stupid. I stripped as much of the extra gear off of the tactical suit as I could, which left me with the base black bodysuit, one breast pocket that could hide the shielding unit, my med kit, a detachable pocket with Emily's work things, and the holster, which I reconfigured to hang under one arm. Over the suit, I donned a pair of slacks and a loose blouse with a high collar that would hide the black base layer. The holster went between the blouse and the leather jacket I put over Emily's professional clothes, then I tossed a sports jacket in my saddlebags for good measure and squirmed into a pair of sweatpants. I'd learned from hard experience that business casual didn't survive long if it was exposed to the extremes of motorcycle riding. That done, I paused to marvel at the difference between Emily Scott's wardrobe and Talia Carmen's. Talia wore printed t-shirts that didn't require protection from the motorcycle. Emily had a professional wardrobe mostly comprised of slacks and button down shirts that would get torn to shreds by the wind.

Ms. King might have been a backstabbing monster, but I had to admit that she'd prepared me better for these last few years than I ever could have hoped. She hadn't covered everything, but it was enough. It had bought me time to learn how to become someone else.

I reviewed my other weapons stash locations. If these next few hours went badly, I would pick up my weapons and flee the city. My cover as Emily Scott probably wouldn't hold for very much longer. I knew that. I knew I should just pick up what things I needed and just leave, while the Organization wasn't on my tail, but I refused to abandon Emily now. There was no evidence that the Organization had ever connected me with this identity. If I could hold on a few more days, I could set up another identity in another city before I had to run.

Plus, Emily Scott was a nanny, and I didn't want to abandon her kids without giving the Tanner family at least a little notice. They would have to make arrangements for someone to watch the kids while they were at work, and those arrangements took time.

If that wasn't enough, today was pay-day, and the extra money would go a long way toward helping me disappear again.

I rolled my motorcycle out of the garage and straddled it. The motorcycle at the gas station was as good as gone. The Organization had likely picked it up the moment they'd traced the Drivers-Ed car to Ben Davis High. Replacing it was going to be a pain—but better than getting hauled in by the Organization.

I revised my plan for keeping the kids occupied today as I drove toward the Tanners' house. It was best if I stayed indoors and out of the line of fire for a while. I'd kicked a hornets nest by calling in the Organization tac team to solve my problem, so I needed to keep my head down. Still, I didn't regret it. Those two police officers would survive.

Like at the school, I parked a block away from the Tanners' house, stowed my leather jacket and sweats in the saddle bags, pulled on my sports jacket to hide the holster, then walked the rest of the way. I let myself into the house using the key in Emily's work pocket.

Mr. Tanner was pacing at the end of the entry hallway with his phone held up to his cheek—odd. Usually he was out at the law firm. His work times and mine coincided perfectly, so I barely ever saw him. Still, it was always good to be polite to my employer. I fixed him with a grin and waved as I stowed my shoes by the door. He nodded back to me and kept pacing along the hallway.

Politeness taken care of, I stood in front of the coat closet on the right side of the hall, listening for the rustle of displaced coats and the giggling of an excited little girl. Nothing. Jasmine was getting better at hiding, but she was still predictable. I jerked open the door to the coat closet—expecting little Jasmine to barrel out at me like she usually did. The closet was empty except for the line of assorted coats and jackets. I frowned as I stared at the neat line of hangers. That was another statistical anomaly. I wondered if she was up in her room.

I turned back to go upstairs and check on her—it wasn't completely unknown for her to get in trouble in the morning and then spend the whole day pouting—when I stopped. A chill ran down my spine.

Mr. Tanner stood in the middle of the hallway. He dropped his phone into the inside pocket of his black suit coat and looked at me, his expression grave.

"Mr. Tanner, are you alright?" I asked. What had happened to make him come home so early? Were the kids alright? Was Mrs. Tanner ill? The silence shrouding the house was oppressive.

I started running calculations in the back of my mind, and they didn't look good. Something was very off, and I couldn't pinpoint what.

Mr. Tanner shook his head. "Emily, can I talk to you for a moment?"

I swallowed hard and followed him through the house. "Where are the kids?" Had the Institute found them? Had I put them in danger? If those kids had been hurt because of me, I would never forgive myself.

Mr. Tanner didn't respond. Instead, he walked silently up the carpeted stairs, past the childrens' rooms, and stopped in front of his office door.

"Mr. Tanner?" It was hard to keep the trepidation from my voice.

His lips twisted into a less severe expression as he opened his office door. Mrs. Tanner was sitting demurely on the velvety couch against the wall that faced Mr. Tanner's desk. She smiled and motioned me inside. I swallowed hard as I looked at the office that was starting to look more and more like a prison—windowless, with locks on the doors sufficient to keep any ordinary burglar from accessing the confidential files Mr. Tanner occasionally kept in there.

"We just want to talk, Emily," Mr. Tanner said. There was a fluctuation of sorts in his surface thoughts. I tried to use my gift to evaluate it, but stopped as a sudden headache cracked over my skull. My abilities weren't recovered enough for this sort of extended use. Manipulating Mr. Grangy earlier, reading Houston and Nick, and searching the area around Emily's apartment were all taking their toll. I grit my teeth and reached for the numbers circulating the back of my mind.

There was not enough information. I synthesized everything I'd learned about the Tanners to try and predict what he was going to do, but he was a closed book. He just stood there, patiently waiting to see if I would enter the room.

I clenched my fist. It was hard to keep my worries as Crystal Farina separate from the ordinary cares of Emily Scott. How well did I know my employers, anyway? I was supposed to care for the kids. Mrs. Tanner was usually around, but engaged in some quiet activity in their basement library, or her own office downstairs. I'd seen her three dozen times in my time working here, and never for very long—although she always had a kind smile for me. Mr. Tanner, I'd seen perhaps twice, and now they were both ambushing me in an office.

Finally, I looked down at the floor. Ms. King said that the closest thing to a surefire way to tell if someone was leading you into a trap was to lie. Change something—react unexpectedly, and then evaluate how they respond.

"Um, Mr. Tanner. I'm a little claustrophobic, and that's…" I coughed into my hand. "That's a very small room."

Mrs. Tanner frowned and held out a hand to her husband. "I'm sorry, I didn't realize. Sweetheart, would you—"

Mr. Tanner left his post at the doorway as Mrs. Tanner struggled to get up. She was favoring her right hip. Her face screwed up into one of pain, and she took a sharp breath as she shifted wrong.

"Oh, please don't. The doctor won't like it," Mr. Tanner said. He put a hand on his wife's shoulder. She glared at him.

"If Emily wants to have this meeting downstairs, then we'll have the meeting downstairs. I am not broken." Mrs. Tanner's voice was the most annoyed I'd ever heard her. She was usually a sweet little thing. But pain made even the most gentle people testy.

Mr. Tanner shot a pleading look over his shoulder. "Please, Emily. It won't take very long, and my wife—well, she may not be helpless, but her hip is most definitely broken."

I looked for physical evidence of that, but doctors couldn't exactly put a cast around someone's hip. The pain on Mrs. Tanner's face certainly looked real, plus, an accident like that would certainly explain Mr. Tanner's presence and how quiet the kids were.

I swallowed hard and stepped over the threshold against my better judgement. I had absolutely no evidence to suggest that the Tanners were affiliated with the Organization. Their reaction to my little lie seemed genuine.

"What happened?" I asked as I tried to dismiss my growing dread. Mr. Tanner moved back to the doorway. "Are the children alright?"

Mr. Tanner shut the door. I jumped a bit—for the sake of my cover—and stared at the walls that were starting to close in around me. I may not have truly been claustrophobic, but the tightness in my chest wasn't an act. The only exit from this room was being guarded by Mr. Tanner, who stood with his back to the door, arms folded, watching me with an unreadable expression. This was not good.

"We thought it best that the kids weren't in the house. They went to their grandparent's," Mrs. Tanner said.

"A few things happened in the last day and a half that have made it so it won't be possible for you to work for us anymore." Mr. Tanner said. I heard the lock click behind him, either activated from the outside, or Mr. Tanner was tele-kinetic, because his hands were still crossed over his chest in an attitude that was becoming increasingly hostile. Any semblance of the doting husband trying to keep his injured wife from having to go back down a flight of stairs was gone.

I looked at Mrs. Tanner, expecting some sort of clar-ification, but her face was closed; controlled. I'd seen that expression before on a dozen tactical operatives. Mr. Tan-ner's gun—I'd known from the beginning that he was armed, but the Tanners had always been careful individuals, and an old-fashioned slug thrower wasn't a threat to me except at close range—was in his hand. I replayed the moment in my head and, while his hand had shifted, his gun had traveled of its own accord from his hidden holster to his hand. The metal bullets I'd disparaged would be more than sufficient given that the muzzle was only two inches away from my spine. I grabbed for the gun beneath my jacket, then stopped as I felt cold metal pressed against the side of my head. Mrs. Tanner held an energy pistol in one steady hand. A single twitch, and I would be everything-but-dead.

"You're with the Organization?" I asked.

"Drop your gun, or we'll shoot." Mrs. Tanner replied. "We have that authorization."

I scanned for a way out, but found nothing. I could try to dodge the first bullet from the gun in Mr. Tanner's hand, but even with my speed I'd have to settle for taking the shot in someplace less lethal. I could ignore the pain—my abnormal pain response hadn't changed when my mind had healed—but I would have to absorb the momentum carried by the bullet, which would slow me down. To get away from Ms. Tanner's weapon, which was the more pressing threat, I would have to set my head against the side of the gun and spin. If I could turn in time and take Mrs. Tanner hostage, I might have a chance. But then what? My numbers now showed that the Tanners were the most talented liars I'd ever seen. They were most certainly intelligence or counterintelligence—Medina's department, either way, and he trained his agents well. Mrs. Tanner's hip was probably fully functional. Even if I *could* subdue the Tanners, the Organization knew I wouldn't leave their children without parents. I wasn't prepared to do that.

I had no other choice.

My hands rose, empty except for the pulser rings I always carried. The gun hadn't even made it halfway out of its holster. It settled back in silently. Mrs. Tanner grabbed it from where it hung under my arm and tossed it against the wall. I winced at the clatter. "Were you working for the Organization the whole time?"

"On your knees, 32." Mr. Tanner instructed. His voice was cold.

I sank down slowly, very aware of the two guns that followed my motion. Despair clutched at my chest. What else was there to do but comply?

I let Mrs. Tanner handcuff my hands behind my back and slip the pulser rings off my fingers.

A new plan presented itself. I could burn Mrs. Tanner's hands to a crisp and take out Mr. Tanner before he could get a shot off, but at what cost? So far I'd managed to avoid killing anyone other than Superiors and their Instructor counterparts. I couldn't be responsible for the death of an Organization agent.

No. I let opportunity pass and closed my eyes.

"I know how this works, and I give you my word that I will do you no harm." I said. My voice was flat, and my throat was tight. Who knew what the Organization would decide to do to me, now? They'd nearly killed me earlier, and now they had the opportunity to finish what they'd started. While the Organization wasn't as trigger happy as the Company had been, they wouldn't have any regrets.

What would Mom think when I never came back?

There was a sharp jab in my arm as they injected a sedative, and the world faded.

CHAPTER SEVEN

My head throbbed when I finally started to regain consciousness. For a moment, I wondered if something had happened at work. I had been at the Tanners' house, and then—

I jerked upright, only to find my hands cuffed to a table.

The Tanners had been working from the Organization from the beginning. My lip curled as that realization settled into my mind like hot coals. I had been too desperate for a job to question why they'd hired Emily when she'd only had one, faked, reference from Tolden. They'd looked like a nice family. Sure, their mental walls were high, but there were plenty of turnips with high walls. Like Nick, Talia Carmen's boyfriend.

I clenched my fists. I thought I was so clever, but they'd been watching me the whole time. The Tanners had been reporting back to the Organization the same way Nick had been. Were all of my friends reporting to the Organization?

I slammed the walls up between my emotions and logic. It was the same thing that happened when I brought the lines to the forefront of my vision before my confrontation with

Ms. King, and it still had the same effect. Adrenaline flooded through my system, the pain receded, and I was instantly more alert.

The Organization was a collection of highly specialized individuals. Of course they had been able to find me. They had the best of the best—people who perseverated on the minutiae of procuring another identity and maintaining it. People like the Tanners. I'd had the basic course from Ms. King. That was enough to vanish off of any government radar, but evading the Organization was another set of equations altogether. Medina wasn't the only one among them who had mysteriously anonymous sources of information, and if he could find me, others within the Organization could too.

Just because they possessed the ability to find me didn't keep me from being annoyed that they had. I'd blown up a Superior base every other weekend—a full month's work for any strike team—and I'd cost them exactly nothing while I'd done it. If their true objective was destroying the Institute, they should have left me out there instead of sedating me and chaining me up in an interrogation room.

I jerked the handcuffs that linked me to the table again, testing them. Within a fraction of a second, I had determined the weakest link and the amount of force required to break it. Alternatively, I could pick the lock with the hair pin in my pocket. Extracting the little metal tool would require some contortion, but it was possible, and I'd already constructed a mental model of the lock's internal mechanisms.

Rather than break out, I directed my attention to the rest of the room. This was the spitting image of the place I'd gone to interview D, down to the false mirror on the wall across me. It let me see every pore on my face that held just a smudge of dirt on one cheek, and a fleck of blood—whose was anybody's guess—on the other. I could see shifts—tiny little motions that would be invisible to someone without my abilities—in the mirror, and straightened my spine. Someone was behind that glass, which meant I was about to have a visitor.

As I'd thought, a man opened the door twenty-point-two seconds later and closed it behind him. He held a folder in his hand, and I curled my lip further as I felt the thought frequency buzzing around his walls. He was a low level telepath—low enough that I could read him even with my tattered gift.

My teleprojection abilities had healed up enough while I was sedated that flexing those mental muscles brought only a twinge of pain. My walls were a fraction higher than they had been—which only made sense. The brain was a muscle just like any other, and using it made it stronger.

I tested my abilities just a bit longer. I wiggled into the low level telepath's mind, then withdrew. The person watching from behind the mirror was still as unreadable as one of the synthetic neural shields the Institute and the Company deployed. My gift was healing, but not fast enough. At this rate, I would never regain my former abilities, even if I lived a long and fruitful life—which was far from certain at the moment. I clenched my jaw and moved my attention back to the low-level telepath in front of me.

His presence told an interesting story. Evidently, the Organization didn't know how much higher my teleprojection rating was now than when they'd taken my biocard from me. Or maybe they just didn't have anyone else to send? That scenario was unlikely. I was in one of their bases, which meant they had plenty of personnel to send. This telepath was here because whoever was in charge of this interrogation wanted him here. I pulled his name from his mind.

"Taylor Scott. Funny, one of my covers was a relative of yours." I crossed my legs and leaned back in the chair—ignoring the way the chains around my wrists pulled with that motion. They hadn't given me very much rope. Perhaps they knew just how dangerous I was. "I assume you have some questions for me."

His eyebrows shot up. Whether or not his bosses knew about my rating was still debatable, but they certainly hadn't told him.

"Crystal Farina. At one point in time, you were Agent 32. Correct?"

I restrained the urge to roll my eyes. What a useless question. "You've got a picture of me in that folder you're holding. You tell me."

The man pressed his lips together. "Just answer."

I twisted my lips into a smile fueled by sheer frustration. This conversation was useless. I wanted to talk to Medina or Ms. Green—someone who could actually answer my questions."I'm Crystal Farina, Agent 32. Before my biocard was taken, I was a PS6.5 almost PS 7. Then I shot up to probably a PS 13. I was taken down to a PS 2 and now I'm resting somewhere between a PS3 and PS5."

There was no clearer way to inform everyone that I could, indeed, read my interrogator. It was something like repaying a favor—considering that they hadn't shot me outright. Now we were even.

I ignored the man in front of me and, instead, arched an eyebrow at whoever was behind the glass. "Is that enough information for you?"

The fluctuations in the half-silvered mirror weren't enough for me to reconstruct exactly who was watching me, but I was getting closer. If I could get them to shift around a bit, maybe I could ID them. My bets were on Ms. Green or Joseph Medina. "No? How about this. I've taken out more Superiors and Institute bases singlehandedly than the entirety of the Organization has in its history. I think that gives me the right to ask a few questions." I slapped a hand on the table with a crack. The interrogator flinched. The person behind the glass didn't so much as shift. "Why did you bring me in?"

I watched the glass, but the fluctuations in the mirror had stopped. Well, so much for that tactic.

The interrogator recovered quickly, and tossed a few pictures of Houston in his new face down on the table. "Do you know who this is?"

I looked at the pictures with disgust. He looked so innocent in the pictures, staring out at me with those blameless hazel eyes. I shuddered. "I'd lie and say no, but whoever's monitoring my thoughts in there would know. That's Doug Houston. A murderer, probably a rapist, and works for the Organization. Oh, and you gave him a new face so he could spy on me."

"When you attacked him, you knew he worked for the Organization?"

I snorted. What kind of an idiot was this guy? Of course I knew. I'd just told him that. "You'd have been angry, too. He's tried to kill me on more than one occasion. You can't blame a girl for punching him in the face. I didn't do any real damage, and you know it. Next time, pick someone who I know a little less well to watch me."

"He tried to kill you? When?" The interrogator asked.

I scanned his thoughts, but he wasn't kidding. He honestly had no clue about my history with Houston. "Before I worked for the Agency, he was trying to kill a girl on her grad assignment named Tabitha Smith. I came to her defense, and in response he and his friends—in hindsight, I think they were Company watch-dogs—attacked me. The second time was when we tried to take him in. He'd just killed Earl West, the Company's recruiter at Martial Academy, and I was impersonating a Company operative. I was unarmed, and he put two bullet holes in me right here." I twisted my bound hands around to point at my abdomen. The tiny blemishes the Agency's medical pods had left were still there. The memory of Houston's boot pressing me into the dirt while he pulled the trigger and laughed at my moans was just as vivid as the day it had happened. I blinked the images away. "Not only did he try to kill me, but the rest of Tac 47 as well. It's all in the mission report."

The interrogator paled just slightly. Yeah, he'd heard about Tac 47. They were one of the few Agency teams to survive the merge mostly unscathed. Vera Hunt had joined them as the Company's representative in the team, and politics had been satisfied.

I leaned forward on the table and lowered my voice so anyone would have to strain to hear. People tended to pay more attention to information they had to work for. "I would have been completely and totally within my right if I had shot him, but I didn't. I threw him against a wall and socked him. If you'd like to see the events through my eyes, I would be more than happy to share them with you. If you've read my file, you know of my mental capabilities. Bring me an interface device, and we'll do it here and now."

The interrogator shook his head, spun his chair around, and straddled it. In response, I pulled on my speed and sat forward to match his posture—although the handcuffs prevented me from turning my chair around.

He didn't even pause. "Why were you even in that club?"

"An untraceable, encrypted email. InDep got it, 18 hours and 29 minutes ago." I thanked the fact that the sedative hadn't put me far enough out to completely disorient my clock. "The data is information pulled from an Instructor. It's the same intel your guys were there to pick up. I had technology they didn't, so I pulled it first and sent it over. Too bad I'm on some of your kill lists, or I would have handed it over personally." I looked pointedly at the people on the other side of the glass. "Any more questions?"

I could feel the annoyance wafting off the interrogator, but I didn't acknowledge it. I was faster and smarter than any operative they had. I knew it, and they knew it. The fact that they sent this low power idiot in meant that the real interrogator was on the other side of the glass.

"One more." The interrogator was obviously listening to the nearly-invisible earbug he wore. I was severely tempted to ask the person evidently dictating the question to ask me to my face, but I suppressed the impulse at the last second. I didn't really need to tick off any more people than I already had. "Have you ever killed another agent of the Organization?"

I raised my eyebrows and looked at the mirror. "You obviously don't know me too well if you think I came here willingly. I have one rule, and I have never broken it. Superiors? Instructors? They're fair game, but I have never and will never kill another human being. It's a good thing for your agents, too. Being hunted down like an animal tries a girl's patience."

The interrogator nodded and gathered the pictures back into the folder. A few moments later, I was alone. That solitude didn't last long, though. Exactly fifteen minutes later, Joseph Medina walked through the door in a white collared shirt and dark jeans—looking the same as the day I'd met him. At one point in time, he'd been the director of InDep. He'd been feeding Tolden and I information as he found missions the Organization either wouldn't or couldn't accomplish by themselves. After his phone call earlier, I hadn't expected to see him here, but he'd never really been one for predictability.

"32. You're in some deep water." He sat down in the chair opposite me, and straddled it the way the interrogator had. I was instantly wary. Medina ran InDep, which meant he had a whole lot of mental tools, and probably more practical ones for interrogation.

"Yes, sir, I know that. I don't see why you brought me here in the first place, though. I wasn't doing you any harm and, let's face it, you got a whole lot of intel while I was out there on my own."

Medina regarded me coolly. "No. We got a lot of unsubstantiated, anonymous data."

I bared my teeth. "It was better than nothing—and let's be honest. If any of the Organization's agents had even tried to go up against that Instructor, they would have all died horrible, excruciating deaths. I got you the intel, didn't I?"

"This isn't about intel, Farina. This is about your lawlessness. No one in the Organization knows what to do with you. After that incident with King, you went off the reservation. You're cocky, arrogant, and some people think you're more dangerous than the Superiors are."

My eyes flashed. "There's no argument about that. I *am* more dangerous than the Superiors are, and that's a good thing. Sir, I don't know if whoever's running the Organization now knows what the Instructors are trying to create, but when they finally manage to make an Alpha-Superior, we're going to be in a land of hurt. If I'm all you've got, then you'd better take me, and hope that more people like me show up. We're the only thing you've got. Telepaths and Telekinetics aren't going to slow these Alphas down in the slightest.

"Remember Ms. King and how she registered on our scales? She tripled them. The Alpha-Superiors will quadruple them, and they're mass-producible. You need me, and you had better tell the others that, too."

Medina leaned in. "And what if they don't believe you?"

I looked him straight in the eye. "Then we will all be taken by the Institute and be *evolved*. Ask Briggs how much he liked that." I clenched my teeth in pain as I thought of the light fading from Briggs's eyes after Tabitha shot him. For just a moment, I could feel his blood running over my face. The Institute killed my friend, and then forced us to destroy his body. Medina didn't understand what that was like to look at the walking corpse of one of the few people that had been kind, and then shoot him. No one could. But if dragging up this old pain could shock Medina into understanding what I was saying, it was worth it.

Medina's expression didn't change as he scrutinized my face. It was like he was trying to stare into my soul. I couldn't tell if he was inside my head or not, but I wouldn't be surprised.

Finally, his eyes glazed over as he listened to a projection. He pulled a ring of silver keys out of his pocket and unlocked my handcuffs. "You've got a second chance, 32. Don't mess it up."

I arched an eyebrow. "I'd better not, sir. If I do, we're all dead."

CHAPTER EIGHT

Medina held the door open, and I saw the agents outside the door. "Stand down, and escort Miss Farina to her quarters."

I counted the agents as they relaxed their energy rifles. There were four. I smiled. Had I decided to leave, these agents couldn't have stopped me, but at least they took my danger rating seriously. I stretched and yawned. My muscles were cramped from my awkward sitting position while I was sedated, and my left leg tingled sinisterly. "If we hurry, you can still hit the mess before it closes."

There was no reaction from any of the agents, and I shrugged. I was likely on some sort of probation until they needed me so much they couldn't afford to keep me benched any longer. This was the closest thing to a vacation I'd had in over a year. The thought struck me as funny, and I smothered an adrenaline-fueled giggle.

The guard escorted me down the hallway, and it was only after the second turn of the base, into a hallway that shouldn't have existed, that I realized that we were not under Martial Academy. I made a mental note to figure out where we were just as soon as the opportunity arose, and started working on a map. I was so engrossed in synthesizing mental hallways and labeling doors that I nearly missed it as a tac operative—this one in full strike gear, helmet and all—walked up to the group and mentioned for us to stop. He exchanged some words with one of the agents, and they changed spots. The original agent jogged down the hallway. We made it almost to the lift before another agent traded off for another helmeted figure. I grit my teeth and ran the numbers. They came back borderline inconclusive, but my gut told me that this wasn't going to be good. When the third tac operative switched off, I prepped for violence.

Preliminary numbers spun in my mind. There was only one reason for grunts to be switching off like this, and it was internal politics. I started another round of analysis in the back of my mind to try trying to calculate the possibilities, but I didn't have enough background information to get an accurate conclusion.

The most likely scenario was that the helmeted strike operatives were Company agents, and they were getting ready to subdue me. I was still on the kill lists, and the Company still really, really hated me—or I wouldn't have been here to begin with. When we exited the lift, the final agent switched out, and I stiffened. If anything was going to happen, it would happen now. Then the analysis that had been running in the back of my mind finished. Movement patterns, musculature, and voices all combined to make me grin. I released my martial stance and shook my head.

"What is this, a party? You'd better not be planning any sort of initiation," I said. The new agents removed their strike helmets so I could see their faces. Suddenly, I was surrounded by friends I hadn't seen in a year. Tac 47 was here. The relief was enough to make me weak-kneed, but I held it together and turned to Tolden—who had been the last to arrive. I flashed him a smile. "I'm glad you're not in lockup."

He shrugged. "I was for a while. Medina released me—said they'd managed to straighten things out."

"What about the helmets?" I asked. Last I'd heard, Flex Tactical Teams weren't being issued Strike gear unless they were responding to an inherently violent situation.

Steele waggled his fingers at me, a flush already creeping up his freckled face.

I punched his shoulder.

"Hey, what was that for?" He gave his best injured expression, and Hunt laughed.

I just shook my head and pivoted so I could see each of my friends as they crowded around me. Hunt was taller than I remembered and just as intimidating, but she grinned at me as I met her eyes. Something in her had—not softened, exactly, but relaxed. She wore an easy grin in place of her usual unreadable expression. Steele's hair was shorter, but still just as bleach white. The only one who hadn't changed was Black. He was still tall and broad-shouldered, and he still wasn't smiling, even though I could feel how pleased he was.

"It's good to see you all," I said, "I have to say, you do have a way of making a girl nervous; switching out with Medina's agents."

Hunt put her hands on her hips. "Nervous? You were spoiling for a fight."

Tolden laughed. "An honest fight would do you good, Crystal. I'm tired of watching you take on a dozen Superiors at a time. You can always guarantee that someone is cheating. Now come on. Before we can get to that, Medina has asked us to make sure you get to R&D safely, and then stay safe."

I pursed my lips at his words. The fact that Medina had sent Tac 47 to make sure I reached my destination safely meant that my fear of the agents switching out wasn't totally unfounded. "Thank you, sir." I looked around, still uneasy. "I think we should go. Lounging around in the hall is fun and all, but I have to admit, I'm a little anxious to get down to nerd town." In my year on the run, any tinkering that wasn't directly related to my survival had taken a back seat. I had a pile up a mile long of archived designs. The thought of finally being able to revisit some of them made goosebumps prickle up on my skin.

"32, they're giving you your biocard back." Tolden said. I wondered, for a moment, about the significance of having a biocard installation taking place in R&D instead of Medical, and then dismissed the thought. While the Organization kept quite a bit of the Agency's framework, they had also changed a lot.

I arched my eyebrows. They were giving my old mental abilities back? "How did you manage that?" The last time I'd had my biocard, I'd broken the first cardinal rule for strong teleprojectors. I'd frozen Ms. Green's agents, and implanted information directly in her mind. My gift had been so strong that even her walls couldn't keep me out. For a few, brief moments, I had been unstoppable. That had terrified the Agency and, according to Medina, it still terrified the Organization. So why were they giving my abilities back?

Tolden's eyes were guarded. "I didn't do anything. You're a bit of a legend in the Tac section, though. There hasn't been another 32 since you left. When we moved central operations to Indianapolis, they moved all your stuff from Academy Base to your locker here. Someone knew you were coming back."

I blinked. Could it be that Medina had always planned to bring me back in, and that Houston had made a good excuse? Or was there another game being played here?

I thought about voicing my suspicions, but I bared my teeth instead. "I'm glad to hear that. I've got a couple things to get in the production stream as soon as I get back on my feet." I followed the arrow that pointed towards R&D.

In the new silence, I swallowed some bitterness at the fact that we were in Indianapolis. The forward tactical base for the Organization had been under my nose the whole time, and I'd missed it. I thought I'd been hundreds of miles away from their operations. I thought I'd found my own playground. The truth was that I'd been invading theirs the entire time. No wonder they'd come after me with such persistence after I socked Houston. They had probably assumed I had known I was playing in their sandbox. Suddenly Medina calling me arrogant made far more sense. Who else would have had the gumption to assault one of their operatives, less than three minutes from their center of operations, then think she could get away with it?

"I've heard tales of some sort of shielding unit." Steele said to break the silence. He turned with a wink. "How's the software working? Does it need an upgrade?"

I smiled. When I'd first designed the module, it had needed software I couldn't just hardwire in like a rube-goldberg machine so I'd briefed Tolden, who'd told Steele about the project. A thumb drive with the software I needed showed up on Emily's doorstep a few days later. "It's saved my bacon multiple times. If you want to tune it up a bit, go ahead."

Steele skipped a step down the hall, then pulled his tablet out and succeeded in nearly running over an unwary tech in R&D off-white as he started typing. Tolden grabbed him out of the way, then mouthed an apology at the R&D tech, who grinned. Steele ignored the entire exchange, still focused on his new project.

"Will the shielding unit be widely used?" Hunt asked as the poor R&D tech got out of hearing range.

I shrugged. "Depends—but I'm thinking so. It's done good things to help me. It will probably have fewer functions, though."

Black snorted. "Is this the thing that sent half the base to the medward?"

I winced. That explained the rest of the reason why they didn't want me out on the street. I'd only intended to take out the people who were pursuing me, not a base full of telepaths.

"I can see why that particular function won't be widely used. Talk about friendly fire," Steele said.

"You're one to talk," Black grumbled, and smacked Steele on the back of the head.

Then we were there. Tolden opened the door and I entered the room. It looked just like the one at Martial Academy. Only the people standing there were different—well, everyone but Robbins, who was at the head of the group. I hesitated. The last time I'd let him into my head, he'd messed with my memories.

"Tolden, you and the others will be here, right? You'll be monitoring me?" The thought of laying there, helpless while these people messed with my brain was enough to make me wish I was armed again. I had no idea where their loyalties lay. I could be on any one of their kill lists, and never know. Of course, people in R&D didn't have kill lists, but it was the theory of the thing.

"Paranoid much?" Hunt asked.

"A year of being hunted by the people in this building would do that, yes."

Tolden slipped his fingers through mine and squeezed. "We'll be here the whole time. You acted as a barrier between the worst of the Institute and us. For these few hours, we can be a barrier between you and the Organization. When you get out, you won't need our help anymore." There was a note of anticipation in his voice. In just a few hours, Tac 47 would be whole again—the top tactical team playing the big game in the fight against the Institute. I would be back on the team, and we would be unstoppable.

I smiled my first real smile of the day. "Thank you, Tolden. For everything." Then I released his hand and surrendered myself to the R&D medical techs.

CHAPTER NINE

I awoke to chatter so loud it split my head with pain. I covered my ears and groaned. A million different voices wailed in my head—building like a siren. Something was wrong. Really, really, wrong. I pried my eyes open, but I was alone in a white-washed room, empty except for the dark, silent monitors next to my bed and the cabinets lining the right hand wall. Words so loud they were unintelligible screamed at me, like lunchtime at Martial Academy had been recorded for a year, then replayed all at once through a speaker cranked up as high as it would go. I covered my ears, tried to sort through the sounds, but the noise only grew. It had to be my telepathic ability. I focused on the silence and tried to bring up my shields, but nothing was working. The control that allowed me to change the frequency of my walls were gone. My mental fingers tugged futilely at the air, grasping nothing. The voices only got louder. My mental fingers disintegrated. Pressure built in my mind, splitting my skull.

I screamed.

I needed help and I needed it now. My eyes landed on a red button on the wall between my bed and the cabinets. I swung my legs out of bed and stumbled toward the button. I smashed it with my fist as a high pitched scream obliterated every thought but pain. Agony like a knife slid through every cell in my body, but I was helpless to stop it. I collapsed to the ground, curling in on myself. Everything hurt too much! An alarm blared at the edge of my hearing, quickly drowned out by the press of voices.

People rushed into the room. Hands grabbed me—checked for injuries, but they were looking in the wrong place.

"R&D…Neural Dampers…hurry." I managed before my throat spasmed shut in a single decimating wave, responding to the agony in my brain. The man who had reached me first relayed the order and one of the people hurried out. He tried to ask me a question, but I didn't even have enough focus to try and read his lips. The structures that had automatically handled tasks like that were gone. I couldn't find them while I was trapped inside this haze of agony. I tried to communicate what was happening, but the message was garbled.

"Too much…no shield…fractured."

I didn't know if the words had actually been said out loud, but he must have gotten some of it. He yelled something to his assistants as he helped me back into the bed. After two excruciating minutes, the assistant hurried back in with a piece of technology in her hand. She fiddled with it, but couldn't seem to get it to work.

I held out my hands, and the woman placed it there. I flipped the switch and twisted the dial past safe limits—grateful that my shaking hands could do that much, at least. A couple of the people in the room looked like they were going to pass out as the field blanketed the room and they went mind blind, but the noise in my head lessened to a garbled chatter, and I remembered to breathe.

The pain receded. I lay there, sweating, panting, as someone I should have recognized stared at me. He had a kind face that was twisted into a worried knot. One hand held onto the bottom corner of my bedpost for balance. A telepath, then. His name was still out of reach.

My mind felt sluggish, as if I'd just had a seizure, but I could speak. "Close the door. Telepaths…shouldn't be here. Damping field can hurt."

The doctor, easily identified by his white coat with Med-Dep emblazoned in silver on the pocket, nodded to the two nurses leaning against the counter for balance. They fled. The doctor looked at the telepath, also in a MedDep coat, who was holding onto my bed. The telepath shook his head.

"Robbins, you can't tell me this won't be a problem," the doctor said.

Robbins? His face flashed in my mind, overlaying with the man I saw standing there. His face was slightly pale— understandable given that his teleprojection abilities were almost as strong as mine had been before they took my bio-card. Standing in the same room as my neural damper had to be excruciating.

"I said I'd take care of it. Anyone who knows how to help with a problem best solved by neural dampers is going to be impacted by the field, anyway. You have other patients," Robbins said.

The other doctor shrugged. "Fine, but don't say I didn't warn you." A moment later, he was gone and Robbins and I were alone in the room.

"What happened?" he asked.

I thought for a moment, but the instant analysis I'd grown used to during my time running from the Organization didn't come. I focused and pulled the blue lines onto my vision. They limped around, nearly as slow as the time Mr. West had given me a concussion, evaluating the data my brain sent at snail speed. My fingers curled into fists.

"I—I don't know." The admission was bitter on my tongue. The words were globular; undefined. The blue lines moved to try and make sense of the sounds, but it was useless.

Robbins used his free hand to rub his temples. "The damping field is helping, so whatever it is has to do with your gift. What happened when you woke up?"

That analysis, at least, was ready. I opened my mouth to explain—I *knew* the lines had finished that work—but the words didn't come. I clenched my teeth and opened the report that blinked on my vision.

A white screen filled with data opened on my vision, like I'd held a paper up to my face. Robbins stared at me, patient as always, as I read the data off. "I've got a huge surge in data input from the moment I woke up—most of it undefined. It swamped my analysis capabilities, triggered a pain response. A subroutine activated and re-routed all available processing. When reinforcements still couldn't handle the load, additional pain response was activated. The overload blew out a dozen processing channels, and I started bleeding data. What I couldn't process, I tried to discard. I couldn't discard enough, and it blew a few more channels."

Tears rose to my eyes as I watched the deceptively simple stream of numbers that described my brain's self-destruct. "The blown channels only further overloaded the still functioning ones. The last entry here shows an emergency subroutine coming into effect, routing all processing to manual and shunting all excess data to the archive to be overwritten."

Robbins was unfazed. "Can you tell if there's any permanent damage?"

I closed my eyes and tried to access the blown subroutines. Data drifted in a dark abyss like the scattered corpses of dreams too good to be true. Nothing moved in the graveyard of my mind. No machinery came to put the data back together. It was dark, silent, and cold.

I shuddered and shoved the image away. "I don't know. Yes. Maybe."

Back in my working mind where blue lines still struggled to sort information and complete the preliminary analysis, a dozen reports blinked for my attention. My head still throbbed. A dull ache eating away at my mind. "What could have happened to create so much data?" I asked.

Robbins's face twisted again, but I couldn't interpret the expression. "You said before that you were a PS2 after we took your biocard? You were back to a PS4 by the time we brought you back in?"

I nodded. Blue lines started working on another problem, but I couldn't tell what.

"My guess is that the additional stress caused by your last year as a low level teleprojector caused a net increase in your abilities. It isn't unheard of for a teleprojector's abilities to increase even while their shields remain constant. When we boosted your abilities again with this new biocard, you may have outstripped your shields—which were likely still damaged from the first removal. Without the ability to protect your mind from the excess data generated by your gift, your processing centers took damage. It was a protection mechanism. Without it, you would have probably gone insane."

I wanted to scream. Robbins said it so simply—like this slow, stupid feeling was a good thing. I wanted my mind back. I needed to feel that lightning fast connection of solving a problem. Now *algebra* took three-point-two seconds to compute!

"I'm fractured." I couldn't hear the defeat in my voice, but I didn't need to. Black despair filled every vein in my body. Tears I was tired of fighting rolled helplessly down my cheeks as revulsion chased despair. I never cried, especially not in front of others—and not in front of *Robbins*, who had invaded my mind twice and stolen my biocard from me.

But the tears just wouldn't stop, and my muscles were so tired I couldn't even wipe them away. I just layed there, helpless.

None of this would have happened if the Agency had let me keep my biocard. None of this would have happened if the Organization had just kept their distance. I had been doing just fine! Now I was useless, slow, and stupid.

The door flew open as Robbins opened his mouth to give me empty consolation. Tolden stood in the doorway with the rest of Tac 47. "32, are you alright?" He asked. He was breathing hard, like he'd just run here. He started to enter the room, then caught himself in the doorway as the damping field shut his telepathy down.

Another tear rolled down my face. How could I tell him that my mind was a graveyard of useless, broken programs? I looked back at Robbins, then at Tolden. I'd come here ready to get my psionic abilities back and, instead, I broke. I couldn't fight the Institute like this.

Robbins turned and said something I couldn't see, much less decipher. Then he left.

Tolden's eyes were hard. He waved Hunt inside, then shut the door behind him, leaning on it to keep from falling over.

Hunt sat on the side of the bed, eyebrows knit together with something between confusion and concern. "Was it an overload?"

I nodded as another tear rolled down my face. I couldn't stop them. I was just so broken. "Think of the worst overload you've ever had and then triple it. My mind fractured to protect itself, and now I'm slow." My analysis ability was gone. My brain was sluggish. My muscles were weak. Everything hurt. I couldn't handle this.

Hunt slipped her hand around mine. "How slow? As slow as while you were at Martial Academy?"

I shook my head. "Worse." I couldn't ever remember this kind of idiotic slugishness. My blue lines could barely hold themselves together. I had to force them to complete their tasks, and then they just laid there. I had been slow during my year at Martial Academy—compared to my mind after the fight with Ms. King, anyway—but this was far more awful.

Hunt's face shifted, but I couldn't tell what emotion was written there. "We'll get through this. Yeah? We'll do it together. Your mind is one of the most brilliant things I've ever seen. And your abilities are still coming back, right? It takes time for things to heal, but once your mind starts coming back together, you can use your wonderful little tools to heal your mind the rest of the way."

She didn't understand. There was no way to tell how much of this was permanent, and how much of this was not. I couldn't heal my own mind if I couldn't even understand it!

I scraped enough of myself together to give her a fake smile. "Maybe." I doubted it, though. The Social Niceties program was blinking in the corner of my mind. I stifled a groan. Not again! I'd spent years with that program prompting my words and actions. Mom had helped me put it together, and it *did* help. It was also the single most annoying program in my rubbish pile of a brain. I took a deep breath. "Thank you, Hunt."

Hunt stepped back and let Tolden take her place at my bedside.

"What can we do to help?" he asked, which only sent another wave of guilt through my system. I should have been able to analyze the situation, work up a damage report, and create a plan of action. I should have been able to create a roadmap to recovery. If I couldn't even do that, what hope was there?

I'd told Medina that I was the only hope the Organization had. Without me, the Institute would walk all over them. I wasn't just slow, now, I was putting everyone in danger. If I couldn't stop the Institute, who could? What chance did we have against the Institute?

I was a failure.

The thought pounded at my mind with an inevitable rhythm. Everyone was depending on me and I let them down. The Institute would win, and it would be all my fault.

I shrugged helplessly. "I don't know...I—I can't do this, Tolden. I'm supposed to protect everyone. I can't do that if I'm fractured."

He shook his head. "You *can* do that if you're fractured. You can't do that if you're a mess. If you could beat Ms. King fractured, you can beat Superiors fractured. You've got a much higher rating now."

I wanted to protest, to tell him that I hadn't been fractured when I took down Ms. King, in fact, that was the only thing that had saved me, but I didn't. Complaining wouldn't be of any use. And what he'd said about a higher rating was probably true. If I was in any condition to test the card, I would know for sure, but I couldn't. In order to test my card, I would have to turn off the neural damper. My stomach twisted at the thought.

Still, a PS 13? Who had ever heard of such a thing? That was one of the reasons they had taken my biocard to begin with. Now, it was the only thing that could compensate for how slow I was, but I couldn't use any of that power. Instead of just taking my power away, the Organization had used it as a weapon to cripple me.

I stifled another sob as I looked at the neural damper clutched between my frail fingers. This was now a permanent fixture in my life.

CHAPTER TEN

I drowsed for the next two days, drifting in and out of sleep, sifting through subroutines, adjusting information flows, fighting the blue lines Mom had helped me create as a child. They weren't nearly as versatile as I remembered them being, and I couldn't tell if that was because I'd grown used to a happy, whole mind, or if the overloaded processing channels had created some sort of error. Probably a mixture of both.

The neural damper turned all the chatter in my mind to a tolerable drone, so when I grew tired of fighting to fix my brain, I stopped to listen to the conversational buzz around me. Most thoughts were inane and fractured by distance. Food. Friends. Occasionally a tactical officer with a chip on her shoulder would walk by. Apparently something was wrong with her biocard, so R&D had been pestering her with tests. She was stuck here until they were all done because the Organization didn't let tactical officers leave the base unless they were fully operational—which didn't make me feel any better. As soon as I sorted through enough of the chaos in my mind to become functional again, I wanted to start preparing for missions again. Using the annoyed tactical officer as a measuring stick, though, I wasn't going to be set loose any time soon.

A new conversation caught my attention as I trudged through the tar pit of mental voices that coated my mind. Tolden was right outside my door, with…Joseph Medina? I focused on the conversation as best I could, and caught the words drifting from their minds even before they said them. Walls were no barrier to my telepathic gift—not with this neural damper, anyway.

Tolden was the most agitated I'd ever felt him, and Medina was calm, although a morsel of guilt was starting to eat at his mind.

A surge of anger from Tolden. "Don't tell me she'll be alright. You haven't seen her."

"I assure you, Robbins gave me a full report. I'm entirely aware of Miss Farina's situation."

"Sir, respectfully, I've seen Farina get shot, blown up, and kicked out of the Agency. Not once did she cry. I don't think you understand just how badly she's hurting in there."

The outer layers of Medina's thoughts stilled like the eye of a storm as deeper thoughts I couldn't quite reach raged. "Agent Tolden, are you attempting to make a point?"

"Yes sir, I am." Tolden's words were biting. "You advocated that she be ejected from the Agency. You didn't want her messing up your brilliantly laid plans to take out the Institute. Then, on a dime, you bring her back here and have Robbins put that thing back in her head. Did you know what it would do to her?"

Anger lanced through Medina's mind like a lightning strike, and dissipated just as quickly. He measured his words, then doled them out deliberately—each word carefully put in its place. "Miss Farina does not deserve to be caught up in this fight—but she insisted, and here we are. I have no control over who the Director orders detained, and who he does not. Personally, I would prefer to have her staying in the tactical wing rather than the prison ward. Wouldn't you?"

Tolden was silent for a moment. His anger cooled abruptly, and I felt a small measure of shame creep in. Medina was one of his superiors. He shouldn't have spoken like that. "She's hurting, and I don't know how to help." The words were inadequate to express the mix of guilt and fear at his core. What if Crystal never recovered? He was the one who had sent her to that club to get that data. He was the one who had put her in Houston's crosshairs. He was the one who had taken her to R&D, then assured her that everything would be alright. This was his fault, more than anyone's, and he didn't know how to make it okay.

Medina's thoughts softened. "It's never easy to see our friends go through difficult times. All you can do is stand by her—and protect her as best you can. She'll get through it. She comes from strong, stubborn stock."

The words, formed in Medina's head just before they were spoken, made me jerk up. I pictured Mom in my mind. She wasn't stubborn. Mom was kind, and gentle, and good at heart, but no one would ever mistake her kindness for stubborness.

Did Medina know my father?

"Yes sir," Tolden responded. His thoughts were slightly stiffer now.

Medina's thoughts hardened again, and I could imagine him leveling a stern look at Tolden. "Good. Now, it would be best not to throw accusations like that around. The Organization is far from stable, and upsetting the wrong person could prove…dangerous."

Medina moved on without waiting for a response.

Tolden stood in front of my doorway, wondering whether he should enter, or if I would still be asleep. After a long time, he turned and walked away. I closed my eyes again against the constant pain in my head. I shouldn't have spent so much time listening with my gift. I made a mental note to boost the power to the neural damper so I could shut out the jabbering voices more completely. Then I stored the conversation for later analysis and hoped that it would still be there once my lines got sorted out enough to actually do what they were supposed to be doing.

The lift door opened with a hiss, and I moved onto the R&D floor. One hand traced the wall in case a bout of dizziness tried to knock me down again. I'd managed to make it from Medical to here without falling, and I wasn't going to break that streak. This new base was organized in levels, without a central gathering area like the Rotunda. The Medical section where they'd moved me after I'd fractured was only two levels below R&D, and one level above Tactical. If I could make it up two flights of stairs, I could finish getting down the hall.

The ball in my hand pulsed as another telepath came into range, and I moved on quickly as he leaned against the wall to keep his balance. It had been almost two weeks since I'd fractured, and this was my first time outside of the medical ward—for a reason. The damper field was cranked up enough that high power telepaths couldn't be in the same room without temporarily losing their ability. For someone who had come to rely on telepathy for almost everything, it was both disorienting and painful to suddenly lose access to that power. I knew exactly how much that impacted everything. That was why Steele had gone ahead to clear out most of the non-essential telepaths from R&D bay 1.

"I think we're almost clear," he reported, after a moment.

His lips moved like lightning, and then he stuck his head back inside the research bay. The doors closed behind him, hesitated, and then opened back up as I approached.

Some of the people in off-white lab coats stopped to stare at me as I entered, but I didn't recognize any of the faces, and no one said a word. I made my way to one of the empty workstations and pulled some pieces from the box at the end. This room was set up very much like it's Academy Base counterpart, down to the separate workstations, and the array of materials kept at each. This wasn't the same as the workstation I'd left abandoned at Academy Base, but it was close, and everything I needed was within grabbing distance.

As I started to lay out the pieces to match the blueprint my blue lines presented, a voice rang across the room. "Hey, who are you, and who gave you the clearance to be here?"

I turned at the sound, and watched the man's lips.

"Sorry, I didn't catch that." I repressed a surge of self-hatred. One moment, sounds were just fine, and the next, I was back to lip reading.

"Who are you, and why are you in here?" The man was tall, and wore a supervisor's lanyard, which suspended an I.D. card labeled Carson Reed. "Your damping field is disrupting the normal functioning of this lab."

I frowned. Why couldn't Cal have been on duty? Another thought followed, and I swallowed hard. Had she even survived the merge?

I looked back at Reed, flicked a look up at his eyes, and then bent my head to study the floor as my gift surged up to try and get inside his head. Voices started to scream, and I winced. Two breaths later, they had faded again. I formed a response. "I'm Agent 32. Sorry. I've got to—" There was another surge of voices, and the words I had lined up in my mind scattered. I grit my teeth, wishing that he would just leave me alone so I could work. "The damper. I've got to restrict the field."

I saw Reed stiffen out of the corner of my eye as I turned to resume my work. I lifted my eyes just enough to see his lips. "There is no Agent 32. There hasn't been since Farina went rogue and disappeared. I'm going to have to call security." He reached for a button on a silver cuff at his wrist, but Steele stepped in front of him. I released a breath in relief. I didn't have the processing space to deal with security right now.

"Sir, I apologize for the confusion. I'm Agent Steele from CIS—er, C-DAD. Occasionally, I help out as a software engineer down here."

Reed nodded for him to continue, and Steele released the breath he was holding. "Agent Farina was actually just recalled from the field. She was behind the disturbance in med lab 4 a while ago. I'm sure Security would verify it for you, if you want."

Reed squinted at me. "You're Farina? For real?"

I nodded.

He snorted, but his hand went back down to his side. "I thought you'd be taller."

I was six feet tall. I brushed the incongruity of his statement aside. It was probably just due to shock. The voices receded. I could think again. "Sorry to disappoint. Now, can I get back to my project, or do I need to worry about Security showing up?"

Reed flushed just a bit. "You can continue. Just hurry. If my boss comes down here and sees this, you're not going to be the only one in trouble."

I nodded, and turned my back to him so I could see the

table. I grabbed an extra power pack and wired it to the current damper. The voices died and, for the first time in years, the world was silent. Reed leaned closer to me, trying to get a good look at what I'd just done. I waited to see if I could feel his leaking curiosity through the field, but there was nothing. The Social Niceties program pinged, so I explained what I was doing. It would be good to have friends down in R&D again.

"I'm putting together a sort of headset for the neural damper," I said as I pulled another spool of wire from a drawer beneath the table. "It should reflect the damping field and focus it so that I can get rid of this infernal buzzing without making other telepaths in the room go mind blind." The nice thing about R&D workstations was that every workstation was kept individually stocked, so no one had to be wandering around the room the whole time. That was even more convenient when the person working at the station had almost no balance, and walking across the floor had more in common with walking a tightrope blind. I kept a steady hand on the desk in front of me and let it support my weight as I worked.

In a few days, my balance would be more-or-less corrected, when my blue lines finished fixing the processing relay that accepted information from my inner ear. As of now, most of that was going shunted to another relay, and information was being lost in the bypass.

Reed moved to the other end of the table and peered at the apparatus that was rapidly taking shape in my fingers.

"It certainly doesn't look like much," he said.

Steele gave him a lopsided grin. "That's alright. The device that disabled every telepath in the entire city a few weeks ago didn't look like much, either."

I took a moment to glare at him, and then bent all of my

focus on assembling the device. As much as they joked about it, I had a feeling that this device would really come in handy. I couldn't control my own shields, so the field would have to become my shield. I would have to have the ability to control how powerful the field was, at exactly the right moment. Before I'd attached the amplifier, I'd had the field turned all the way up, and my projection strength had still been bouncing around the PS 4 frequencies—just a little lower than where I'd been before they gave my biocard back. The difference was that I had been able to hear every low frequency thought in the room and the hallway beyond it—which was better than the alternative. If I turned the damping field down at all, the buzzing at the edge of my mind swelled into a deafening roar. I hoped to be able to decrease the field, given some time, but this was where it would have to stay for now.

"Farina," a voice from outside my head called for me, but I didn't hear it.

"Farina," The voice grew a bit more insistent, and I looked up from the nearly completed device.

It was Steele. "Everyone else broke for lunch two hours ago, and Black's been trying to get ahold of you for almost as long. You need to take a break."

I looked back down at the mass of wires and metal. My blue lines ran an analysis, and I grinned. "Give me sixty-eight more seconds." I was almost done, so leaving it unfinished would be silly. Plus, having the device would allow me to walk into a room of telepaths without half of them having to leave because they'd gone mindblind.

"Still as accurate as ever," came a dry voice.

Steele tapped me on the shoulder, and I turned. "Robbins?"

My fingers curled into fists as I looked at him standing

there, absolutely calm. He was Medina's pet teleprojector. He'd checked in on me a few times in Medical, but he couldn't do anything about my situation—not without getting inside my head, and I was never going to let him do that again. The last time I'd let him in, he'd wiped every image of D, the Instructor the Agency had captured, from my mind and given me a month's worth of headaches. Then he'd taken my biocard out, and now he'd put it back in, which had crippled me. I didn't hold him responsible. If the Organization as a whole hadn't ordered it, he wouldn't have done it. That said, he was a meddler, and I was a fair way toward hating him right about now.

"What do you want?" I tried to keep my voice level, but there was no way to tell if I'd succeeded.

"I just wanted to come by and make sure you were still doing alright. I hear that one of your tac team members couldn't get a hold of you."

I frowned. While he could be here of his own volition, the blue lines on my vision told another story. Medina had asked Robbins to check up on me.

"I can still take care of myself, you know," I said. The last thing I needed was to appear weak in front of these people.

He nodded. "No one said you couldn't. Just be careful, 32. The Organization is different than the Agency was. Not everything is as it appears."

Then he just turned, and walked away.

Steele hissed. "That was some message. Hurry up, Farina, and let's go find Black."

I nodded. Now was not the time to be caught alone in the Organization. I didn't know who I'd angered, or how, but whoever it was held enough power in the Organization to make Medina nervous.

CHAPTER ELEVEN

My head banged against the mat, and the blue lines scattered again.

"Come on, Farina. You're never going to beat a Superior like that." Black helped me back to my feet.

"Do you think I don't know that?" I turned away and stalked towards the bench. Anger, undiluted and unrestrained ran through my blood like lava. I was getting so tired of being thrown on the mat like my first year at Martial Academy. I'd gotten over that. I'd gotten faster, and now I was back to square one.

Tolden frowned. "Farina, we need Tac 47 out there—get your head in the game."

"So clear me, already," I snapped. After I'd finished the damper device, it had been two weeks of nonstop combat training and tests, and I was sick of it. My aim was still fantastic, but that was about it. I was slow, tired more easily, and my response time was roughly half what it had been at Martial Academy. I couldn't beat anyone in hand-to-hand, let alone Black, who had just been facing me on the mat. He was supposed to be helping me recover my old speed, but it didn't feel like helping when he tied me up in knots and then smirked as I struggled to untangle myself again.

My abilities weren't going to change anytime soon. It just took too much time to look at the data my blue lines outputted, interpret them, and then react. Not just that, but my blue lines were slower than they had been since I was six! Half my processing relays were still down. I'd managed to put two of them back together, but even that had barely increased my processing time. My abilities still fluctuated, in spite of the more powerful damping field. My teleprojection was out of control. Yes, I was the highest level telepath in the building—but I was also the slowest of them all.

"I can't do that until I know you're not going to get yourself—and us—killed in the field." Tolden didn't budge an inch, and his frown only deepened. He was our AIC, which meant that we didn't go out until he gave the green light.

"I'm not going to get anyone killed. I know my limits. I know I'm slow. I know my shields aren't healed, and I know there are dozens of people in this building that can beat me in a straight fight. That said, I'm not a child. Things aren't getting any better out there." I couldn't sit here, useless, as turnips were being taken off the street.

I wiped the sweat off my forehead with a towel from the bench as I watched Tolden think. Unfortunately, his thoughts weren't headed in the direction that would take Tac 47 off the bench. I focused my abilities. I'd learned more than combat skills in the year I'd been away from the organization, and finess was one of the most valuable things I'd learned. I may have been a glorified empath, but even empaths could get things done if they pulled on the right thought train.

"I'll find an easy mission for you," he finally agreed.

I arched my eyebrows even as I fought down an internal cheer. I wasn't completely helpless, after all! That wasn't an approach that would work in combat, and it wasn't an approach that could protect me from the bloodthirsty instincts of the Superiors, but it was better than nothing.

"You might want to think about that answer for a moment, Agent." A new voice entered the conversation, and I turned to identify the newcomer. Medina. And he hadn't missed that little bit of tampering I'd done. His face was closed, and his eyes were dark. Without my gift, I couldn't tell just how much trouble I was in.

Tolden spun around to look at his superior, and then jerked his head back to me with narrowed eyebrows as he realized what I'd done. I shrugged. There were a lot of things I'd learned out there in the big, bad, real world, and how to suggest things to others was one of them. There was only so much I could do as a PS 2, but I'd made the most of my gifts.

"Thank you, sir. I don't know that I would have caught that, otherwise." His voice was a careful monotone, but I could still feel his annoyance. Manipulation was a tricky subject, and manipulating someone on my team was beyond rude.

My cheeks flushed. I shouldn't have given into my impulse, but I wanted to get back out there so badly it hurt. I had to prove to them that I could still be an asset.

Medina shifted his attention from Tolden, to me. "That being said, I have a job for you and your team."

I stiffened. Really? That was great news! "Thank you, sir. I won't—"

Medina gave me a quelling stare, and my words died in my throat. "Miss Farina, I'm going to need you to surrender your weapons."

Miss Farina? That was hardly good. He usually called me Agent—or, he had while I worked for the Agency. And surrendering my weaponry? What kind of mission required that?

A sick feeling started in my stomach. What was Medina doing giving us a mission, anyway? He was with InDep, and we were a tactical team.

I clenched my teeth and considered the weaponry I had on me. There wasn't much to hand over. All I was allowed to keep on me outside the shooting range was the electric pulser on my tactical glove, and the only reason I had that was because I'd smuggled out a demonstration model I'd made for R&D.

Medina held out his hand, but I didn't budge. I didn't hold any illusions about my status in the Organization, or my ability to defend myself without a weapon. Black had just proved that I wasn't going to be beating anyone in hand-to-hand. Going around unarmed in this facility would quickly end with me being very dead. The only reason there hadn't been an attack yet was because Tac 47 had been taking turns on guard duty. I hadn't been alone since the moment I'd set foot in this facility.

"Sir, are you sure this is a good idea?" Surely he had to understand the danger I was in. Was he trying to get me killed?

Medina's lips thinned. "Perhaps not, but this is the only way you and your team will be getting off the bench. The alternative is you being transferred to R&D on a permanent basis."

Once upon a time, I would have welcomed that change with open arms. Now, I hesitated. The fight against the Institute was so much larger than me. Even without my combat capabilities, I would be useful in the field. More than that, I didn't trust the Organization to handle the situation by themselves.

This whole thing stunk of internal politics, and I wrinkled my nose, still thinking. What was my alternative? The thought of defying Medina while I was like this—slow, and armed only with an electropulser—was enough to make me shiver. I had very few allies in this fight, and Medina was the most powerful one I had. I grit my teeth as his words came back to me. I didn't have to be buddy-buddy with him. I didn't even really have to trust him. The most important quality in an ally was that he had power, and was willing to use it against our common enemy. I just had to be aware—and nimble—enough to stay out of the crossfire.

I still stripped off my glove and handed it to Medina. He met my eyes, and I could feel a deliberate amount of approval drifting from him. Hooray. I'd satisfied my ally. Now I just had to stay alive for long enough to make use of that connection.

"Now, the rest of Tac 47 is not to be in the same room with you until I say otherwise." He looked at Tolden. "The nightly guards will cease. Understand? We're all working on the same side here. Miss Farina is in no danger."

My teeth clenched as he called me that again. It was a deliberate message. I wasn't an agent again in the Organization's eyes. I was more like a stray puppy with abilities. When he said I was in no danger, he was lying through his teeth. If I couldn't follow orders, they would break me to heel.

Tolden's mouth opened, then closed again. He stiffened and met Medina's gaze. "Yes, sir."

"What's the mission?" I asked.

Medina projected a sense of irony as he looked at me again. "The mission is getting you off the bench. Now, I'm sure I don't have to tell you this, but you are to follow all orders from those higher than yourself in the chain of command without question, and without hesitation."

Which, for me, included everyone. I swallowed. Medina wasn't really one for spelling things out. A lot must be riding on this mission for him, and whatever was coming wasn't going to be good.

Already, I regretted giving Medina my electropulser.

I pushed back into the inside of my mind, found the recently reconstructed PREP module, and deliberately locked it into the larger machine where I couldn't remove it without going through a dozen other modules. When the time came, I was going to need it.

When that was done, I met Medina's eyes. "I hope you know what you're doing," I said.

His gaze softened just a bit. "Me too, Crystal. Me too."

He left just as quickly as he had come. Tolden jerked his head at the rest of the team, and they left too. Then it was just him and me. His eyes met mine, cool, without the rage I had expected—although I couldn't be entirely sure why I expected him to be angry. Tolden had never had a quick temper. He was a logical kind of guy, who valued thoughtful action above hasty reaction. Lack of anger aside, I could tell he was composing a speech in his head, and I pressed my lips into a line. I didn't need a lecture now, when I had just been disarmed and practically told to expect an attack at any moment that I was forbidden to defend myself from.

"At least you know I'm capable of *some* manipulation now. I won't be a liability in the field," I said.

Tolden's mouth closed on whatever he was going to say. "That's not what I'm worried about."

"Then what is it?" I crossed my arms and stared him down. They all looked at me like I was broken. They were right. I was. Just because I was broken, though, didn't mean I was helpless. If I continued focusing on what I couldn't do, I would never get back in the field.

Black was certainly trying his best to cripple me during training, and there was nothing I could do to prevent it. I rejected that evaluation with every fiber in my being. I wasn't going to stay broken. I might not ever get my old skills back, but I was not going to be a victim. I was going to prove that I was useful if it meant shoving every single one of their faces into the mat.

Of course, that was no longer an easy task.

Tolden held up a hand. "Look, I know you're frustrated, and hurting, and scared, but you're not helping your case."

Scared? Fear wasn't what made my fingers tremble when I got up in the morning; that was rage. How dare they drag me off the street where I could do some good, and confine me in this compound? How dare they disarm me and make me play their stupid little games!

"Crystal, look at me." I met his eyes again. They were calm, like Mom's after I'd cleared the fires in her mind. "I can't pretend to know what you're going through, but believe me when I say that blustering about your abilities isn't going to get you where you want to go. You're smart; so is everyone else here. You have your expertise, I have mine, Steele has his, Hunt has hers. You're no more special than anyone else in the Organization.

"I feel bad that you're hurting. I want to help so badly, but I can't. My brain isn't like yours. I don't process my emotions the way you do. I can't watch numbers dancing in my head, and I can't build a plasma pulser. I can give you a little bit of advice, though. Lashing out in anger might feel good, but it only tears those around you down. Some people here are your enemy—I don't doubt that—but most of us are your friends. We want to help you. If we can't fix your mind, then we can damn well guard your back while you figure it out yourself. But we can only do that if you stop pushing us away and, for goodness sake, stop making more enemies! You've got tools in your head. Use them. If you can find Robbins's tampering in your memories, you can fix anything in your mind. It might take some time, and it might take some patience, but standing there and yelling at the world is only going to make that road longer. You're an analyst: quantify the problem, break it down, and start working toward recovery. We'll have your back while you do—I don't care what Medina says."

He finally took a breath, and watched my face carefully.

I watched him back, trying to absorb his words. Memories of Mom started flashing through my head so fast I couldn't make out any of her words. I watched as she held me. I watched as she handed me notecards with her handwriting scrawled over it in smeared black ink, trying to teach me some rudimentary understanding of how society worked. I had gotten angry then; angry at her, and angry at the people who constantly chattered at me like I could decipher their words. They thought that because I looked normal, their words should make sense. Well, they didn't. Now, I knew so much more. I'd built a little model of society in my head and I watched it while I was asleep. Words weren't hard anymore because I'd learned to look at lips. But the Organization? It twisted and contorted itself in an effort to do things that made no sense. It hurt me—just to see if it could. So, just like a child, I'd lashed out. I'd manipulated my friends in a desperate grab for control.

Tolden was right. I'd only started to understand society when I'd learned to communicate my anger in a constructive way. Now I had to do the same thing with the Organization.

Inside, numbers locked into place, framing equations in

my mind and assembling into another module. FIX. The processing relays in my mind were broken. The first step to recovery was fixing them. That took active attention. If I could mechanize the process, I could integrate the FIX module into a subroutine that would run any time I had extra processing space. My mind would be back to where it was when I first walked through Martial Academy doors within a week and a half—if I could synthesize the information I'd gotten from fixing the other two relays into a cohesive, constructive module. When I had most of my analysis capabilities back, I could set up an automation that could start gathering extra data on the Organization's actions. Once I understood why they were doing things that made no sense on the outside, I could take steps to protect myself and my friends from more idiotic orders—like this mission Medina had just given us.

I looked back up at Tolden, who was watching me like an interstate device, wondering if he could get clear of the blast range before I exploded. I twisted my lips into a smile and pulled the Social Niceties to the forefront of my mind. Options—polite ways to answer Tolden's words—arrayed in front of me like sparkling jewels. I selected options, building an answer in my mind while I continued to work on the new module.

"You're right, Tolden. Anger isn't helping anything. Thank you for watching out for me. I need to think about this and make a plan." I gave him a wry smile. "Unfortunately, I don't think I can talk while I finish the analysis required. This plan's going to take a while to figure out and automate."

Some of the tension left Tolden's muscles, and he returned my smile. "Then you'd best get going and," he looked around, "I'd best get going, too. Be careful, Farina. Something's coming down the pike, and we're not going to like it when it gets here. Medina thinks you can handle it, or he wouldn't have sent it our way. Just try to hold onto your temper?"

I nodded, and he turned to walk away, only to pause.

"And Crystal?" His eyes pierced mine. "If you need help, yell. Organization or not, we'll be there. You are not alone."

I awoke to a bright light in my eyes and hands grabbing me. The PREP module cycled, starting threat analysis; the FIX module retreated, freeing processing space; and my blue lines sprung to life. The light shifted, bringing tears to my eyes. Piercing pain in my head faded as the PREP module shunted it to the back of my awareness and kept trying to pin down the shapes of my attackers. Without that model, I could do nothing. The light shifted. My pupils tried to constrict, but it was happening too slowly. The additional programs I'd built as a child to help speed the process were still scattered in pieces around the void of my mind. I located the primary section, which was mostly intact, and shoved it into place. My mind screamed at me. Pain response activated. I groaned. My eyes still didn't adjust. Blue lines continued to piece together miniscule pieces of information.

The hands pulled me out of bed and made me stand. The thought of resisting came and went. I looked away from the light and continued to work on the broken program. What was I going to do? Fight blind? Medina's warning was fresh in my mind, and Tolden's warning only compounded it. Being reactionary right now would get me killed. No. I needed information before I resisted.

"Who are you?" I forced my voice calm as the light shifted to glare right in my eyes again. The blue lines were doing their job, though, and I had rough outlines of two of my attackers. It wasn't the full model I wanted, but it would have to be enough.

"We have orders from Director Carlisle to bring you in for questioning," a voice answered. It had notes of familiarity, so I ran my mind past his. Every muscle in my body stiffened as the blue lines incorporated this new information into their model. Two ghostly faces outlined in blue stared back at me. One was square and hard with piercing eyes that didn't bother to hide his arrogance. The other was softer, made by the organization to make him seem less of a threat. The softer face attached to the rough outline of his form that quickly defined itself in light of this new information.

Houston.

I grit my teeth.

Suddenly, Zachary was in front of me, fist coiled to strike. Blue lines sprung to my vision. I jerked against the people holding me—then stopped as the blue lines flashed. I wasn't at home. Zach wasn't here. The person in front of me wasn't Zach, it was Houston.

What was he doing here? Was this the mission Medina had mentioned? My thoughts were sluggish as I tried to think through the problem.

I turned my attention to the other models that were starting to complete. Out of the six people around me, I recognized—at least vaguely—all of them. These were all the people who had cause to hate me the most. They were the Company agents I had helped Tac 47 imprison or transport during my time at the Agency.

Cold, hard metal pressed up against the base of my neck. The muzzle of a gun. "Try to do anything but walk, and I'll blow your brains out, you—"

I tuned out the rest of her words as she started into a stream of increasingly profane descriptions. Yes, I remembered her. She was the one who had made me create a program that could selectively destroy sound files stored in my brain instead of relying on the haphazard filing system to lose them for me. I'd never heard such foul words before in my life, and I'd hoped never to hear them again.

"Please, Inora, keep it to a minimum." Houston rubbed his temples absentmindedly. "That said, she is right. You're a bright girl, Crystal, so you know by now that there isn't a single one of us here who wouldn't love to tear you limb from limb. Please give us an excuse. I still owe you for that headache you gave me the other day."

"Of course." I loaded my words with as much sarcasm as I could handle, then winced as they jerked my arms behind me. Human arms weren't designed to move that way, and I was still sore from my sessions with Black.

Houston secured the handcuffs tightly so that the metal dug into my wrists, cutting off circulation. My fingers started to tingle.

There was no doubt about it, this was why Medina had taken my electropulser—although I still couldn't fathom what maniac would send this group of agents to bring me wherever we were going. Did they want one of us to be dead by the end of this?

My blue lines said something different, though, and I believed them. This was a test—and not a gentle one. I couldn't wait to see the head of the Organization so I could spit in his eye. He'd caused me a year of continuous trouble, and I was fed up with it.

Houston opened the door, and led the way into the dimly lit hallway, even as I set my blue lines to work on the problem more deeply. The situation inside the Organization was getting a bit more tense than I'd anticipated. If I got an opportunity to escape, I would take it. Even fractured, I would do more good working without the Organization's hindrance. Figuring out the politics at play here was a waste of processing space. I couldn't fight the Institute if I was worried about the Organization stabbing me in the back or dragging me off in chains.

We moved up two floors and started into the labyrinth of hallways that was the Interrogation portion of InDep when Houston finally opened a door and led the group into a room. It wasn't the interrogation room I'd anticipated, but more like a meeting room. The extra agents waited in the hall, but Houston accompanied me inside. I scanned the room as Houston took a place at my shoulder and finally got out of the way of my vision. There were a dozen chairs scattered around the room, and only a few of them were filled. About halfway into the room was a set of two chairs next to each other. Medina sat in one, but I didn't recognize the man sitting next to him. Could this be the new head of InDep? Tolden had mentioned that Company agents had taken control of both InDep and TacDep.

"Miss Farina, thank you for joining us," the man said, and indicated a chair.

I sat awkwardly, perched on the edge of my chair where I could stand easily if it came to blows. My hands were still secured behind my back, pushing my balance forward. If I had to fight with my hands tied, it was going to be a very short fight. I wished for my old speed back. Even the speed I'd had when I first came to Martial Academy would turn this into a much more equitable situation. "I didn't exactly have a choice."

The man's eyes flicked to my still bound hands, and then back to my face. He arched an eyebrow. "Then you shouldn't have resisted."

Resisted? I had done nothing when they attacked. I opened my mouth to respond hotly, but restructured my argument at Medina's warning glance. "Respectfully, sir, I think our definitions of resist differ. If I'd tried to resist, then someone would be dead." If Houston's attitude was anything to judge by, I would be one of those people.

He and Medina shared a look.

"Still as cocky as ever, I see," was Medina's only response.

I pursed my lips. "Sir, is there a reason I was abducted from my quarters at this time of night?" He'd known this was coming. I was sure of it.

Just then, a portion of the wall behind Medina and his superior slid back to reveal a new form.

I gasped as my blue lines came to life. The man had golden eyes that narrowed as I watched him. His hair was as black as mine, and a scar, now barely a pale line down his cheek, ran at a slight angle from his temple to his nose.

No, it couldn't be! The eyes, the face, the hair, it was everything I'd remembered during my battle with Ms. King.

Pulsing blue lines traced his figure. Ninety-eight-point-nine percent match.

This man was my father.

He watched me stiffen, then frowned.

"Ah, so you did manage to remember. That's unfortunate." He met my eyes as he fully entered the room.

My mouth opened, and then closed again. I'd known he was alive, but this? Working for the Organization? Projector or not, I'd never anticipated this. Suddenly I understood why the Organization had been so touchy about Steele's search. My father didn't want to be found, and he had enough power to remake reality and disappear. Now I was being brought to him at gunpoint. "Who are you?" And what kind of father went to these kinds of lengths to hide?

I felt fingers in my mind, even through the damping field. I clenched my teeth and tried to shift the frequencies in my thoughts, but my control center was still broken. The only defense I had was the damping field, and he cut through it like a hot knife through butter. What rating was he, to be able to get inside my head this easily? Who, exactly, was this man?

Abruptly, my vision dimmed, and his face blurred. What was happening? I squirmed in my seat as his fingers in my mind multiplied into a billion ants shifting around my head, biting some places and trampling others.

"I'm Director Carlisle." His voice sputtered in and out of my hearing, and I couldn't seem to focus on his lips. I tore my gaze away. Something about the information was wrong, but the blue lines wouldn't come to the forefront of my vision. He'd done something to temporarily disable them. This person was the director of the Organization? My fath—

The thought faded as quickly as it had come. He was Director Carlisle, and nothing else.

"Remember you?" A voice echoed outside my head, just out of reach. "What did you do to her? Carlisle, stop this. She's your daughter!"

My vision grew fuzzy as the fingers in my mind ruffled through my thoughts, and my head drooped.

"It is of no consequence, Medina." I knew this voice from a long time ago—that was certain. But from where? Who was he?

"Sir, respectfully, she's still injured. We need her to combat the Superiors."

The pressure in my head started to increase, and I tried to grab my head, but my hands were still bound. My wrists twisted against the restraints. I couldn't move. The pressure reached its critical point. My skull felt like it was splitting, like his mind was splitting mine with an axe. I couldn't look away. The pressure tripled in an instant. He was turning my mind to goo!

I screamed.

What was he doing? Who was he?

The pain obliterated those thoughts.

"Lyle!"

"Sit down, Medina!" That unknown voice cracked with authority.

My vision was completely gone. The world was nothing except pain as I writhed, trying futility to get away, to make it *stop*, and then even that faded.

CHAPTER TWELVE

I opened my eyes to see someone standing over me. His name, Director Carlisle, was written above his head in blue. I was curled up on the floor, but why? I tried to pull footage of what had happened but the last two minutes of my memory didn't exist—like time had suddenly skipped. I had been talking with Medina one moment, and I was just here the next.

"Agent 32, are you alright?" Medina asked. His voice was sharper, now. Was he worried about me? But why would he be worried? What had just happened? He was crouched by my side. One hand hovered hesitantly over my shoulder, as though he wanted to help, but was too afraid to actually touch me. I groaned and sat up. His jaw tightened. He grabbed my elbow to help me to my feet. Then he released me and returned to his seat—his face a complete mask once again. Any worry I thought I'd seen had been stubbornly wiped away.

"Yes, sir," I finally responded. I blinked again, trying to make my modules fill in those blank two minutes. The modules were incredibly responsive—moving with a speed I hadn't felt since before I'd fractured. They still couldn't find anything. I looked back at Medina. "What happened?"

Medina opened his mouth to answer, his eyes dark. Then he stopped, and looked over at Director Carlisle. His eyebrows narrowed. He closed his mouth.

The new Director of InDep, sitting next to Medina, frowned. "Nothing, Agent. Would you take your chair, please?"

The metal cuffs around my wrist unlocked themselves and drifted back to Houston's hands. I sat in the chair they indicated, then turned back to Director Carlisle. What had been happening?

I pulled the footage again and skipped past the black parts. Director Carlisle had been introducing himself?

I searched my mind for suitable phrases to resume the conversation. The Social Niceties program presented an option, and I took it.

"Director Carlisle, it's nice to meet you." I clasped my hands in my lap. There were red marks around my wrists, like a friction rash. It was painful as I touched the irritated skin. Well, that was strange. I'd only been in cuffs for a few moments. It almost looked like—

The thought went away, and I looked back up at Director Carlisle. It was rude to ignore people who were talking, and I had to look at him to understand what he was saying. Besides, Director Carlisle's face was more interesting than the red marks on my wrists. His face shifted as I watched, defeating the matching program that was running on overdrive in the back of my mind. The Director was unquantifiable. An unsolvable mystery. I shouldn't even try to evaluate him. That would just be a waste of resources.

The director was nodding. "Yes. I'm sure you're wondering why I brought you here. Honestly, it was mere curiosity. I wanted to meet the famous Agent 32."

I looked back at Houston. "Mere curiosity?" Then why the handcuffs?

Director Carlisle let out a belly rumbling laugh. "I'm afraid I didn't specify that I wanted neutral agents to retrieve you. I apologize for any inconvenience that may have caused."

I frowned. That didn't seem like the kind of thing he could simply forget.

Director Carlisle's eyebrows narrowed but, just then, there was a knock on the door. "Ah, that must be the refreshments."

A man wheeling a cart entered the room, and I let my blue lines flick over him. Refreshments? Did the upper echelons of the Organization have stewards to serve them? At two-fifty-one in the morning?

One of my lines flashed red and the world devolved into chaos. I reacted as the line sighted the threat, and was between Director Carlisle and the steward before anyone else could fully see the gun in the steward's hand. The blue lines blinked in surety. He was an assassin. I reviewed the memory as I moved, consciously cross-checking the lines. I saw the steward reach into a pocket and produce a tiny two-shot derringer. Cross-check complete.

I was in front of him. My blue lines plotted courses. I followed them. In one fluid movement, I took the weapon from his hand and threw him to the floor. I brought my elbow down on his temple. He was unconscious before anyone else could move.

I straightened and let my blue lines survey the rest of the room as the silence stretched thin. Another line flashed red as the whine of an energy pistol filled the room. The weapon was leveled at my chest and Houston's finger was on the trigger. The percent chance that he would actually pull the trigger was nearing ninety percent. It continued to tick up as my blue lines revised the number in real time.

This wasn't good. His eyes were fixed on the assassin's gun, which was in my hand. According to the lines on my vision, none of the escape routes the PREP module calculated upon entering the room would do anything but increase my chance of death. I had only one option. I released the gun and stepped slowly out from around the limited cover of the steward's cart.

The sound of the steward's gun clattering against the floor echoed from every wall. An alert flashed across my vision—too late. The gun didn't have a safety switch, and a stray shock could set the thing off. The size of the weapon came at the cost of security. The derringer didn't fire. I noted its location in case I needed it later, then refocused.

I watched Houston like he was a snake, coiled to strike. If he thought he could get away with it, he would pull that trigger and laugh. I remembered the way his eyes looked two years ago when he'd cut at me with his knife just so he could watch my futile struggle for life. His eyes were the same now.

I looked around the rest of the room with a quick flick of my eyes. Something was blocking me from computing the chance that Medina or one of the other two in the room would interfere, but I could only hope it was high enough to keep me alive. After all, I'd just taken out an assassin bent on killing them—or two of the three of them, anyway. There was no third bullet in the gun.

"Don't shoot." I kept my voice level, and focused on Houston, but the only thoughts I could catch reeked of anticipation. I flinched away from past memories of laying there helpless under Houston's smoking gun. I wasn't helpless.

"Get on the ground." He spat the words.

My jaw hardened, but I sank to my knees. This was why Medina had reminded me that I had to follow all orders. He knew this—or something like it—was going to happen.

"I'm not a threat, Houston. Put your gun away." This was a charade. He was humiliating me in front of the Directors just because he could—because holding a gun made him feel powerful, and watching me get on the ground was the closest he could come to making me beg. I knelt on the ground, still tall and defiant as I stared at him.

Houston's face twisted into a snarl. He jerked the pistol. "Get on the ground!"

I pressed my face against the cold stained cement floor and went prone as a flush crept up my neck. The directors looked on with interest.

This was pointless. We all knew this was a farce, but pointing that out would just give Houston an excuse to shoot me. He would take any opportunity he could get, just to watch me scream.

Pain lanced through my back as Houston planted a knee on my spine, and jerked my arms behind me.

"Director Carlisle, hasn't this gone far enough?" I arched my eyebrows as I realized that I could recognize the voice. It was Medina.

I dove into my own mind, assessing the wreckage recovery operation. Three of the once-broken processing relays in my mind were mostly repaired. That was work that should have taken weeks, and it had been completed during those two minutes I couldn't remember. How was that possible?

"Yes, I agree. Houston, get off her." That was Director Carlisle's voice.

I didn't wait for him to get off me. Instead, I pulled my lines to the front of my vision, and rolled out from underneath him.

I stood with some measure of satisfaction. While I wasn't exactly sure what Director Carlisle had done—or really, if he'd done anything in those missing two minutes—but whatever it was had sped up my mind to where it had been before I'd entered Martial Academy. While I was still fractured, and my psionic abilities hadn't recovered in the slightest, I was moving much faster.

"I suppose I should thank you, Agent," Director Carlisle said as he motioned for Houston to put his gun away. "As you can see, not everyone is happy about the Company and Agency's merger. I'm glad to see that you're one of the supporters."

So that's what this was all about. I kept my voice carefully blank of all emotion. "I suppose it would be a bit more strange if I were against the merge, sir. After all, Tac 47 went to the Company and built a team to subdue Ms. King, which opened the Agency up to the possibility of working with the Company. We alerted the Agency to the danger the Institute posed, and set things in motion so the merge could happen. You could say, I'm the reason the Organization exists. But," I held up a hand, "At the end of the day, I fight to protect the innocents the Institute wants to hurt, not for the Agency, not for the Company, and not for the Organization."

The director of InDep's eyebrows narrowed, but Director Carlisle didn't even pause. "Of course, Agent. In light of your actions over the last year, I would be surprised if you had declared allegiance only to us. Now, I do believe you have a tactical team to return to. No?"

I looked past the director to Medina. He inclined his head just enough for me to notice.

I nodded. The Social Niceties program pinged. "Thank you, sir. This meeting has been very educational."

The processing relays had come together impossibly quickly. I sorted through them as I strode down the hall—I could do both at the same time now, due to those same relays. Director Carlisle had done something, or I had done something, or *someone* had done something, and that was the only thing I knew. I slowed down the footage of those precious seconds before the *event* and examined it with all the blue lines in my arsenal, and they revealed exactly nothing. Those memories weren't just gone. They had been obliterated. I shoved down the urge to go back in there, throw Director Carlisle against a wall, and demand answers. He wouldn't answer any questions he didn't want to answer, and he had a whole lot of fire-power backing his 'no'.

I strode down the hallway, racking my memory as I went. Sure enough, those two minutes between talking with Medina and finding myself on the floor were completely blank. One moment, my timestamp read 02:45, the next, it read 02:47—like the time had been erased. It wouldn't be the first time my memories had been altered, but I couldn't find any tampering like Robbins had left behind. Plus, why would someone erase two minutes at the beginning of a meeting? That wasn't enough time for me to hear or see any sensitive information.

Why were Medina and the InDep director there? The only one who had actually done anything was Director Carlisle. Medina's presence wasn't that hard to explain—he was Ms. Green's representative. But the director of InDep? If the director of TacDep had been there, I would have attributed it to a meeting of all the offensively oriented department heads, but he—whoever he was—hadn't been.

Then there was the assassin, and Houston. It should have been obvious to any outside observer that I'd just disarmed an assassin, thereby saving the heads of the Organization—but

Houston had treated me like an enemy. That wasn't surprising. Houston and I had a long history which mostly consisted of him trying to kill me. The first time, I had stepped in to save Tabitha Smith. The second time, I was with Tac 47, trying to bring him back to the Agency after he'd murdered Earl West—who was the Company's recruiter before Ms. Graff.

I shook my head. Why did Houston even work for the Organization? It made no sense! He'd tried to kill people who worked for the Company and the Agency alike and now, as I examined the memory, I could tell that Ms. King had been pulling his strings. His head had been filled with thoughts of becoming stronger, and faster, and more powerful than he was then. It wasn't a far leap to guess that Ms. King had promised him a rebirth as a Superior, without explaining all the gruesome details.

Which brought me back to my first question. Had the Organization failed to connect the dots? Did they simply not know that Houston worked for the Institute? I couldn't bring myself to believe that they knew and were choosing to ignore it.

But, then, was that really any different than what they were doing with me? They knew I was fighting against the Institute, and they still jerked me around with little tests and tortures designed to make sure I was a loyal little soldier.

I shook my head. What a load of crap. I was an agent, and they were treating me like a cat toy. What if Houston had shot me? Would they have just shrugged and moved on with their day? Director Carlisle had wanted to see how I would react when my interests didn't quite align with his. He didn't just want to know if I would shoot at Superiors, but whether I would allow the Organization to get caught in the cross-fire. It all came back to that question they'd asked when they first brought me back. Had I ever killed an Organization agent.

That was the litmus test, and I had passed. Now they were trying to dial in on the limits of my patience.

I shook my head again. I was an agent, not a toy. I wasn't going to play their games, and I wasn't going to let them make me angry again. I had a plan that had just been jumped forward by a few weeks. When my brain was fully functional again, I was going to leave. This time, I would do a good enough job of disappearing that the Organization would never find me.

"Agent Farina." Medina was behind me. I stopped and turned to face him.

"I see you made it through relatively unscathed." He nodded towards my chafed wrists. My eyebrows narrowed slightly. I'd forgotten all about them. That was strange. I looked back up at Medina, but his face was as blank as it had been the day I met him. No clues there.

"Agent Houston doesn't even have another bruise. I'll admit to being impressed," Medina finished.

I pursed my lips. So I'd been right. It was a test.

I folded my arms. "You know Houston works for the Institute, right?"

He didn't even blink. "We all have a past, Farina. His is a little more…colorful than most."

Colorful didn't even begin to describe it.

"He killed Earl West, tried to kill Tac 47 and now he's free to roam the facility? He's being sent out on intelligence gathering missions?"

I had seen his eyes, and the bloodlust was still there. He wasn't a Superior, but he was the closest thing to it I'd seen that was still human.

A ghost of a smile touched Medina's lips. "We have ways

of keeping wayward operatives under control."

"What kind of ways?"

"Ways that involve a very small room and a very powerful teleprojector. Trust me, Houston isn't a threat any more."

I snorted. "Maybe not to the Organization, but he would gladly cut up anyone he got his hands on just for fun."

I could still see the pleasure in his eyes as he fired his weapon into my abdomen all that time ago. I could still see his grin as I screamed.

Medina arched an eyebrow. "Your personal investment in this matter is admirable, but it has been taken care of. We keep him on a short leash."

"Obviously not short enough," I spat. He had almost shot me in there, and no one had even tried to lift a finger.

Medina raised a hand. "Since the Organization's creation, has he taken any action to permanently harm you?"

I grit my teeth. "No." Just taken pleasure in my humiliation.

Medina spread his hands. "Well, then there's not much I can do."

I snorted. Of course he couldn't do much. He'd helped concoct this entire situation. "Is this 'mission' over, or are you keeping my electropulser?" I couldn't quite keep all the challenge out of my voice.

Medina arched an eyebrow. "I've taken the liberty of having it placed in your locker, along with a certain duty weapon we recovered from a civilian apartment rented under the name Talia Carmen. What was it doing there, I wonder?"

That news was almost enough to wipe away the cloud hanging over my mood. Almost. I still had too many unanswered questions to be completely satisfied. "Am I now officially a full agent, or am I still provisionary?"

Medina's lips twitched. "Your rank has been restored, and you will be receiving back pay at combat time rates for every day you were on an Organization kill list and one of our agents was within eight square miles."

I nodded. That was going to be the best apology I could expect for over a year of being on the run—and I certainly wasn't going to be thanked for all the intelligence I'd provided them during that time. Still, it was bound to be a neat sum. Maybe it would even be enough that, if I squirreled it away, I could spend another year on the run. "Is Tac 47 still on the bench?"

"The team has been reentered into the duty roster, with missions dependent on the AICs approval. In light of your updated records, you are officially the next senior member of the team—simply by virtue of having the most combat time."

I shook my head. That was saying something, seeing as Black had been working for the Agency for longer than I'd been alive. Still, a year of nearly straight combat time would more than offset that. Looking back on it, that was about where I'd been, too. It had been a hard year of dodging both Superiors, and the Organization, but now it was over.

Medina turned to walk away, "Welcome home, 32. Now go get those wrists checked."

I stiffened. This wasn't home. They'd destroyed my home when they took my biocard away from me. Still, the Social Niceties icon blinked in the corner of my vision. "Thank you, sir." I turned back down the hall that led to my locker, wrists forgotten yet again.

CHAPTER THIRTEEN

U n-benched or not, Tac 47's routine didn't change. I watched tactical teams go out, and come in bloodied while we continued our training exercises. When I asked Tolden about it, he said that we were running one person short, and no one could find another person with a "suitable personality" to join the team. It was just another delaying tactic, though. Between Tolden, Black, Steele, Hunt, and I, Tac 47 was at full strength. Vera Hunt was a brilliant infiltrator, as shown by the time she'd spent as a double agent for the Agency and the Company before the merge. Neal Black was our weapons expert, but every one of us could reasonably go up against a Superior and expect to live through the encounter—now that we had a good grasp of their capabilities and weaknesses. Perhaps Steele and I would need a little help from our gadgets, but we would survive. Now that my blue lines had figured out which way was up, Steele and I could handle any analysis between us, and Tolden was as brilliant a strategist as he'd been before the merge.

No, this was just one more excuse to keep us inside the Organization compound. The question was, why? What could they possibly gain from keeping us out of the field?

I didn't have an answer to that. The longer upper management delayed, the less I understood Director Carlisle. If his goal truly was destroying the Institute, why didn't he make use of the tools he had? Was he even the one calling the shots? The only contact I'd had with the Organization's upper management since that meeting with Director Carlisle was through Medina—which was strange, because Tactical 47 was still listed as a tactical team, and that was far from Medina's job. I wondered if it was because of our history. He had been working with me since the first time I saw a Superior and, while I didn't understand him, he was a familiar face.

My thoughts kept going back to the intelligence I'd taken off the Instructor earlier. The directions for how to obtain it had come from Medina, so it had to have been important. I hadn't been able to decode it with the general software Steele had slipped me while I was setting up my illicit operations after my biocard had been taken, but what if he had physical access to the data? He would make short work of the encryption, and then I could analyze the data. Info that important had to provide the foundation for some sort of mission. I could slip out of the base, take out more of the Institute's assets, and be back before anyone realized I was gone. They would know I was competent, and the Organization would have to take Tac 47 off the bench.

I tried to push the thought away. It was too risky. Getting caught breaking into the Organization's servers was a great way to be put on the bench and never taken off—or worse. I wasn't entirely sure how far the Organization would go to protect their secrets, but they weren't above putting a few holes in someone to prove their point. They had access to the Agency's pods, so it wouldn't be irreparable. People tended to be less restrained about causing massive trauma to the human body when they knew that the equivalent of an hour in a tanning bed would fix everything.

No, while getting shot for overstepping my bounds would be unpleasant, what Medina had mentioned about how they were ostensibly controlling Houston was far more concerning. One thing was for sure. The Organization had far fewer scruples than the Agency I'd left.

But the thought wouldn't leave me alone. It was joined by a second thought. I didn't have to break into the Organization's servers to get the information I was looking for, I had a copy of it on my phone. Unfortunately, that was the same phone the Organization had confiscated when they first brought me in, then never released. It was being held with the rest of my things in the secure lockers next to Interrogation.

Tolden had warned me not to be rash; going off half cocked because I was mad at what the Organization was doing would only get everyone in trouble. I monitored my mental state for a moment, and decided that I wasn't angry. This was a logical step. Tac 47 could help, if we only had the information to put together a mission. We needed to prove to the Organization that we had as many people as we needed. What would communicate that better than a successful mission?

At breakfast, I found Steele in the cafeteria and waved him aside. He didn't take too much convincing. Apparently, I wasn't the only one who was getting bored with the Organization's arrangement.

"What happened to only wanting that chair in CIS?" I asked him as we walked toward Interrogation together. It had only taken him a moment to pinpoint the location of the locker we needed.

"They changed the name. They left all the other departments more or less the same, but CIS apparently wasn't good enough anymore."

I couldn't help myself. I laughed. "So because it isn't a chair in CIS anymore, you don't want it as much?"

He shrugged. "Central Data Analysis Department doesn't have the same ring to it. Who comes up with the acronyms, anyway? C-DAD? Why would I want a workspace there?"

"Because you can sit in a comfy chair and eat fries while you destroy bad guys with your pet drones."

He shook his head. "Naw. They've downgraded the chair quality, too. Something about funding being tight now that half the Agency's donors have pulled out. Apparently, the Institute has connections in high places, and they've persuaded those high places to stop giving us money. Does Tactical suffer from the budget cuts, though? No. It's all us tech heads sitting in—well, whatever they decide they want to call our department—and saving the world with our brains."

"We're saving the world with our brains, too," I said.

He twisted a few long strands of bleached blonde hair between his fingers, suddenly serious. "Maybe you are, 32, but I don't know about the rest of TacDep. It's a different place, now. The only info they give tactical agents are the mission briefs, and they don't like people who ask questions, either. Even Tolden has to be careful, and he's one of the most senior tactical agents we've got."

I held up a hand as we turned a corner. There was a desk in front of us with three tactical types with InDep embroidered on their tactical suits. They eyed us as we approached.

"Names and business?"

Steele tapped something on his belt.

"I'm Agent 32," I said. The neural damper was as low as I could set it without losing control of my shields, and I applied the thinnest possible layer of coercion. I was better at manipulation, now. A year of only the smallest amount of teleprojection power had taught me how to make the most of my resources. The guard's wariness dropped just a touch as he had me input my code into the computer.

I held my breath as it processed, but the hack Steele had just activated held. The guards waved us through.

::That went much better than my last attempt to infiltrate InDep did,:: I projected to Steele.

He offered me a tight lipped grin. *I'm just that awesome. Now hurry. There's always the chance that someone will see us where we aren't supposed to be. I'll stick my neck out for you, sure, but I'll haunt you forever if this goes badly. No technology will ever work for you again.*

It only took a moment for Steele to point out the locker we needed. It was an old-fashioned key lock. Steele stuck his tongue out at it. "I hope you know how to deal with this, because I'm not touching that thing."

"Ms. King was thorough in her training," I said. I pulled the lock-pick set out of its spot in my tactical suit and set to work. It only took a second for my blue lines to reconstruct the internal structure of the lock. A moment later, the pins were out of the way and the lock clicked open.

I scanned over the contents of the locker. Most of my tools had already been carted down the R&D to see if their engineers could reconstruct them. The ones they couldn't figure out, they had me build for them. Mostly, that left my phone—useless to the Organization, but essential if I wanted to run quite a few of my toys—and my street clothes, which they only kept from me because I couldn't exactly run around in public wearing a tactical suit. Civilians would stare and, more importantly, I'd light up on every single camera the Organization had access to. Plus, I was pretty sure there were a few tracking devices embedded into the tactical suits they'd given me.

I debated taking the clothes back to my assigned living space, then disregarded the impulse. It was beyond stupid. They would know we'd been in here, and I'd tip my hand. I could figure out how to get clothes when I left. If I left. If Tac 47 wasn't taken off the bench. If things didn't get better.

I wanted things to get better.

Steele grabbed the phone and jacked it into his tablet. A moment later, he pursed his lips in a silent whistle.

"The whole file is a list of names, locations, and dates starting three weeks ago when you lifted the intel, and going until—looks like next week." He pressed another button, then handed the tablet to me. The entire file flashed across the screen faster than I could follow. My blue lines started sorting the data. In a few minutes, I would have a coherent file sitting inside my memory.

"Good work, Steele." I put the phone back in the locker and swung it closed with a click. There. No one would even know that we'd been here.

I stiffened as I felt another mind coming. Whoever it was had higher shields than I could penetrate without turning the neural damper down past safe levels, and had a tight hold on their surface thoughts.

::Steele, hide!:: I projected.

I looked around for somewhere to go, but it was too late. There was nowhere to go. The door slid open and Doug Houston stood in the hallway we'd just come from with an energy pistol in one hand.

"Crystal Farina. Somehow I thought I'd find you here," he drawled.

I took a step toward him, only for Steele to catch my arm. "Careful, 32," he whispered.

"Listen to your tech head. You have no idea how annoying it is having to keep tabs on you. One more step, and you'll solve all my problems."

I spread my arms, palms out. "Nobody's going to be happy if you shoot me here."

Houston bared his teeth. "I would be, and that's really all I care about. Now, what are you doing here?"

My thoughts raced as I grabbed for a lie. "Medina—"

"Cut the crap, Farina. Medina didn't send you here, and neither did anyone else. What are you looking for?"

"Nothing," I said truthfully. I'd already found what I was looking for, and Steele's program was set to destroy the information off his tablet the moment I was done looking at it. There was no evidence to say we were looking for anything. We had tactical gloves on. Our prints wouldn't show up anywhere.

Of course, the lack of evidence would only help if the Organization cared about things like that. They'd found us somewhere we weren't supposed to be. Worse, Houston had found us somewhere we weren't supposed to be. They knew we were looking for something, and the fact that there was no evidence to support the fact that we'd found it wouldn't matter. As far as they were concerned, we'd gone rogue. Unless my fractured mind and I could come up with an excuse, things might get very ugly.

Houston motioned for us to walk in front of him.

"Where are we going?" Steele asked. His face was pale.

Houston gave us an ugly grin. "You won't tell me what you wanted, then fine. We can find out. That's the nice thing about having the most powerful psionics in the world together in one room. Minds are such breakable things. Right, Farina?"

I didn't respond. I wouldn't let him see my fear.

Suddenly, Zachary was standing in front of me. His eyes looked like Houston's—or maybe it was the other way around.

I clenched my jaw and moved through his ghost. Zach wasn't here. He was in a wheelchair far, far away from here. I couldn't help the way my fingers trembled, but I could refuse to believe in things that weren't there. Zach had no place in my life anymore. That didn't keep him from showing up where he wasn't welcome.

Houston escorted us to an office, and I bit my lip as Medina answered the door.

Great. Another interview with Medina. This was the second time I'd tried to break into InDep under his watch. Somehow I doubted he was going to be as forgiving the second time.

But he just stood in the doorway looking at Houston as something passed between them. Finally, he sighed. "Agent Steele, your electronics please?"

Steele handed the tablet over. Medina just looked at him.

Steele pulled his phone from where it sat on his belt, a small cube from a tactical pocket, his watch and, when Media arched an eyebrow at him, a small pen from a nearly invisible pocket on his pants.

"Thank you. Return to your quarters and wait for orders."

Steele's eyes widened. "Really?"

"Consider yourself confined."

Steele looked at me, then back to Medina. Evidently he'd been expecting something much worse. "Thank you, sir." He looked at me, still concerned.

Medina gave a long-suffering sigh. "You and your bodyguards," he said to me. "Farina will exit my office in one piece, Agent. That's more than I can say for you if you don't leave."

Steele's face whitened at Medina's acidity. I pushed at him with my thoughts. I'd survived interviews with Medina before. He didn't scare me nearly as much as he should. Steele nodded at me, still worried, and then hurried off.

Medina stepped out of the doorway, and Houston pressed the muzzle of his energy pistol into the small of my back, like he thought I was going to resist. I just ignored the threat. It was nothing new.

Medina must have thought the same, because he looked at Houston. "You won't be needing that."

Houston jammed it back in its holster with ill grace, then pushed past me into the room. I followed, and then Medina closed the door behind us. He looked at me.

"You can't stay out of trouble for a week, can you Agent Farina?"

I counted up the days since my last clash with Houston, then shrugged. "Six days is almost a week and, if I remember correctly, you're the one who got me handcuffed and dragged in to see Director Carlisle."

"This isn't funny."

"I didn't say it was, sir. I was merely stating facts."

Medina massaged the bridge of his nose. "Some people find facts inconvenient, Farina. You would do well to remember that." He looked to Houston. "What is it this time?"

"I caught her and the drone kid sneaking into the InDep lockers. They looked to be finishing up when I got there."

Medina put the tablet he'd taken from Steele on the edge of his desk. "What could you possibly have needed Agent Steele for?" He asked as he moved around to his computer.

A moment later, a hologram of those same names, dates, and locations Steele had decoded for me displayed above his desk.

I swallowed.

"That's what I thought." Medina killed the hologram. "Agent Farina, it's getting dangerous to have you around the compound. This data is small-time compared to some of the things you and Agent Steele could have done if you'd put your minds together, but the fact that you went after it at all is going to anger some very powerful people."

"I wouldn't have been looking for the data—which I retrieved, by the way—if you would just let Tactical 47 go out and do our job in the first place. I didn't come back just to sit at headquarters and watch everyone else go out and get hurt. I jumped through your hoops. Tactical 47 is ready to go out!"

Medina gave a slight smile. "Oh, I know. Unfortunately, your Agent In Charge is intransigent. He thinks he's protecting you."

I blinked. What did Tolden have to do with this?

"Oh, I'm sure his tactic will work in a few weeks when we've had a little more time to study you and your behaviors—or, it would have before this little stunt," Medina continued, "but I'm afraid even Carter Tolden can occasionally miscalculate."

"I don't understand," I said. "What has Tolden been doing?"

Houston scoffed and started to say something, but he bit it off when Medina raised a hand.

"As you've no-doubt been told, Tactical 47 is running a person short."

I glared at him. "We are not." We didn't have as many people as some flex teams, sure, but we were a cohesive team, and we could handle anything the Institute decided to throw at us. The only thing that would come from them tacking a random person on the team was another fiasco like Boston.

"You are, though. Your mission positions are all filled—all except one. You, Agent Farina, need a watchdog. Director Carlisle refuses to clear your team without one."

I scoffed. "You would waste a full time agent just to keep tabs on me?"

"It would still be a reduction from what we were using. The Tanners and your Nick are being quite helpful out in the field, by the way."

I grit my teeth at the reminder that they'd been using four full agents to watch me, all while I thought I was invisible to them. "Who is the watchdog?"

"Really, Farina?" Houston said. He waved a hand at me. "I thought you were smarter than that." His smug grin told me everything I needed to know.

Medina was trying to get Houston put on Tac 47. Had the Organization learned nothing from the incident in Boston?

"No." The one word was cold. It was so idiotic, I couldn't believe that the Organization had even thought of it. Houston being assigned to watch me while we were in combat?

Medina chuckled to himself. "Somehow, that's what Tolden thought you would say. Which is why Tac 47 is still here in the compound."

I pointed a shaking finger at Houston. "I am not working with him in the field. How do I know he's not going to shoot me in the back?"

Houston grinned. "The thought has occurred to me."

Medina glared at him. "Agent Houston will take no action to harm you because he values his mind. He knows exactly what horrors will be waiting if something untoward were to happen to you."

For just a moment, I could see a kernel of fear deep in Houston's eyes. Then he snarled. "Stay out of my head!"

"See?" Medina handed the pile of Steele's electronics back to me. "The choice is yours. Accept Houston on your team, or stay here."

Somehow, I got the impression that staying here didn't mean as an agent. He meant here in InDep. They had a pretty little cell with my name on it.

"Fine." I spat the word.

Medina's grin widened. "Great. I'll let Tolden know. Do start reviewing that data you retrieved. It will look familiar in the mission brief."

Tolden gathered us in a briefing room after lunch. When I got there, he was watching Houston from the corner of his eye, careful not to be combative, but even I couldn't miss the disgust in his posture. The others were nowhere to be found.

I turned the neural damper down just enough for me to slip inside Tolden's mind. The ambient sound increased, but it was bearable.

::I think I might have messed up, earlier,:: I confessed.

Tolden didn't move, but I could feel his frustration. *You should have come to me. I'm your AIC, and beyond that, I'm your friend.*

I bit the inside of my cheek. I should have at least warned him before I took Steele to try and find that intel. What did

I think I was going to do once I found it, sneak out alone? I was going to need his help eventually.

::I guess I'm not very used to having Big Brother watching my every move. For a year, I went and did what I wanted to. If I wanted to blow up a Superior base, I could do it and be home by dinner. This enforced waiting is killing me.::

You have to learn to play nice, Crystal. Going off half-cocked is going to get you killed. Especially now that your mind is fractured again. He turned to meet my eyes.

I looked away, and instead found a chair at the large oval table in the middle of the room, as far away from Houston as I could manage. Tolden was right. According to Medina, I had only needed to wait a little longer, and we would have been back in the field without this walking liability next to us. Even if Houston didn't pull the trigger, he was in a position to do a massive amount of harm. Medina wasn't going to be happy if we had to carry him back from our first mission in a body bag, which meant all he had to do was walk into a danger-ous situation and watch what happened to us while we were trying to defend him. He would gladly stand by and watch while Superiors gutted us, but we couldn't exactly watch them do the same to him—no matter how much we wanted to. My blue lines computed the consequences of that situation, then presented me with the numbers. Sixty-eight percent chance of me ending up behind bars if Houston didn't survive this mission. The rest was unknown.

Crystal, can I count on you? Tolden asked from across the table.

I nodded. ::I've learned my lesson.:: I was going to get through this mission, and then I was going to disappear again. Fractured or not, I was done working with the Organization. I had hoped that I could acclimatize to living here. I didn't want to leave my friends. I didn't want to spend the rest of my life alone. I couldn't let the Organization keep treating me like this, though. I wasn't their toy. I'd warned them, but they'd kept playing with me. Well, it took two to play, and I was done. When we got back from the mission, I would take what I needed and leave.

I didn't let those thoughts leak to Tolden, though. He wouldn't understand. The Organization was fighting to protect innocents, which was all Tolden wanted to do. He wasn't jumping at every shadow, wondering if the person around the corner had orders to hurt him. He was secure in his place here. This was his home.

Well, there might have been a world in which this place could have been my home, but this felt nothing like the Agency now. The Agency had been wandering around in the dark wearing the Institute's blindfold, but they'd been trying their best. Better, they didn't target their own agents.

Hunt, Steele, and Black arrived a moment later. When Hunt saw Houston, she crossed the room in a flash. Tolden must have seen it coming, though, because he stepped between them before she could reach Houston.

"Murderer!" she spat at him.

Houston leaned back in his chair and put his feet up on the table, whistling silently to himself as he ignored her.

"What is he doing here?" she asked. She didn't take her eyes off of Houston. Her muscles twitched as she stared at him. I wondered how she'd recognized him through his new face.

Tolden pointed to a seat next to mine. She ignored the instruction.

"You should be in prison." Her voice was gravelly.

"Vera, sit down. Please?" Tolden's words didn't reach my ears, but I could see his lips move.

Hunt looked at Tolden, who stood so close they were almost touching. "He killed Earl West."

Tolden nodded. "I know you were close, and I'm sorry. But we've got to work with him." His finger pointing to the chair hadn't wavered. Hunt took a deep breath and sat next to me. Even that far away from him, and even starting seated, it would only give us one-point-six seconds to intercept her before she reached him. Tolden gave me a warning glance.

Watch her.

I crossed my arms. Tolden was asking *me* to keep Hunt from killing Houston? If I hadn't been sitting across from a murderer, I would have laughed.

My first inclination was to merely not get in the way. I couldn't harm Houston without the Organization crushing me, but that didn't mean I had to protect him. I understood the rage behind Hunt's eyes far too well to stop her. My blue lines computed my chance of survival if I sat here and did nothing, though, and it wasn't good. I clenched my teeth.

::Fine.::

I reached into Hunt's mind as the buzzing in my ears increased. It was almost time to turn the neural damper back up, but that would take me out of the mental conversation.

::I get it, Hunt,:: I projected to her. ::I would sleep a lot better if he wasn't running around with a gun—::

I could feel her cataloguing Houston's hidden weapons as I said that. Her anxiety shot up, tripling her rage in an instant. I shifted forward, ready to restrain her if need be. Her emotions hit a wall. The fury of battle left her eyes. She gave a mental sigh. *Who decided arming him was a good idea?*

::I'm not sure. The last person I talked to about it was Medina.:: Privately, I wondered at what I'd just seen. How had Hunt gained that amount of control? It was like she'd done something similar to how I put up a wall between my logic and emotions, but it had kicked in automatically.

Medina? She was shocked at that. *He's always been a stable sort of person. I can't imagine he's behind this insanity.*

::Well, I bring out the crazy in people.:: I forced a chuckle, then focused back on Houston. ::Just try not to kill him. The Organization's being awfully protective.::

Hunt's thoughts sharpened. *I can't believe you're alright with this. You knew him too.* Her thoughts turned to Earl West, the man who had been her other handler while she'd been a double agent. *Houston didn't just kill him, he destroyed him.*

I remembered the teacher's face, then blinked the image away. He had been a kind, just man before Houston murdered him. It didn't matter what I thought, though. Tolden asked me to make sure Hunt wouldn't cause a problem with Houston, so that was what I needed to do.

::Medina said they have him under control. Something about a very small room and a very powerful teleprojector.::

Hunt thought for a moment, then nodded. *Fine. But if he steps a toe out of line, I'm going to kill him myself.* The anger I'd felt vanish earlier reappeared in a single iron bar of forged rage. For just a millisecond, Vera Hunt had a plan. She would launch herself across the table and drive the knife on her belt into Houston's throat. She wouldn't laugh. She wouldn't enjoy the feeling of blood under her fingernails, but Earl West would be avenged and Houston wouldn't hurt anyone ever again. That would be enough.

I started to move. My blue lines started to plot intercepts to keep her away from Houston. I would be too slow. Maybe if I had been whole, I would have had a chance.

I was halfway out of my chair before I realized that

Hunt hadn't so much as shifted and the plan in her mind had vanished without a trace—except in my memory. That one moment had been so intense I'd mistaken it for reality. She looked at me sideways, a fraction of a smile on her lips—which were painted red like blood.

::You can be disturbing, you know.:: I projected to her.

She dipped her chin. *Disturbed, perhaps. I'll admit that much. But, then, we don't all have the luxury of second guessing ourselves. Make no mistake. If he steps a toe out of line, he won't survive.*

I almost applauded her then and there, but my blue lines flashed a warning. I was still on thin ice. It was best not to stomp around.

I returned my attention to Tolden and turned the neural damper back up. The buzzing of unfiltered thoughts faded, and I took a deep breath. Having Houston in the room felt like dinner with Mom when Zachary was sitting across from me. I tried to hold still, to keep from drawing attention to myself. I tried to take deep breaths. I'd gotten over this during my first year at Martial Academy, so why were the feelings coming back now? I tried to remember all the progress I'd made in becoming a teleprojector. I could defend myself now. Neither Zach nor Houston would be able to hurt me. I wasn't weak like I was before I came to Martial Academy.

So why did it feel like I was drowning inside?

I took another deep breath—like the oxygen would help this time, even though it hadn't helped yet—and sealed those thoughts away. I didn't need to think about Zach. I didn't need to think about Houston's leering eyes, or how he still stared at me from across the table. I put all those thoughts in a box in my mind, locked it, and buried it under layers of half-repaired modules.

Instead, I focused on evaluating my mind's progress. Most of the processing relays were more-or-less put together again, but it would still take some time to fix them all. Once they were whole, I would have to go through a series of optimization tests for each one, then integration tests, then start in on the emergency shunts. Only once my mind was fully functioning could I even start searching for the root problem behind my tattered shields. Once those were whole again, I might have a shot at figuring out how to fuse my fractured mind back together again, but even that wasn't guaranteed. It would take me months before I could work without the neural damper, and years—if ever—before I had completely regained what I had lost after Robbins put my biocard back.

Another wave of despair crashed over my head. I shoved those thoughts away too, and focused on Tolden's briefing.

"A few weeks ago, the Organization received a list of targets, kidnapping locations, and times," Tolden was saying. "We have been doing our best, but we've only managed to intercept half the chosen targets. The Institute has the others. So far as we can tell, these individuals are highly functional, non-psionic neurodivergents in non-prominent positions in society. In other words, civilians who may be missed, but won't instigate a nationwide manhunt if they go missing, and look at the world just differently enough to cause the Institute a major problem. Now we're not entirely sure if that's the only reason they're being taken, but that's the working hypothesis."

His eyes swept the room. "We have just been tapped as a retrieval team. The mission is simple. Get there early, learn the terrain, identify the target, then sweep them up before the Superiors get there. If we have to engage the Superiors, our primary goal is protecting the civilians and retrieving our target. Farina, that's your job. Black, Hunt, you'll play guard duty. Steele, you've got lookout. Houston," Tolden bared his teeth, "you get to babysit the target if Farina is engaged. Black will evaluate your skills and assign weaponry as needed."

In other words, Houston's first mission with Tac 47 was going to be a lot like mine. There was no way Black was going to clear him for a weapon.

That tidbit wasn't lost on Houston, and his eyes widened. "You're going to send me out there defenseless?"

Tolden quirked an eyebrow. "You're hardly defenseless. I've seen what your telekinesis can do. Now let me be very clear. If I catch any hint that you're planning on using your talents for anything unnecessary, I will cut you from the team. Until that point, consider yourself our new kid. You will follow any and all orders established members of Tac 47 give. That includes Farina. Is that understood?"

Houston looked up at the ceiling. "Sure."

"Sure, *sir*," Black growled.

Houston picked his feet off the table and sat back up. "I'm not here as your lackey. I've got a very specific job, and that's to watch Farina—sir."

Tolden grinned good-naturedly. "You can do that from down in C-DAD with a camera feed from one of Steele's drones, or you can work as part of the team."

"As if. Medina gave me this spot, and you can't gainsay him."

"But I can bring you up on charges for insubordination. Like it or not, I'm your AIC. Watch Farina all you want but, if you're on Tac 47, you've got a real job to do. Got it?"

Houston scrunched his lips into a snarl. "Yes, sir."

"Very good." Tolden pointed to the door. "Grab your gear, folks. The chopper's on the hot pad. We lift in five."

CHAPTER FOURTEEN

The school across from the cafe where I lounged was a tiny building in a tiny town near the Illinois-Missouri border. If Tabitha had been there, I had no doubt she would have been able to hear the Mississippi from where we sat—but she wasn't, and my ears weren't that good. My eyes, however, swept over the front entrance of the school, which was motionless except for a pair of highschoolers necking under the trees next to the parking lot.

The street itself was free of cars, giving us a clear view into the school. Steele and Houston had blocked off both sides of the road with construction cones to divert traffic while Hunt, Tolden, and I watched the exits. I sat across from the front entrance—which was the most likely exit point for our target. My phone showed feeds from Steele's drones with footage of the other exits, just in case.

I could see why they'd sent Tac 47 to deal with this particular situation instead of one of the other four abductions scheduled to happen around now. The kid was in classes. When the bell rang, he would exit the building inside a mass of highschoolers.

Even if we were right about his most likely path to get back home, identifying the kid the Superiors were here for without my blue lines would have been a headache. Even Steele's drones, hovering around the school, would have only had a sixty-seven percent chance of catching him when the bell rang and the horde of kids flooded out. With my blue lines, the chance of reaching our target before the Superiors did shot up to a whopping ninety-two-point-six percent.

The target was Hardy Quell, a Senior at Jersey Community Highschool. According to Steele's research, he was two months away from graduating in the top one percent of his class and moving to Silicon Valley for an internship. As I watched the school, I couldn't help but wonder where I would be now, if I hadn't ever met Zachary, gotten kicked out of public school and enrolled in Martial Academy. Hardy Quell was only two months younger than I was. Could I have been preparing to go to University instead of staking out a highschool to protect a clueless student from genetic experiments?

I remembered a time when I had dreamt of going to college and getting a Ph.D. I wanted everyone to know I was the best—that my brain really could think up all this miraculous technology. I thought the only way I could accomplish that was through education. If I had letters in front of my name, then everyone would know that I was as brilliant as I felt. I would be accepted by other engineers. I would be able to build whatever impossible things my brain came up with.

I could pull the memories and watch videos of my life before I knew about psionics, but it was surreal. Everything was so easy back then. I worried about whether the kids at school liked me—whether they were laughing at me, or at some unfathomable mystery of the universe. I tweaked my blue lines for maximum efficiency, and revised mental blueprints of technology I knew I'd never be able to build.

Zach had burned that life and dangled me above the smoke to watch it die.

I had still wanted to get to University, but he had made that impossible. Universities didn't accept kids who never finished highschool, no matter how intelligent they were.

Now, looking back, I couldn't bring myself to wish it had turned out differently. My work fighting the Institute mattered. I'd built my impossible technology, and I'd learned to take care of myself. I worked side by side with people like Cal, who had multiple degrees. Even without that piece of paper hanging on my wall, they accepted me. They helped me hone my brilliance. They let me build the fantastic things I created in my mind. With or without University, I had found a release. I had still become an engineer.

If I could change one thing, I would find a way to bring Mom with me.

Immediately, the warning flashed on my vision, obscuring everything else with its urgency. Mom could not know about the neurodivergent world I lived in. If she found out, she would die. The percentage hovered at ninety-nine-point-nine-nine percent. I shoved the message away, but it remained, blinking at me with awful finality. I grit my teeth, martialed my lines, and sealed it away.

The message still came every time I thought about Mom. I hadn't seen her in a year. My chest ached when I thought about going home—how worried she would be, and how happy she would be to finally see me again. If only Mom didn't have an Instance—a sort of tool in Mom's mind that would unravel if it spent any time in the neurodivergent world. The message embedded in my consciousness reinforced that fact. If the Instance unraveled, Mom would die. It was a built-in barrier to keep her away from me and the world I lived in. I clenched my fists and wished the warning away. If only the

Instance had never existed! Then I could bring her with me when I next fled the Organization. But, then, even that had its drawbacks. My delicate mother could hardly handle being torn from her home only to travel halfway across the world to avoid the Organization's ruthlessness.

"Heads up," Steele said across the mic. I locked the WATCH module alongside the PREP module as the bell rang and the once empty school entrance became an ocean of teenagers. Students poured out of the doors like some sort of non-newtonian fluid. They stopped and bunched up in places as students gawked at classmates, and sped up as some students hurried to get home. Once, a crowd like this would have hijacked my blue lines and it would have taken an eternity to get them back under control. Now, I occasionally flicked the BYE-BYE module, but shoved all extraneous calculations to the back of my mind.

"Superiors are here," I muttered as I saw a woman strolling down the street. On the outside, she moved like anyone else, but the muscle load on her limbs was different. Her bone structure was almost correct, but she was taller than someone with her proportions should have been. Her forearms were longer. Her limbs rotated as she walked. I didn't know what the height was for—other than giving the Superiors an edge during a fight—but that was another constant across all the variations of Zeta-Superiors I'd seen.

Another Superior appeared from around the next corner, and then I stiffened as a car parked in front of the school.

"Steele? Houston? Where did the car come from?"

There was a hiss in the com as I stood and started strolling toward the Superiors who were piling out of the car. My vision was covered in red as I saw even more Superiors appear from down the street. Sixteen…no, twenty-two, and they were still coming.

"Um, we've got a problem," I said. Then I identified Quell, the target. I dropped the damping field just long enough to project the kid's location into everyone's head. When I pulled it back up, my head was starting to pound.

"Black, I need you to link up with Hunt like we've been practicing. Separate the Superiors from the kids. Farina, how loud can you yell?" Tolden's voice crackled over the comms.

I could feel the intent behind his words as I turned the neural damper down again and the buzzing started at the edge of my mind. My blue lines flickered. This wasn't going to turn out well if Tolden couldn't get here in time. I wasn't as fast as I used to be, and the Organization hadn't let me bring any of my toys except the electropulser. Maybe if I had my shielding unit—

I stopped that thought before my blue lines could finish calculating how much that would have increased my survival chance.

"Oi, doggies!" I shouted at the top of my lungs. Some of them turned. "Remember me?"

They turned, anticipation battering at my vulnerable mind. Yeah, they recognized my face. The Instructors still wanted me. If they could bring me in, they would be rewarded. Suddenly, Quell wasn't their only target.

I checked the charge on the electric rifle slung over my back. Not my favorite weapon, but definitely the one for the job. This was a Superior-killer. If a human got a full shot and then got to a hospital they would survive it. If they caught the nimbus, they could walk it off. A Superior wouldn't, though. It targeted the modifications that happened in their brain when they were changed.

Half of them snarled and charged. I swallowed hard. Fifteen Superiors were definitely enough to saturate my defenses, and the other fourteen would rip through those high school kids like they were dolls.

"Tolden, tell me you have a plan," I said as I dropped to a knee, kicked the rifle into automatic, and opened fire. I only had three magazines for this thing—which should have been more than sufficient. That was before Superiors started coming out of the works. When I was out of charge, life was going to get a whole lot more difficult.

"Don't try to catch them," Tolden said. There were notes of humor in his voice I could catch even over the comms system.

I started to ask for clarification, but then I saw the first Superior clawing at the ground as it lifted off the school's sidewalk and started flying toward me. He landed in a pile of fellow Superiors like a bowling ball, and they tried to untangle themselves as the next Superior started flying.

Hunt and Black must have access to the interface device we'd used to take down Ms. King. Neither of them was a high level telekinetic, but the device let them multiply what power they had. Working together, they were the equal of an Instructor.

I grinned as I tossed the first clip aside and jammed the second one into the bottom of the weapon. The Superiors were learning, though, and they were starting to thin out enough that dodging was effective.

I snarled and set my blue lines to calculating their evasion patterns, but that decreased my rate of fire by half.

The first Superior reached me, and only eight were down. I rolled out of its way, sprang to my feet, and lit the electro-pulser glove. I couldn't have taken seven of these things on my own even before my mind had fractured. I shoved away panic and focused on following the cues my blue lines gave.

"I've got the kid. I repeat, I have Hardy Quell," Houston said. "Heading back to the chopper."

"Steele, check to make sure his path is clear," Tolden said. I could hear him panting on the other side of the com. Students were scattered every which way. I dropped a Superior just before it could finish trying to rip a kid's head off. A running tally in the top corner of my vision revealed that the kid I'd just saved was in the minority. Most of them had gotten away. The ones that weren't safe yet were being protected by Black and Hunt, still standing on the cafe's roof behind me.

Steele swore. "DEXDA puts another ten Superiors that way. Houston, take the kid to the secondary vehicle and get out of here."

"They knew we were coming," Tolden said. My blue lines blinked an agreement just moments before I cleared them with a savage swipe.

I propelled the side of my booted foot into a Superior's knee, slapped the electropulser on its face, then spun in time to dodge green claws. My blue lines seized on that image and started running a match program.

"They're running with sedative-laced claws," I warned. "Don't get hit."

"I thought this was supposed to be a retrieval mission," Black said. "Thirty Superiors for a civi?"

He was right. This was too many Superiors for them to just be grabbing one kid. They'd showed up in force, ready to fight the Organization.

"Well, they obviously either knew we were coming, or spotted us and have a base close enough to respond," I said. I'd rooted out all of the bases I could find in Indianapolis proper, but we were a ways away from there, and I hadn't even started in on the surrounding area. They had dug into this area like termites, and they weren't letting go.

"Houston got to the car in time," Steele said, then cursed again. "Black, there's a sniper on the roof. Tolden's down."

"32!" Black snarled. "I won't get there in time. Go. See how bad the damage is."

I got another shot with the electric rifle off, then tossed it aside. It was out of charge. About as useful as a club right now. I caught the glare from a plasma cannon off the mirrors of the parked car. Black had joined the fight, but there were still too many of them.

I drew my semiautomatic and finished fighting my way to Tolden. A moment later, Black joined me. He held the Superiors back while I checked Tolden, but there was almost no blood. I figured out why when I saw the dart in his throat. I jerked the needle free and sniffed the substance they'd injected into him. The same sedative as laced the Superiors' claws. They'd knocked him out? Why?

"You've got the most combat time, kid. We need a plan," Black said.

I nearly choked. I was in charge? In the middle of this mess? My blue lines flickered up, and a moment later I had recovered. Black was right. Steele's brain might be able to handle more sheer data than mine could, but I had the ability to make a plan and then execute it in the middle of this changing situation. Black was great at combat, but his plans usually consisted of "blow it up. If it's still moving, hit it with a cannon". Steele was too cerebral, and Hunt was a berserker in battle. That left me.

"Hunt, we need a ride out of here. There's a base on the outskirts of St. Louis. If we can make it there, their auto defenses will take care of the rest."

"On it," Hunt said. "Southwest corner of the school—"

the comms units fizzled out and started smoking. I jerked mine from my ear and stomped on it to extinguish the flames.

"We're being jammed—hard," Black said. "Get him up, I'll cover you."

I holstered my weapon and pulled Tolden over my shoulders. He wasn't nearly as light as Mom was. I staggered under his weight.

"Hold it together, kid. Get him to the car."

It was slow going, but six minutes later, I found the car Hunt had hot-wired. Steele was in the driver's seat, and Hunt was firing the last electric rounds she had brought.

"Steele," I shouted as I got in the car. "Can you blow the chopper from here?"

His eyebrows drew together as he ran through a series of computations. "So they don't get our supplies cache. Tac-Dep's going to throw a fit at the loss of resources, but I'll get it done."

I looked back at Black, who was trying to hold the Superiors off. His plasma cannon was down to half charge. I felt the Superiors intention as they lunged.

"Watch out!"

But I was too late. The Superior locked its jaws around Blacks leg. Hunt's last electric rifle round knocked the Superior off him. It rolled away and shook off the stun, slowed, but still fully functional as Hunt leaped at it. Black made it to the car. Hunt was down on one knee, bashing the Superior's head with the butt of her rifle.

"Get in here, crazy!" Black shouted. A moment later, she was inside and Steele was driving like a madman through the Jersyville streets. Hunt regained some reason in her eyes and ripped the medkit off of Black's tactical suit as he groaned.

The suit's leg had contracted to try and staunch the bleeding, but the Superior had ripped out a chunk of the suit, along with his leg. There was blood all over the seat, turning creme suede crimson.

She dumped a handful of antiseptic powder over his wound then slapped a self-sealing bandage on his leg. Almost immediately, it started to darken with blood. "He needs a hospital soon, or he's going to need a pod," Hunt said.

I pulled up an image of the base map and read off longitude and latitude. "There's a med bay there."

"That's not home base," Steele protested.

"But it's the closest one we've got," I said. Black needed medical attention. He hadn't let me die when Houston shot me, and I wasn't going to let him bleed out now if I had anything to say about it.

Black pushed himself up and rolled down the window so he could stick the barrel of his plasma cannon out.

I grimaced. We'd taken down thirty-six Superiors—but the ones chasing us brought the total count to fifty-three, and they were persistent. They barreled toward us on all fours like awkward wolves, snapping at the back bumper of the car or clawing at the tires. Their claw marks were scratched into the aluminum car body above the wheels, but Steele's fancy driving had kept them from puncturing a tire.

"Steele, I need you to broadcast a message to the St. Louis base we're headed for. If they don't know we're coming, we're going to read as hostile and our own autodefenses will take us out."

Black fired three more plasma rounds out the window. He nailed one Superior, but it wasn't enough.

"I can't believe I gave up my chair in C-DAD for this!" Steele complained.

I clenched my jaw. "Really not the time, Steele."

I could feel his concentration increase, and he stifled a curse. "Not yet. Somebody's jamming us, and every time I figure a way around it, the frequencies shift. They've got a neurodivergent on the other end of their jammer."

I looked back at the mob of Superiors coming after us, then pulled up the image of the Superior Hunt had hit with the electric rifle blast. A direct blast like that should have killed it, but it had rolled and kept coming. Had the Superiors already started adapting to our weaponry?

A more detailed analysis showed some sort of high-tech armor. It was nearly invisible. I clenched my teeth. Of all the times for them to come up with a brilliant technological advance, this was the worst. Where was all this crap coming from? Every time we deployed a new weapon, they found some way to counter it! I scanned the crowd of Superiors in pursuit. Sixty-point-two percent of them were in that body armor. Additionally, they were faster, stronger, and had grasped the concept of 'a trap'. A quick catalogue of our weaponry showed that only Black's plasma cannon had a hope of damaging them. This, right here, was why the Organization hadn't already defeated the Institute.

I watched as Black's eyes started to roll back in his head, and slapped him.

"Don't you dare pass out on me," I shouted, but he had lost a lot of blood from that gash in his leg. I slapped another self-sealing bandage on top of the last one, but there wasn't much else I could do. The bandage was soaked almost as soon as I laid it down.

"Here." Hunt held out a hand, and I pried Black's plasma cannon from his grip and handed it to her.

"Careful with the charge," I warned. It had to be close to

empty, and that was the only weapon we had that could do a thing against them.

She only grinned and stuck the barrel out the window.

A moment later, there were six fewer Superiors, and the cannon was out of charge. Hunt pulled the weapon back inside the car. "Well, that was fun. What's Plan B?"

I looked from Black, who was somewhere between conscious and unconscious, to Tolden, who was still sleeping off the sedative.

"We have to let the St. Louis base know we're coming, or it won't matter what happens to those Superiors. If we come in this hot, they aren't going to check for Friend or Foe. The auto defenses are going to blast us into very tiny pieces."

Hunt looked through the back window. "They've been running full out for over fifteen minutes under heavy fire, and they still aren't tiring. I hate to sound disloyal here, but why can't the superhuman soldiers be on our side for once?"

I understood what she meant. I reached into Steele's head.

::Can you get those doors open, or not? It's not going to be pretty when the defense systems activate, and we're almost out of gas.::

They're jamming us in a way I've never seen before. I can't figure it out. I can't hear the base, and they certainly can't hear us. I'm doing all I can just to keep DEXDA from bursting into flames, just like the comms. The frustration was evident in his thoughts. *If we don't let them know we're coming, then our own missiles will take us out! We weren't supposed to get anywhere close to this base during the course of the mission, so they don't even know we're in the area.* Then an edge of humor entered his thoughts. *You know, this was not what I intended when I said that no tech would ever work for you again.*

I frowned as my blue lines spat out alternatives. None of them were good. I clenched my jaw and turned to Hunt. "Give me five minutes. If I'm not back, then start thinking my name as loud as you can. Understand?"

Hunt's eyes narrowed. "What are you going to do?"

Something unbelievably stupid. I hesitated a moment as I saw the worry in Hunt's eyes. I'd detached my consciousness from my body more times than any other projector telepath in the Organization, and I'd made it back every time, but the process was far from safe. The last time I'd done it, I was in full control of my gift, and I'd still gotten lost on my way back. If it wasn't for Tolden, I would never have made it.

Now, my gift was far from healed, Tolden was unconscious, and I was barely in control. My blue lines gave me a thirty percent chance of survival.

This was my only choice. I was the reason we were out on this mission. I was going to get us out of this mess.

I reached up and turned the dial on the neural damper all the way off.

Lights and sounds erupted in my mind, all fighting for attention. Superiors threw off bloodlust and adrenaline from the chase that crashed into me like a tsunami, followed by pulses of pain that came and went with the beat of Black's heart. Hunt tried to put on a brave face, but she couldn't hide her terror. The feelings and thoughts mixed with the fear taking root in my own mind as I tried to fight through the suffocating layers. The grasses and bugs were all shouting about sunlight, and food, and warmth. Even farther than that, there was a numbing watchfulness from microorganisms too small to see—but not too small to add to this disordered cacophony of thoughts. The world was painted in bright, flashing colors that made my head explode inside my skull. There were no blue lines to save me from the pain, here. I was alone.

I pushed past the colors, and cast my mind out. I moved quickly, propelled by the need to stop all the noise as I soared across the road, and skimmed off the surface of the sky. There! More minds.

I fingered through them, ignoring their thoughts as best I could until I found the one I needed. The woman bore a sense of power, and assurance, but even as I touched her mind, the woman tried to wiggle away. I held her fast, driven in part by the clamoring outside my head. If I let go, there was no telling where I would end up.

::Stop fidgeting, and listen.:: I shouted above the noise.

Pain lanced through the woman's mind, and I realized my mistake. The woman couldn't hear all this other excruciating clamor. I sent a feeling of brief apology.

Who are you? This woman wasn't a projector telepath, or even if she was, there wasn't a whole lot for her to communicate with. I was fading.

::I'm Agent 32 with Tac 47. We're coming in hot, with fourteen Superiors on our tail. Electronic communications are jammed, and I can't stay here long. Track us as best you can—::

Pressure was building in my skull as the world took it apart. This was too much!

Slow down. You're who? Confusion and fear washed over the woman's mind in equal parts.

::Not much time. Have the gates open for us when we get there—:: A gust of fear dislodged me from the woman's mind, and I flew into someone else's mind, dug in my fingernails, and launched back toward where I thought I'd come from. The sound of my heartbeat was low beneath everything else that fought for my attention. It was slower, now. When it stopped, I wouldn't have a body to go back to.

Another gust of bloodlust pushed me off course. I could feel my mind fading. Thoughts were being stripped away with every sound. The pain was gone. I was too tired to feel pain. Too tired to fight through this noise. It would be so easy to just slip away.

Darkness—numb and welcoming—surrounded me. Beyond that, an echo of remembered agony. Colors. White, blue, green. Red. The color of blood.

Black was dying.

Hunt was crying.

Tolden slept, blissfully unaware of the pain around him. How much easier would it be to slip into the dark? I was so tired.

Another mind was there. Familiar. Dark. Unknowable. Laced with pain I couldn't see. He held his identity deep inside the folds of his own mind as he swallowed me. The noise faded. The lights dimmed. For the first time in a long time, my mind was silent. Safe in the confines of this other being.

The other mind left, and the cacophony was back. Hate. Anguish. Agony. It pushed me like the winds of a hurricane as I tried to orient myself.

Crystal—Crys—don't go!

The words punched into me. I felt Hunt near. Black was incoherent. They were closer now. I stitched my thoughts together and forced my mind to function. Below me was a body. It had lost its customary golden skin tone. Its hands were limp. Its eyes were dead.

I felt its heartbeat stitched into the lining of my mind.

That person was me. That body was mine.

I clawed my way toward it in one last act of desperation—and sat up, gasping for air.

"Oh, Farina. Thank goodness you're alright!" Sound came rushing back through my ears, and I shuddered away from the pain that cracked over my head. The world was pulsing in shades of black. It was like someone had taken a nail and hammered it through my skull. The invisible torturer set a second nail against the back of my head and began to drive it through my brain. I reached up to cover my ears to drive out some of the sound, but it didn't help. The noise was still there, above the sound of my heartbeat, above the sound of the hammer.

Hunt was waving at me, but I couldn't tell what she was saying. I reached a trembling hand toward my head and jerked the damping field to full. The noise faded away, leaving only the beating of my heart.

"What happened?" Hunt asked. The worry in her eyes was palpable.

I shook my head and immediately regretted it as acid started to climb my throat. I held a hand up.

"Steele," I croaked, "the doors are going to open for us. Are we going to have enough fuel to make it?"

"Yes, Ma'am."

My stomach knotted, and I grabbed for the window, Hunt shifted out of the way in time for me to empty my stomach contents all over the road. I righted myself, panting as a Superior's claws passed through the air my head had just occupied. Now was not the time to be sick, no matter how badly it hurt. "Get us there."

I couldn't help but think about that mind that had rescued me. Who was it? Who was he? I closed my eyes and went back in my memory, but there were no clues. The mind hadn't said a word. It had just deposited me on top of my body.

I nearly died.

The realization should have frightened me, but I was past fear.

"The jamming has dropped off, 32. We're coming into the base's short-range missile envelope." Steele reported.

Sure enough, portions of the road slid open to reveal a dimly lit ramp.

I gulped. "Take us in, and alert the base that Black and Tolden need medical attention."

CHAPTER FIFTEEN

I stepped out of the vehicle and ran an eye over the pair of white-coated medics with the name of their department stamped on the back carting Black away. Another set was tending to Tolden, but unlike the medics tending to Black, none of them seemed particularly worried. The mix the Superiors had shot him with really was just a fast acting sedative. Black was the one I was worried about. The man could handle a lot, but he'd lost a lot of blood. When the medics lifted him onto the gurney, he had been frightfully pale.

He was in good hands, though. The Organization would take good care of him. Unlike me, Black was a good soldier. When they told him to jump, his only question was "how high?"

I looked over Steele and Hunt for injuries, but they were only a little scraped up. I started to breathe normally again. We'd made it out alive. The adrenaline started to filter out of my bloodstream, and I nearly collapsed. I caught myself on the side of the scraped up car, panting hard as any pain I'd shipped to the back of my awareness dumped back into my conscious thoughts. My muscles trembled.

A white-coated medic hurried up to me, but I waved her off. I would be fine in a few moments. I sorted essential sensory input for the unessential input and shunted everything I could into my back brain. I needed to think. I couldn't do that if I was curled up in a ball of pain, and I couldn't do that if a well-meaning medical technician shot me full of pain killers.

Pain killers.

I fumbled for the little white pill in the top pocket of my tactical suit and crushed it under my tongue. The rest of the pain receded. I set a timer for when the meds would wear off and hard-wired a notification that would trigger ten minutes before the timer finished. I would get to medical before the meds wore off. Until then, I had to be functional. There was too much that didn't make sense. I started reviewing the footage of the mission.

Why had there been fifty-three Superiors there to begin with? The only other places I'd seen that many Superiors was at their bases, like the one I'd taken down a few weeks ago. I hadn't seen any signs that Jersyville contained a Superior base. Maybe they had known we were coming?

It was tempting to think that the Organization had a traitor in their midst that had told the Institute our mission objective and timeframe—and even more tempting to think it was Houston. Wouldn't that be a great setup? Houston escapes with the kidnapping victim while the rest of the team goes up against overwhelming force? The Superiors got their target, got me, and killed the others. Houston could arrive at the nearest Organization base empty-handed and report whatever he wanted. There would be no evidence to gainsay him.

Somehow, that story didn't ring true. Medina said that the Organization had been inside Houston's mind, and had done something to keep him from working with the Institute. If he'd broken that training, he would have tracked me down. It burned at his mind that I had escaped him, not once, but three times now. If he was working with the Superiors, he would have cornered me and exacted his revenge. At the very least, he would have stayed to watch the Superiors dismember us. No, Houston wasn't working with the Superiors.

Something just didn't add up. It wasn't just the question of why there had been so many Superiors, but also why they had laced their claws with sedatives instead of poisons the way they usually did. Superiors liked to play with their food, but sleepy victims weren't any fun. Better would be a paralytic, so they could transport us without the fuss, and then take their time without having to wait for us to wake up. Superiors weren't patient creatures. If my year of hunting them had taught me anything it was that they had very few priorities. First, they obeyed the Instructors. Second, they were easily bored. Third, they enjoyed pain. The only one of those things would explain the sedative, so why did the Instructors direct the Superiors to sedate us and bring us in?

"Agent 32?" A woman's voice jerked me away from my thoughts. I turned so I could see her face. "Thank goodness. It looks like I got to Command fast enough."

I furrowed my eyebrows. Who was this person? I longed to reach a tendril out and brush the woman's mind but, even with the pain killers, it was all I could do to stand up straight. Turning the neural damper down right now would be debilitating, and even the woman's surface thoughts were unreachable behind her walls. I rubbed my temples. "Who are you?"

She frowned. "Agent 69—Jane Doe. You're the one who contacted me."

I blinked. Right. Of course she could tell that I was the one who had grabbed her mind. Any telepath worth their salt would be able to recognize that. Conversely, I should have recognized this woman the moment I laid eyes on her. It was a testament to my sheer exhaustion—and the damage my mind had taken—that I hadn't.

My blue lines surfaced of their own volition and flicked over the woman's body. There had been a subtle shift—so subtle I'd almost missed it. This woman was primed for violence. There was a weapon of some sort hidden in her sleeve, just out of her grasp.

Great. Trust InDep to tell that something was hinkey.

"You're the mind I grabbed. Right." I showed the woman my palms. Now was not the time to be getting in fights with InDep supervisors. Director Carlisle and the Director of In-Dep hardly trusted me as it was.

The woman's eyes widened, and she projected the image of a harmless little valley girl. "I don't understand."

I shook my head, and then berated myself once more as the pounding in my head increased. "I kind of took hold of a random mind that felt like it would have some sort of authority. It was plain, dumb luck that I grabbed you. That being said, thank you for getting those doors open."

Jane Doe didn't relax in the slightest. "What kind of projector doesn't have basic control over who they communicate with?" Her tone was harmless, as if the answer to her question wouldn't trigger an assault if I answered it wrong. It was the kind of voice that Ms. King had us practice to disarm opponents by making them think we weren't the sharpest knife in the block. Jane Doe was sharp enough for both of us.

The deception made my head hurt even worse, and I pushed down a wave of irritation. "The kind that has to wear a neural damper so she can block everything else out. Check my file. I'm sure all the information is there."

A paper thin electronics pad appeared in the Doe's hand almost immediately, and she ran her eye down the page. Time passed, and she relaxed. The blue lines of my vision receded. My headache worsened. I kept one steadying hand on the side of the car, careful to avoid places where Superior claws had left gouges of metal above the wheel-well. Those ridges were sharp enough to cut.

This war with the Institute had everyone on edge, and I was no exception. The only difference was, that if I wasn't extremely careful, I could end back on an Organization kill list. I'd met Director Carlisle, and he didn't seem like the kind of man that one angered, and then escaped.

Director Carlisle. The name triggered a storm of memories that tore at my mind. The blank two minutes; the chafing at my wrist—forgotten twice, now. And something else. Something recent.

My vision faded to black for a moment, like I'd blinked. I shook my head to clear the cotton balls that had inserted themselves between my ears. Maybe I needed to go to Med-Dep sooner than I'd anticipated.

Doe's mouth curled into a grin as she finished perusing my—rather extensive—file, and she dropped the girlish demeanor. "Well, I can understand why you were so defensive. Your file is quite the read." She looked up to meet my eyes. "Welcome to St. Louis Research Base, and congratulations for not dying on your way." Another glance down my battered tactical suit and blood-speckled extremities, and her smile became more genuine. "Why don't you follow me down to R&D. Our MedDep is mostly designed to fix accidents—I'm sure you've noticed by now that we're not exactly a combat oriented base—so your two teammates have filled up our beds already. Luckily, there are some advantages to being a Pod research facility."

I took a hand off the car and managed to keep my feet as I followed the Doe down the hallway, around one corner, and through the standard blast-proof glass sliding doors that separated R&D from the rest of the facility. The room was a bomb of sensory input, with chattering researchers, six drones hovering in the back corner, the stench of burning metal mixing with antiseptic, and the taste of microscopic copper shavings that stuck in the back of my throat. I coughed to try and get rid of the taste, and the resulting surge of pain stole my vision and left me gasping for breath.

When I came back to myself enough to look around, I was seated in the back corner that had been buzzing with drones only a moment ago—except the clock in the top of my vision revealed that I'd been out of it for three-point-two minutes. There was a mask over my face with clean air, making it easier to breathe. A few more breaths finished washing the metallic taste out of my mouth. I touched the plastic mask over my mouth and nose, blinking as more spots on my vision darkened to black.

"It's just oxygen. You were having trouble breathing," Doe said. She was standing to the side of where I was seated, looking down at me with unreadable eyes. "The prototype will be here in just a moment."

There was a hiss of the doors opening and then closing again. I moved my head, which was getting heavier by the moment. The timer on my vision that counted down until the stim was at low enough concentrations so as to be ineffective was blinking at five minutes, twenty-three seconds. It was starting to filter out of my system. I spotted the white research coat and the person with a capped syringe in his hand and a plastic sealed needle in the other. He made his way to the Doe's side, his lips pinched into a frown.

"We've done human trials, but not for anything neurological, Doe, are you sure? I mean, the reports on this are going to be ugly, and she hasn't signed the waiver, and I just finished coaxing these little darlings out of the Pod—a process that took two weeks. We're not really going to use them for this, are we?"

"The other tactical agent's taking up the pod, and she doesn't look like she's going to last much longer." Doe tilted her head slightly at the researcher, as though urging him to take the hint and just make use of whatever was in that capped needle he held in his hand. The beady-eyed researcher didn't seem to notice the Doe's look, though, because he was far more focused on the silver-green, viscous liquid in his syringe.

I moved my lips to tell them that I was fine. I just needed another stim, and then to go check on Black and Tolden. This wasn't the first time I'd been hurt bad, and it probably wouldn't be the last.

No sound came out of my mouth, and my tongue was big and heavy. Blue lines crowded up my vision with damage reports from analysis that had started the moment I'd come back to consciousness, and were only now finishing. I didn't need blue lines to tell me that the response time was atrocious.

"She really doesn't look so good, does she?" The researcher looked away from the syringe long enough to lean over the chair Doe had sat me in, eyes squinting at me. "Alrighty, you can use my little sweeties, but only if she gives us a full report afterward. It's hard to find genuine test subjects for this—well, I guess it's in clinical trials, now, for limited use, anyway." He looked at Doe and held the syringe up meaningfully. "This is the most recent batch cultivated from the pod, you know. I think we've almost figured out which signals correlate to the stem nano bots. When we can find that one, I think we can get them to replicate outside of the machine, and then this tech will be viable for more than six hours after they're removed from the pod."

"Kay," Doe's tone had a touch of warning in it. "The human being is dying. Perhaps she deserves some of your attention?"

The researcher, Kay, blinked, then nodded. "Oh, right." He swabbed my skin with something cold and wet then jammed the needle in my arm without ceremony. He watched the syringe with all the intent of a cat watching a mouse den as he depressed the back and watched all his precious silver-green concoction drain away. "Anyway, as I was saying, these little nanos should have your girl all patched up in about half the time the pod would take. She'll be out probably three hours before that poor chap who got stuck with that old dinosaur of a medical machine. Of course, we're unable to replicate all the same safeguards as within the pod, but we don't need them because these ones aren't self-replicating."

The researcher's voice faded in and out as I felt a million little things crawling in my arm, like little needles, and then that sensation faded. The workshop faded from my senses—everything except the sound of Kay and the Doe, which came into sharper focus than I'd heard anything since they'd put my biocard back.

"You know, it's a wonder we haven't got this technology earlier. We would have, if the old neurodivergent council wasn't so self-centered. Before they got all blown to bits, or whatever happened. Keeping this tech out of development," Kay snorted. "Well, once it gets perfected, Director Carlisle might approve limited neurotypical trials, and then we'll really be changing the world. We should have had this decades ago."

Doe gave the kind of long-suffering sigh that said she'd heard this complaint from him before. "The world is controlled through information. Keeping it out of certain hands may be the only way to keep the Institute from causing more problems. I've told you this before. Now, why don't you focus on monitoring your machines? If she dies, the Director and Subdirector Medina are going to have my head."

The researcher looked at me, blinked, pulled out a little electronics pad, and stabbed something on the surface.

Even the sounds faded.

I woke up an hour later, blue lines in working order, and with my head remarkably clear. Researcher Kay was standing where Doe had been, and Doe was in a chair against the wall, dozing with her face propped up by one fist.

"How do you feel?" Kay asked.

I blinked, took a full breath. Nothing hurt—a novel sensation. "Better."

My blue lines started running diagnostics, only for an ache to start back up in the base of my skull.

Kay was frowning down at that electronics pad he held like a single sheet of paper in front of his white buttoned lab coat. "If you're going to take part in a trial like this, I'm going to need more info than 'better'. Fingers and toes move? No, of course they do. Eyes work? Taste? Smell? Come on, you've got to give me something for my notes, or I'm not going to be able to justify this to my supervisor. Doe's not the one in charge of research on this toothpick of a base, you know, and this was a majorly expensive trial."

The blue lines completed their report while Kay was saying that. He looked up from the screen, glared at me, and took a breath to start in again on the importance of getting data.

I held up a hand to hopefully fend off another tide of words. "Diagnostics say that there isn't very much neurological damage, and most of that is part of an old wound I've been working on healing up for a while. I'm not at a hundred percent yet, but most of that is just gift overuse."

Researcher Kay blinked. "Old wound? Well, you should have said so before the trial, this is going to skew all the results! How inconsiderate."

I pushed myself to the edge of the chair and was pleased to find that the world did not try to rotate out from under me, nor did my headache increase considerably.

"You don't have any more details on the injuries the nano bots left alone? It's the least you can do, I think, after you messed up all my data. I'm going to be writing up expense justifications for the next week, not to mention having to cultivate another batch of nano bots from the Pod. Well? What's still the problem? This old injury thing, that is. You don't have another twelve hours, do you? I can try and whip up something to target it if we know what the problem is. But of course you don't have the time. You're a tactical agent, and you're all rush, rush, rush, these days. Something about genetic mutants trying to destroy the world. Well, I guess I don't want to be turned into one of those slobbering dog-things, so I can't really complain—"

"—but that's hardly going to stop him," Doe remarked muzzily from her chair. She blinked sleep from her eyes. Kay whirled around, eyes wide.

"Oh, you shouldn't be awake yet. You were up for 72 hours yesterday—well, not exactly just yesterday—which is hardly healthy. Go back to sleep." He made shooing motions with the hand that wasn't clutching the electronics pad.

Doe glared at him. "I don't know that anyone can sleep with all this chatter."

Kay shrugged and turned back to me. "Anyway, as I was saying. What old damage? I—"

I held up a hand to stop him and, to my shock, it worked. I pulled up the report and read off the info. "I've got one damaged sensory shunt that's about sixty-percent complete, but that won't hold data without losing approximately eighty percent of the load. Processing still has a few sticky spots, but hunting them down is an exercise in frustration. My best guess is that at least one of them has something to do with the incomplete shunt, but that hardly explains all of it."

Researcher Kay blinked. "And that means what, exactly?"

"I'm still confined to using my blue lines for processing and analysis, and my brain's still fractured. The speed of these processes has quadrupled since I first fractured back at headquarters, and is roughly equivalent to the speed I had when I was just finishing my training at Martial academy."

Kay shook his head so vigorously that his double chin continued to wobble even after his head had stilled. "I can't put that in my notes! What specifically is damaged? What neurons? You're using relative speeds for blue lines? What even are those, and what do they have to do with the neurological welfare of your brain? I need absolute medical terms here!"

I shrugged. "Reports don't give me absolute medical terms, that's not how my mind works. I don't have a medical degree. I never even finished highschool."

"Never even—" He looked down at the electronics pad in his hand, squinted for a moment, then looked back up at me. "You're this one, right? Agent 32?"

He flipped the pad around, and I saw a 3D version of myself in tactical black staring back with green eyes that reflected back the light. Under the picture was a list of working prototype technologies and technology derivatives that spanned two pages.

I nodded. "Turns out, book knowledge isn't the only useful thing in the world."

Researcher Kay just shook his head again. "Unbelievable. I don't think I would like a single second in your head. Stranger than most," he muttered.

Doe laughed. "So you say, but I've *been* in your head. Why don't you go finish those reports you love so much. Let me know if your supervisor gives you any trouble, and thanks for your help."

Researcher Kay left, still muttering to himself. I wasted a moment wondering if he ever stopped talking, and then refocused on Jane Doe who had made her way to her feet and was busy combing her fingers through shoulder length blonde hair.

"Well, if there's anything still busted, you should probably go down to MedDep. It's down one floor, and besides, you can badger our medical techs about how your tactical agent is doing."

I flushed. "He's not my tactical agent. I took command when the AIC—Carter Tolden, that is—got sedated by the Superiors. I'm not really cut out for his job."

The Doe smiled just a bit. "Whatever you say, 32. Anyway, when you're done with that, feel free to come back down to R&D. I've heard that some of the researchers are having trouble with some of your technology off-shoots, and you certainly aren't being deployed until your teammates are back to—" she cut off, and pulled a more-or-less normal looking phone from her pocket. "Perhaps not. Agent 32, SubDirector Medina is trying to reach you." Her eyebrows narrowed, but she didn't ask why her boss was trying to reach a tactical operative. "There's a secure room just outside the blast doors and down that hall. Your access code should open it. I'll shunt the call to that screen."

I pursed my lips. Medina was trying to reach me? Somehow that wasn't a surprise. MedDep would have to wait. I thanked the Doe, then strode off in the direction she had indicated.

The secure room was basically a closet at the end of the hall, with a screen embedded in the wall, a cheap plastic fold-up table beneath it, and a card reader to one side. The whole thing was illuminated with LEDs strung around the top corner of the ceiling—which was good. I wasn't sure I could handle close proximity to the constant flashing of an incandescent lightbulb right now. The nano bots, or whatever Researcher Kay had shot me full of, had helped, but I was getting tired of having a constant headache.

I slapped my card against the reader, then pressed my thumb to it a moment later to verify that I really was Crystal Farina, and not some goon who'd stolen her card. The screen flickered to "Establishing Secure Connection" for three-point-six seconds, then blinked again to reveal a close-in shot of Subdirector Medina's face.

New creases were worn into his forehead as he stared at me from the other side of the screen, his eyes dull and hard. Visual analysis showed that a sheen of sweat covered his face, revealed by the way he reflected the constant light of his office. There was a repetitive tremor in his muscles, like he was bouncing his knee beneath the camera, where I couldn't see.

I grit my teeth. I'd seen Medina survive an assassination attempt and look less worried than he did right now.

"Agent Farina, I thought you would want to know that Houston arrived safely with the package." His voice held a note I couldn't identify.

I nodded. The high school student was in Organization hands, then. I couldn't quite be sure if that was good or not, but it had to be better than leaving him with the Superiors. The fact that Houston had returned to the Organization only further fueled my suspicions that Houston was not a spy. The

Institute was up to something, and I wouldn't like it when they finally sprung their surprise.

"That is good to know," I said slowly as I debated whether or not to tell Medina my suspicions that the Organization had a leak. I tossed the decision to my blue lines to see what they would make of it. A notification appeared on my vision detailing the exits I had seen and the security measures in place around this base. This place, unlike the Organization's primary base of operations, was not built like a prison. Slipping out would be simple.

A moment later, the security briefing faded to be replaced by a note I'd written to myself.

This is not home. As soon as the mission is complete, I'm leaving.

I swallowed hard. Tolden and Black were lying unconscious in MedDep. They would both probably pull through, but leaving while they were hurt didn't feel right.

On the other side, though, they wouldn't be able to talk me out of leaving. If Tolden figured out what I was planning, he was probably the only one who could persuade me not to go through with it. Leaving before he woke up was the only way to ensure that I got out.

I grit my teeth again, my jaw so tense it ached. My blue lines blinked with the probability of a successful escape if I waited for the rest of my team to be out of MedDep. Twenty-six-point-nine percent. If I left as soon as I was done with Medina, it shot up to eighty-two percent even. I wouldn't be going to MedDep.

I returned my attention to the original question of whether I should tell Medina my suspicions. The answer was no. If they had a mole, it wasn't really my problem. I would leave, and finally be free of the Organization's control. The mole wouldn't impact me.

What about my father?

The question nearly flattened me. I doubled over, gasping, my fingers splayed on the table in front of me as pain tore through my head. I wasn't supposed to ask that question. I wasn't supposed to think about my father.

"32, what's wrong?" Medina asked, his voice sharp.

I waved a hand at him. The pain was already fading. What was pain, anymore? I spent so much time with my head pounding my brain into mush that it didn't matter. I barely felt it anymore.

If I left, I would never find my father.

My vision blanked for half a second, then I looked up, struggling to pin down my train of thought. What had I been planning?

Dark footprints, like the void had been walking in my thoughts, dotted my mind.

Leaving. I was leaving. I shook my head, trying to pull myself together. I was more tired than I had originally thought, to be having this much trouble—and it was no wonder, after I'd just been healed by some prototype medical technology. Researcher Kay had mentioned that he'd never used his nano bots to heal an injury like mine. Who knew what sort of side-effects there would be?

I assigned priorities. First, I had to get as much information I could get before I left. I wouldn't be able to use Tolden and Medina the way I'd used them before—or risk the Organization finding me again. They wouldn't be so nice if they had to bring me in a second time. No. If I left, I would be on my own until I finished taking the Institute down.

"How did the other retrieval missions go?" I asked. I looked back up at Medina, whose worry had only increased.

He stared at me a long time before he answered. If I'd been sitting across the desk from him, I would have assumed he was worming his way into my thoughts. Even Medina couldn't read my mind from halfway across the state, though, which was good. I didn't need him to feel the echo of irrational pain in my thoughts, and I didn't need him to discover the escape plans my blue lines were busy synthesising in the back of my brain.

"Better than yours did," he finally said. "The Superiors beat one team to the target, but all the teams emerged more or less unscathed. Unfortunately, the Institute launched an attack on headquarters. Our strike teams and quick response teams were all out—dealing with the attack and additional retrievals." Medina's eyes hardened. "We pulled units from long standing surveillance and defensive locations to repost the attack, and it worked. We were able to drive them off with minimal casualties, but calling for reinforcements had other consequences. Our analysis department is still sorting out whether it was deliberate—but that doesn't much matter." For one moment, his eyes changed. Age old regret merged with undiluted terror. "They have her now."

"Have who?" I asked.

Medina pinched the bridge of his nose. "Is the room clear? Is it secure?"

I shot a glance at the solid wood door behind me. The locking light was red. I looked back at the screen. "Yes. Now what is going on?"

There was a sick feeling in the pit of my stomach. Something had gone badly wrong. I'd never seen Medina this talkative, or this flustered. I triggered the BYE-BYE module to clear all thoughts of escaping from my mind. The timer for the medication I had taken earlier cleared away with it. My working mind was clear and ready to address whatever threat Medina revealed.

Medina took a deep breath. "Good. Now I want you to promise me you'll think this through. Don't do anything rash."

Rash?

"What is it?"

Something ugly flashed in Medina's eyes. It was gone just as quickly as it had come. His voice flattened, almost like he was reading off a script. Any emotional attachment I thought I'd heard was gone. "Two hours ago, InDep received word of a civilian kidnapping. We don't know a lot. All we know is that the Institute infiltrated an apartment building and captured an adult female. Director Carlisle handed me the brief personally."

I arched an eyebrow. The Institute kidnapping turnips wasn't exactly new. They needed more test subjects for their serums, and fodder to turn into Superiors. It was awful, but none of it necessitated Medina calling me this soon after a mission. I was hardly great material for a team leader, and Tolden would be up soon enough. Medina should be giving him this information, not me. Especially not when my brain was this messed up.

My blue lines flashed on my vision with a warning. Medina's behavior was inconsistent with every other interaction I'd had with him. For him to have a behavior shift this large? Something was wrong, and it wasn't just a turnip kidnapping.

"Do you have a description of the victim?" I asked. I pushed my blue lines harder, trying to figure out what it was that had made Medina sound so worried. The expected time of completion on that report was six minutes and twenty-three seconds from now. Hardly fast enough to give me any useful information.

"We have video of the abduction."

"Then you can track them?"

Medina shook his head. "We don't have to. We know where she's been taken. It's a reinforcement center run by an Instructor. The number of Superiors there changes depending on the time of year and number of Superiors they need to retrain and how many operational bases they can bleed overflow into. Right now it is packed to the brim. Our analysts put two hundred and fifty Superiors there right now."

I shook my head. "Why would they kidnap a turnip and hold her in a facility like that?"

Shadows crossed his eyes, and Medina shook his head. "We don't know." He was lying. I didn't know how I knew that, but I did. Maybe it was the way his eyes shifted. Maybe it was a note in his tone.

"Well, who is it?"

He swallowed. "You have to promise me you won't do anything rash. Farina, understand. Now is not the time for you to go off the deep end. All the Organization's resources are focused on this retrieval."

The time of completion on the report I'd started my blue lines on jumped forward by six minutes. A moment later, it was finished. I stared at the report icon on my vision blinking at me, and then past it at Medina's drawn face. Whatever he was about to tell me, I didn't want to know. It was awful. I could tell just by the way he looked at me with pity in his eyes.

"Who did the Superiors take?"

"Adalind Farina."

I looked at him for one moment, then another. The words didn't quite register. Adalind Farina. The name tugged at my heart. "No."

The Institute had taken Mom.

"Have you had any contact with her since you left the Agency?"

He wanted to know if I had done anything to drag Mom into this mess. I grit my teeth. "No, I specifically cut all contact. You are wrong, they didn't take Mom. Olivia's mom lives across the street, and she looks a little like Mom. Maybe they took her, and you thought it was Mom. It has to be someone else."

Medina tapped a button, and a camera feed covered his face. There, on the screen, was a picture of the street outside the apartment I had shared with my mother. I pieced together the pixelated image in my mind, and tried to study the scene, but the blue lines in my vision refused to come. The video played through, and I watched as a group of Superiors shoved my mother into a car at gunpoint.

My vision pulsed red, and I could feel minds from outside the room rubbing against my mind—everyone blissfully unaware of my anguish. I grabbed the dial on the neural damper, and tried to turn it all the way up, only the switch wouldn't budge. It was all the way up. I'd doubled the strength of the field, and it still wasn't enough. The Institute had my mother.

"Farina, are you alright?" Medina asked. There was caution in his voice.

My head snapped to his face and the fear in his eyes. "Where is she being held?"

"Not far from your location. I'll send you the coordinates as soon as you finish the briefing."

I turned away and stalked towards the door. The Institute couldn't turn my mother into a Superior. I wouldn't let that happen. I was going to get my mother back, no matter the cost. Images of Mom flashed through my mind with her bright green eyes and dreamy, childlike smile. Mom was the reason I fought this war—so she wouldn't be involved.

The Institute was going to rue the day they'd thought up this scheme. I would tear them apart limb from limb if I had to. When I was finished with them, there wasn't going to be enough left to fill a bucket. "Agent Farina!" Medina shouted, but I ignored him. "Crystal!"

I stopped and turned so I could see his face on the screen. "If they hurt her—" my voice broke. What if I was already too late? What if they had already turned her into one of those monsters?

Behind my eyes, I could see the bullet puncture Brigg's head. I could see the light in his eyes die. I'd already killed one friend who had been destroyed by the Institute.

Briggs's face morphed into Mom's. His strong, muscles body thinned until she was laying on top of me, choking me with her blood.

I shoved the image away, stumbled over a step, retching, then forced my way back to my feet. They would not turn Mom into a Superior. I wouldn't let them!

"I understand, Crystal, but you can't just storm the facility. We don't have complete intelligence yet."

Something inside me stiffened, and I looked him straight in the eye. "I don't care."

"You can't storm that facility by yourself." Medina fought to keep his voice calm, but I could still hear a crackle of fear.

"I can try," I snapped.

Medina slapped his hand on the table as fear turned to sudden anger, and I jumped. "Farina, just listen! Director Carlisle is on his way to the St. Louis base. He's bringing two strike teams with him. He's going to lead the extraction himself."

My blue lines flashed in my vision, showing the likelihood of my survival without Director Carlisle's team. A moment later, it was overridden with the likelihood of Medina lying to me.

I blinked the lines away.

"Director Carlisle won't risk himself and two strike teams to save one woman. She's a turnip."

Medina held up a hand, but I overrode him.

"There's only one reason for Director Carlisle to be coming, and that's because he's the only teleprojector with a hope of stopping me. He doesn't want to save my mother, and he knows he needs me to defeat the Institute. If you think I'm going to wait around for him to rip my mother out of my mind, you are insane!" He'd already messed with my memories once, in that meeting. I still hadn't managed to unravel whatever he'd done. I wouldn't let him do it again. I refused to forget Mom. I refused to let the Institute have her.

Medina lifted a finger. "Not everything is about you, Crystal. He is coming to help you. He doesn't like the idea of a civilian in that outpost any better than you do."

I snarled. "He hasn't saved any of the other civilians. What makes my mom different, Medina? Huh?"

His eyes darkened and he looked down at his desk.

I cut the connection before he could answer. I refused to sit here and wait. The Institute thought I was a threat before? They were going to regret taking my mother. Anger pulsed in my veins, hotter and stronger than anything I'd ever felt, buoyed by fear, and tempered by logic. Blue lines appeared in my mind with percentages. Medina was right about one thing. I needed a plan.

I strode into the MedDep lobby to find Steele and Hunt staring at the floor. Hunt stood as I entered. She flinched back when she met my eyes.

"What happened?"

I grit my teeth. "How are Black and Tolden?"

"The doctors say Black will be out of the pod in a few hours. Tolden will be up and about soon, too, and then they'll run some additional tests to see if the Superiors slipped anything else into that cocktail they shot him with," Steele said.

I nodded, then clenched my fists. "The Institute took my mom. I'm going to get her, but I need help getting out of the compound. Steele, can you take their cameras offline for a while? Unlock the doors?"

"This isn't a sanctioned mission, is it?" Steele asked. He took his tablet from his belt.

I shook my head.

"Then you're going to need supplies," Hunt said. "I saw a prototype motorcycle down in the garage when we came in. It'll be fast. Maneuverable."

Steele nodded. "And there were some shielding unit prototypes there, too."

I nodded. I wasn't as fast as I used to be, but a shielding unit and a bike would go a long way. If I went back down to R&D, I could find pieces to make a grapple, then I might have a chance.

Hunt put her hands on her hips. "I'll get the motorcycle and weapons, if you'll gather what devices you need. How many Superiors are we up against?"

"There is no 'we.'" If they got killed on this mad mission, I would never forgive myself.

"Don't be daft. You need someone to make sure your mother is safe. You can't do that if you're fighting a dozen Superiors," Hunt said.

I swallowed my argument as my blue lines blinked in agreement with Hunt. They were my best shot of getting Mom out alive. Live or die, nothing mattered except Mom.

A chill ran down my spine. Would I really sacrifice my friends to help my mother?

Yes.

Steele stood and pocketed his tablet. "It's settled, then. I'll fire up DEXDA and clear you a way out of here, then get one of the armored cars. Hunt will get the motorcycle and the weapons, and we'll meet you at the exit." He handed me a phone, and another one of the little white pills. I took both, and hoped I wouldn't need the stim. "Cloned your own phone when we were in there to get mission data earlier. It's got all the software you need to run your gadgets. I'll push directions to it."

CHAPTER SIXTEEN

I touched a button on my phone to activate the radio as we came in sight of the compound.

"You get her, and you get out. Understand?" I asked.

"Yup. And just to help us get out of this mess alive, I've removed my computer curse. We're going to need all the help we can get." Steele was on the radio in the other vehicle, a jeep that was really more of a steel cage with wheels. It would defend against electric weapons just fine, but its real strength was in speed and the guns held by its occupants. Hunt and Steele were both as heavily armed as I'd even seen them, with plasma weaponry stuck in anything that could possibly count as a holster.

The social niceties program pinged in my head. An answer to Steele's comment displayed on my vision, something about computers being nice to me. I ignored it. Now was not a time for jokes.

Instead, I nodded and swerved to avoid yet another rut in the road. Black and Tolden were still unconscious in the research base we'd just left, but I wasn't about to wait around. The image of Mom's smiling face was still burned into my vision. The warning that she must not learn about the neuro-divergent world overwrote the image. I obliterated it, found the underlying subroutine, and chained it to the iron solid lining of my mind. I didn't care whether she learned about the neurodivergent world or not. Mom would not pay for my choices.

There were two Superiors guarding the entrance to the Estate, and they both snarled when they saw us. Hunt gunned her little cage of a vehicle into the one on the right side, and pinned it up against the wall. A plasma blast finished it almost before I reached the other one. I thrust a knife through the Superior's suit, angling down instead of up into its heart. The grapple I'd put together from an incomplete model in R&D became a sturdy measure of rope that I used to pin its arms against its body.

"Where's your prisoner?" I asked. My voice was steady despite the adrenaline that made my fingers shake.

The Superior made a sound that might have been a laugh if any humanity had remained. "The Instructor holds the woman, meat."

It was the first time I'd heard a Superior talk, and I blinked. This must be one of the newer ones.

"Where is the Instructor?"

The Superior laughed again. "Why don't we trade? Give me your hand to gnaw, and I shall tell you where to find my master."

I shuddered. For all the fact that this thing could talk, its thoughts were only of food, pain, and power. Riding below all that was the thing I actually needed, though. The Superior's gloating eyes turned to awful understanding as I plucked the location from its mind and grinned.

"Thanks for the help, boyo."

The Superior lunged at me, teeth snapping together in an attempt to bite my nose off, but I brought the knife up and stepped out of the way of its strike. Snarling turned to gurgles.

Hunt looked at me. "Got it?"

I nodded and remounted my motorcycle. "Basement, southwest corner. There's an Instructor in with her."

She nodded. "Go cause some havoc. We'll get into position." She and Steele both activated their mindshield, and the glow of their minds vanished from my awareness—and hopefully from the Instructor's as well.

I led the way onto the dirt path that would take us the rest of the way to where Mom was being held.

The trees on either side of the driveway thickened, and the undergrowth between them tripled until there was no way to tell what was on the other side of the living wall on either side of me. The design was supposed to look natural, but I saw the fences they used to train the plants, and the cameras they hid among the foliage to warn them of newcomers.

"Cameras," I alerted Steele, "One on each side, six meters up. Can you fry them with DEXDA, or do you need more direct support? Maybe twenty seconds until we're in range."

A chemical concussion answered that question as Hunt took out one camera. The second followed it a heartbeat later, and Hunt set the rifle back down. I added *sniper* to her list of useful skills.

Then we were in sight of the gate. It was a wrought-iron monstrosity that might have looked decorative in another age. Now it just looked old, with columns that turned into misshapen leaves and ugly flowers. Worse, it was fourteen feet tall, with no room beneath for me to slide through. I was going to have to jump it, and misjudging the height would leave me skewered on the spikes that protruded from the top. My blue lines scanned the red brick wall on either side of the gate that quickly disappeared into the trained foliage. Another timer counted down. Twenty seconds until I went splat against the wall. Twenty seconds to figure out how to get to Mom.

Three seconds later, and my blue lines highlighted the gate's weakness: a fingerwidth protrusion on the right side sandwiched between the bush-covered fence and the edge of the gate. There were no spikes, and the top of the wall was almost level. It would be just wide enough for me to haul myself over the wall. Hunt might be able to follow me over. Steele wouldn't make it unless he'd packed a jet-pack.

"Find your own way in, and don't get seen" I growled over the speaker, and found my balance standing on the motorcycle seat. The machine wobbled alarmingly as I launched myself at the wall. I caught the handhold with a grunt, and pulled myself the rest of the way over.

There was a clang as the motorcycle rammed itself into the gate, and I hoped my ride wouldn't be too damaged. I flicked a switch attached to my belt that would activate the engine locks. The motorcycle died.

If someone tried to move it without disarming the locks, they'd be in for a shock that would fry even a Superior's brain—which meant it was going to stay right where it was, blocking the gate, until it was time for me to get back out.

"Crystal, don't go in there alone," Hunt said. I didn't miss the warning tone in her voice, but I chose to ignore it as I dropped over the other side of the wall.

Hunt cursed, then told Steele to find them an alternate access to the estate. I shut her voice out as a dozen Superior growls caught my attention, and then I was buried under a flood of blue lines directing my defense.

Alarms blared, and I scowled at the speakers. They thought I was dangerous before they took my mother—and perhaps I was. Killing them and taking apart their bases was just business, though. When they kidnapped my mom, they made it personal. They had no idea how dangerous I could be.

There were three Superiors within easy range of the plasma pistol I'd stolen from the research base. They died in quick succession. The rest of the dozen had longer range weapons pointed through the windows of the largest dwelling on the estate. Rather than play an extended game of dodgeball with the bullets, plasma discharges, and other fun toys they had aimed my direction, I hooked my grapple around an upper railing on the house and swung up onto the balcony. The Superior that had been using the area as a sniper perch shrieked as it fell three stories to the cobbled driveway, then lay there unmoving. It was probably just stunned. Most Superiors could survive a fall like that, although the shock of being thrown off a house by a six-foot tall woman may have done some damage.

The inside of the mansion bore no resemblance to the old world ivy-covered, crumbling brick exterior. The walls were white and blank, the fireplaces filled in with concrete. It was spartan, and modern, and completely undecorated—although not empty.

A Superior that must have been coming to aid the monster I'd thrown off the balcony lunged at me as it came around the corner. I left its corpse cooling on the unfeeling cement floor and reached for my communicator.

"Hunt, Steele, I'm on the top floor. Let me know when I can stop playing Superior bait and proceed to the objective."

"Getting there as quick as we can, 32, but *somebody* abandoned us outside the gate!" Steele kept his voice to a whisper even though I could tell he wasn't happy, which probably meant they were inside the compound.

"And is currently playing Superior bait," I reminded him. "Somebody's got to keep them from seeing you, and I've got the experience. This isn't the first time I've soloed a base like this."

"First time you did it as a frontal assault," he said sourly, "and with an Instructor inside."

Hunt came on the line. "You get her to us, and we'll get her out. Not sure any of us are equal to taking down an Instructor, though."

Not anymore. The thought was bitter in my mind, but my blue lines chimed in to remind me the goal of this operation. Mom was the only thing that mattered. If it came down to it, we could just run away from the Instructor.

I exited the room behind the balcony and turned to see if I could find some stairs and start working my way to the basement, but there were six Superiors already charging toward me.

The blue lines on my vision blinked. Engagement was not an option—not if I still wanted to be fully functional to fight the Instructor later.

I hurled a shielding unit to either side of the hall and spared a second to make sure the shield filled the entire hallway. It wouldn't be a solid barrier between me and the Superiors on either side, but it would give me a few more seconds.

I picked up one of the marble sized pieces of putty Hunt had slipped me.

"How much blast power does one of those gummy-things pack?" I asked on the com.

"More than it should." Steele was breathing hard on the other side. "But the building should withstand it. They've reinforced the interior to deal with rogue Superiors."

I read off the code on the top of the putty and slapped it on the floor. With Black indisposed, Steele had the only remote detonator for the explosives. "Give me five seconds before you blow it."

Steele's only answer was a grunt.

I deployed my last shielding unit to face the blast, and covered my ears as best I could. There wasn't much I could do in five seconds, though, and my world shook when Steele activated the explosive. I dropped through the new hole in the floor as the two shielding units that had been holding back the tide of Superiors died. They lunged for me, claws flashing, but I wasn't there. For a moment, they looked at each other, confused, but they quickly discovered the hole I'd used to escape, and followed me down.

I checked my equipment as I ran down the hall. Miraculously, nothing had taken any damage. Not even the relatively delicate neural damper headset that cradled my forehead. Its dial was turned to seventy-five percent—which was stronger than it had been for the last mission. I hadn't recovered completely yet, but I refused to drown under this flood of voices. I would save my mother whether my gift was broken or not. The blue lines compensated for any mental weakness. Programs spun in my mind, weaving a deadly web of targets, intercepts, and warnings. I would not be stopped.

Stairs were nowhere to be found as I flew past room after room stripped bare of anything except a bathroom that was little more than a drain. Bars took the place of doors—which I wondered at until I passed a frenzied Superior shaking the bars as I passed. It foamed at the lips, and its thoughts were so overcome by the need for pain and food that I almost turned the neural damper back up. Superiors weren't the most highly trained or sane of troops, but the new ones were uncontrollable. The Instructors had no use for soldiers that could not be controlled. This was where they were confined until they became useful.

When I'd created enough distance between me and the pursuing Superiors, I slapped another chunk of putty on the ground and had Steele trigger it.

The new hole in the floor dropped me into the only completely unoccupied floor I'd seen in the manor so far—although the Superiors chasing me fixed that only a few seconds after I dropped from the ceiling.

Steele's voice crackled over the radio. "We're in position."

I changed direction, sprinting toward the basement so fast that I almost missed the Superior waiting for me around the next corner. Claws raked up one arm before one of my blue lines found a large enough opening for me to react. I pulsed my shielding unit long enough to leave the Superior without an arm, and then propelled the now-fizzling unit into its face. I activated the new, explosive, self destruct as I walked away.

I held my arm up to shield myself from the blood spatter as the Superior exploded. "Be there in three minutes and forty-two seconds." I tore open a syringe from my med pack and uncapped it with my teeth. I didn't even slow as I jammed the antidote for the Superior's poisoned claws into my thigh, depressed the syringe, then threw the empty needle against the wall. From the shadows and sounds, my blue lines calculated six Superiors still behind me.

"Be careful. Your intel was right—she's not alone."

"Good. Got an escape route?"

"What do you think I've been doing this whole time? Eating potato chips?"

"Probably complaining," I quipped back.

"Steele, focus!" I heard Hunt snap. "It's rather difficult to glue your head back on if you've been decapitated."

There was a thud and a groan, and then Steele got back on the com. "I've shipped the route to your phone."

I grit my teeth. "Was that a Superior? You were supposed to stay invisible."

Hunt clicked her tongue. "You should know by now that plans and enemy combatants rarely get along. It didn't see us, and it won't be raising the alarm any time soon. We're still clean."

I double-checked my route, then put on another burst of speed. The last thing I needed was for the Instructor to realize that there was another group waiting in ambush. The longer they stayed in there, the more chance that a Superior would raise a second alarm, and then we would be in real trouble.

It didn't take long to shake or kill the Superiors that had been pursuing me, then make it to the room where Mom was being kept. I shot the lock off the door, and assessed my new targets.

There, directly in front of the door was a woman tied to a chair, hand and foot. I steeled myself against the sight.

Mom's clothes were tattered, and her skin was covered in shades of brown, blue, and green where she'd been beaten. Her chin dropped defeatedly, and her eyelids were half closed. She was only semiconscious. Good. She wouldn't have to see what I'd become in order to save her.

Behind the chair stood a Superior, but this one was different than the other Superiors I had killed. It looked just a bit more wolf-like—just a bit more Superior. Its green eyes matched D's, and so did its bone structure. Its mind was different, too. Even through the neural damper, I could feel its power. This creature had every single one of the gifts Ms. King had possessed.

"Crystal?" The word was a half-whisper. It didn't even make it fully past Mom's lips as she raised her head just enough to focus her emerald eyes on me. "Run."

I clenched my teeth and sent my blue lines into a frenzy. Plans spun themselves into existence, to be covered by contingency plans and contingency plans for the contingency plans. Above all of it was guilt that threatened to crush me beneath its weight. This was all my fault. I hadn't been there to protect Mom the way Mom was always there to protect me.

My hands curled into fists as I met my mother's eyes.

Mistake.

Her eyes grabbed me and pulled me inside of her. Everything around me faded out. I flinched away from the pain I'd seen the last time her eyes had grabbed me, but everything was quiet. I was alone with her in an emerald room painted with hope. Safety. Peace. For just a moment, I felt like I was home drinking tea with Mom and none of this had ever happened. We were together again. Happy.

Sounds echoed outside the emerald room, but I paid them no heed. Somehow, Mom's eyes were the only thing I could process. Relays in my mind shifted, growing, shrinking, spinning. I heard the Instance still trapped in my mother's mind whisper unintelligible words.

Fear cracked the emerald sanctuary we'd built together. Mom knew what was out there. She remembered the pain.

So much pain.

Data exploded in the walls. Shifting numbers engraved like impurities in the gemstone flickered, shadow-like. An Instructor passed us. The cracks in the wall grew. I couldn't follow the data trails as a self fulfilling loop of love, hope, fear, trapped me. Then the words stopped. The numbers faded. The Instance vanished. I jerked back into my own mind.

The lines in my vision flashed red. Danger! I froze as I felt the claws at my throat. How had that happened? I looked down at the timestamp in the corner of my vision. It had been almost ten seconds—certainly long enough for everything to go downhill. I started reconstructing what had happened while I stared at Mom.

"Here I thought the one who had felled my sister would be harder to catch. Of all of us, she really was the smartest, and yet I find you to be pitifully stupid. You really shouldn't have come here, but I'm glad you did. When I bring you and this traitorous wench in, my siblings won't be able to look down on me anymore." The Instructor's voice sounded like water crashing against the sand. He still stood behind the chair. There must have been another Superior in the room that I'd missed on the initial scan. This other Superior held me fast. Even through the damper, I could feel its pleasure. The razor edge of its claws pressed into my throat. A trickle of blood ran down the side of my neck as I shifted just wrong enough to cut myself. The Superior behind me stiffened, ready to finish the job. The scent of blood was intoxicating.

The Instructor lifted a remarkably human-looking hand. The Superior froze.

"You think you've caught me?" I laughed. It was a dead, broken sound.

Anyone else would have run. The Instructor pulled its lips back in anticipation of a snarl.

The lines flashed purple—the color of opportunity. I flipped the switch on the last shielding unit on my belt, and the Superior behind me dropped to the ground, dead. My weapon was halfway pointed towards the Instructor when the next line flashed.

"I wouldn't, if I were you." The Instructor's voice was mild as he gestured towards his poison-filled claw poised above Mom's throat.

I paused. Numbers flashed on my vision. I wasn't as fast as I used to be. I would get the shot off, but not before the Instructor killed Mom.

"Good," he purred, "now, lay down your weapon, and I'll pack you both up to go home. Maybe I'll even be merciful and sedate you for the journey. My idiot minions don't enjoy bloodsport with an unfeeling target, you know."

My lips thinned. Just because I couldn't get a shot off, didn't mean I couldn't slow him down.

The Instructor shook his head. "You're set at a PS 4, 5? You can't get through my shields, so don't even try. You've met the Defect. You know what I am."

I cocked my head. "Is that right?" This game was far from over, and I let my mouth curl into a smirk as I caught the fringes of other minds directly above us. The distraction had worked, and the others were in position.

::Now!::

My hand flashed up, and turned the dial on the neural damper all the way off. I braced myself for the influx of sound, but it was muted—like more of the noise was being caught by my shields. Somehow, inextricably, my mind was healing under this additional pressure instead of being torn apart. Whether it would stay healed after I was done still remained to be seen.

The ceiling exploded into a shower of sparks and I poured all my pain and anger into an ever enduring scream inside the Instructor's mind. My vision faded to just shadows, and sweat stung my eyes, but I could see Hunt and Steele faintly in the dust. A timer appeared in my vision.

Seventeen seconds was all they needed to get Mom and escape.

The seventeen seconds were done, and I dropped to my knees. I was still screaming. My voice was raw, but I couldn't stop. It was like my brain had been smashed with a hammer. I squeezed my eyes shut to fight off the pain, but it was useless. Even with better-than-normal shields, the combined effort of stopping the Instructor and fighting off the other minds was too much. Medina was right. I couldn't do this alone.

I could feel clawed hands grabbing me, but I didn't react. My senses dulled as the neural damper turned back on, even without me touching it. Someone else must have—

Rough fingers forced my eyelids open, and I could just make out the form of the Instructor.

"Well that was uncommonly stupid." The sounds penetrated the fog around my mind.

Pain erupted in my midsection, and the blue lines on my vision tried to flare to life, but they just fluttered and died. Air spouted from my throat. I gasped, trying to get a full breath.

I rolled to my knees in an action propelled more by muscle memory and force of will than anything else, then struggled back to my feet. I had to get out of here. She was safe, but I was not. I had to see Mom again one more time, and that wouldn't happen if I was dead.

"I thought you were supposed to be fearsome," the Instructor sneered. "We used to take bets, you know. About who would finally end your pitiful existence. Psycho said none of us would—the Administrators want you alive, after all—but I say differently. The others laughed when I said I would disembowel you and make you watch as your guts spilled out. They said the least of us couldn't possibly do it, that I was too *stupid* to kill the agent that had destroyed—how many of our operating centers? Twenty nine." I could just barely make out the way it licked its lips. "I was going to take you both to the Administrators. I was going to be merciful. Now I think I'll settle for making you suffer an hour for every one of the bases you destroyed and recording it so the others will believe me when I say that I was the one to kill you."

The shadowy figure in my vision lumbered towards me, and I started constructing reality on top of my blurred vision. If I could reconstruct Mr. West's classroom and all its mirrors after nearly being knocked out by an overzealous recruiter, I could reconstruct this plain, old, box of a room. Pain flared. My vision died, but I was still aware enough to feel the way my body crumpled to the floor.

The Instructor's next blow caught my temple, and I slammed into the wall.

I lay there, paralyzed, struggling to get a full breath.

"Oh, come now. You can't possibly be that fragile. We haven't even gotten started with the real pain yet."

Claws raked down my side, but I was too exhausted even to scream. My skin blistered, like the Instructor had set me on fire.

I whimpered. I didn't want to die.

The Instructor laughed. He grabbed a fistful of my hair and yanked me up. I would have been level with his nose if I had been able to see, but my vision was black and useless.

"What ties did you have with that monstrous woman, anyway? There was real fury in your face—before it turned to terror, that is."

He snorted and threw me against the wall again. My head smashed into the wall, setting up a resonance in my mind as I lay there, dazed. The resonance didn't fade. There was pain—suddenly muted.

Something in my head shifted. Clicked. My vision flared to life in full color.

I stared at the Instructor, whose lips were pulled back in a full predatory grin. Bone white teeth flashed in the harsh electric light. "Or—now here's a thought—what if I play with you, record it so my siblings cannot deny my superiority, and *then* take you to the Administrators. Yes, I think the Administrators will be so pleased when I deliver you to them that I might even be able to ask *them* for reassignment, and then I'll be free. No more time as a Superior training dummy for me; one of my siblings will have to take this post, and won't that stick in their craw! The Administrators get another look at your blood, which was—well, let's just say it was interesting. We didn't get it all before the bomb decommissioned itself, but that was enough. You are going to create some deadly Superiors, and I—well, I'll earn some time away from Phren."

I blinked at him, my blue lines suddenly at the ready without me having to summon them. They calculated his next possible moves. He stiffened, shifted his balance, started to lunge forward—claws poised to rake across my face. My blue lines screamed at me and I reacted almost before the warning flashed on my vision. I dove to the side out of the reach of his claws, caught myself on my hands, and rolled back to my feet. I reached down to the grapple on my belt, but it wasn't there. An image of it skidding across the floor flashed in my mind—something that had happened while I had been trapped looking at Mom. It was halfway across the room. I would have to do without it.

The Instructor turned to face me. Its eyes were suddenly alight with the calculation of a true predator. "You might be entertaining, after all."

I didn't know what prompted me to move, but I did. Moments later, there was a clinking sound against the wall.

A dozen flechettes had embedded themselves in the concrete, exactly where my belly would have just been. If those had hit, they would have chewed me to bits. The Instructor's hand had peeled back to reveal a gun the size of a bowling ball.

I cursed. Superiors in their new high-tech suits were bad enough, but this was an Instructor in a suit.

One of the lines on my vision lit up red, and I moved out of the way of yet another spray of flechettes. I slid to the floor, and snatched the grapple up. Another line blinked for my attention, and I fired the grapple at the wreckage of a beam in the ceiling two floors above me that had been exposed by the blast that had freed my mother. I hit a button on the back of the grapple, and it jerked me through the air. The Instructor growled. He was gathering himself to try and jump the distance to the above floor where I'd landed.

Even an Instructor couldn't jump that far, could it?

I didn't wait around to find out. This was a battle I couldn't win now. I bottled the agony of my bleeding side away and sprinted toward the exit. My blue lines flashed, gathering information and synthesizing it without my intervention. The Instructor was behind me. A warning flared. I wouldn't be able to get out of the way in time, but I still tried.

"Hold still, you nitwit!" The Instructor was flustered.

I twisted wildly out of the lane of fire and hit the ground as a ball of green writhing flame passed where my head had been. The Instructor wasn't trying to retrieve me anymore. It could feel me slipping through its claws, and it wanted me dead. That moment of panic, that moment of indecision on the Instructor's part was all that had saved me.

I scrambled back to my feet and kept running. Awareness of the Instructor faded away as I turned a corner and kept running. I vaulted over Superiors that stood in my way, following the path my blue lines laid out for me with no real thought. My fingers fumbled for the white pill Steele had given me from his own tactical suit before we embarked on this mad venture. I had hoped not to need it—not this soon after using the last one—but I swallowed it anyway and kept moving.

This Instructor didn't seem to be the smartest of the bunch, but it was desperate to prove itself and that made it dangerous. I didn't dare stop for a moment.

The double doors of carved mahogany that served as the manor's entrance were open and filled almost completely by Superiors. My blue lines noted the position of the gate directly in front of the main entrance. I wrapped my grapple around the solid iron bars and let it pull me through the crowd of savage monsters.

I smashed into the gate, dazed, but I got a hand over the top bar of the gate and held on as the Superiors howled in frustration. My limbs were like lead as I untangled the grapple and used the last reserves of energy I had to navigate the spikes that topped the gate. I dropped to the ground just in time to avoid a foul-smelling blast of that green flame.

My breath came in gasps. My side was bleeding freely, and my head was so light I was afraid it was going to float away. I reached the motorcycle. The Instructor snarled at me from a shattered window two stories up and pointed its fist in my direction again. I slapped my hands on the locks and revved the engine. The sudden jerk of power nearly unseated me, but my blue lines were already compensating. I followed their directions, adjusted my balance. The ground behind me erupted into green flame. It was all I could do to hold on as I sped away, leaving the frustrated growls of the Instructor behind me.

In the corner of my vision, an icon pulsed. Phren? Psycho? I'd seen those names before.

CHAPTER SEVENTEEN

"**G**et out of my way, Agent." My voice was dangerously low as I stared at the tactical agent in front of the door between me, and my mother's room in MedDep.

His voice was still level. "I was given strict instructions not to let anyone in. That means you, Agent 32." His eyes flicked over my tattered tactical suit. "Besides, it looks like you need a room of your own. Go find a doctor."

I pressed my lips into a line. I'd ridden directly back to the base where my mother was being treated without stopping for medical care. I had a bloodied arm, broken ribs, and a bleeding side that had been reasonably staunched by a self-sealing bandage. I'd taken two of the tactical painkillers—Hunt had met me at the entrance to give me hers, in addition to Steele's that I'd taken earlier, but I still had a pounding headache from my ability, and a man in between me and Mom. If one of those things didn't change, someone was going to get hurt.

I drew myself up to my full six feet of height, and met the agent's eyes evenly. "You will get out of my way, or I will make you."

He tensed, and I could feel resistance drifting from his mind. Wrong decision.

I moved, and moments later he was in an unconscious heap on the floor. Screw Director Carlisle and the Organization. No one was going to keep me away from Mom. If the Institute couldn't manage it, then the Organization most certainly couldn't.

I opened the door.

There she was: Adalind Farina. She lay, still unconscious, on a lone white hospital bed in the middle of a grey room that stank of antiseptic spray. The motley of bruises that covered every inch of her skin didn't look any better than they had when she was tied to the chair, but one quick scan of the room and its facilities reassured me that Mom would recover soon. And then I saw the man sitting by Mom's side. He was hunched over Mom's prone body, whispering things I couldn't hear. He clutched her hand so hard I was afraid he was going to break her delicate little fingers.

He sat up as the door closed behind me. He turned, and the world froze. I forgot to breathe.

What was he doing here?

Jet black hair framed a smooth tan face, interrupted by a slightly crooked nose, and almond-shaped, golden eyes. A scar ran from the corner of his eye, then snaked down to his cheekbone, where it vanished.

My blue lines labeled his figure as Director Carlisle and—something else. The lines pixelated, working, trying to break through some block in the recesses of my mind. The aching in my head doubled, then faded, pounding in time with the beating of my heart, which was far too rapid.

My vision sharpened as the block shattered.

Dad. Director Carlisle was my father.

When I'd seen him last, he'd wiped the realization from my mind by barging through my mental walls and rearranging my mind with agonizing brute force. He twisted my tools to keep them from recognizing him. He redirected my thoughts away from the agony of those two minutes. He did everything he could to keep me from knowing who he was. He was the Projector who'd run away from home and never come back.

The blue lines were working at full efficiency in my mind, pulling flags that had been suppressed all my life. Data streamed in and I absorbed it effortlessly. A file appeared on my vision: Dr. Carlisle.

I scanned the folder with interest turning into anger. It seemed that my father had wiped himself from both my mind and Mom's, then stuck around for about a year to monitor us—to see whether the block he'd put in our memories would hold. That was the real reason I'd gone to see the Psychiatrist Dr. Carlisle, and that was the real reason he'd given me medications.

Another flag presented itself, and I nodded to myself. I was willing to bet that if I'd actually taken any of the pills he'd given me, I probably still wouldn't remember him. My head would have been too messed up for that, and it would have been his fault.

My fingers tightened into fists as I stared at my father. He stiffened, and I could feel his mental fingers reaching out towards me. I slapped them away. "Stay out of my head."

Shock radiated from him.

My lips thinned as the last flag in the queue presented itself. As a child, I'd always thought Mom had destroyed all the pictures of Dad because of her grief. That wasn't the case, though. I could remember that night in all its clarity. The video overlaid reality, and I watched him holding my mother in his arms. Her face was stained with tears. His face was unreadable. A moment later, she recoiled. There was no recognition in her eyes. He pointed to the family photo displayed on the wall beside the television, and she obeyed. There was a lighter in her hand. She moved around the house, methodically burning pictures as he watched. When there were no more photos left, she collapsed into a heap on the floor, unconscious. Even asleep, tears ran down her face.

Mom still loved him. She was desperate to remember everything—the same way I was.

She'd destroyed those pictures because he'd forced her to. He'd coated her mind in his will and used us both like puppets. And now he sat there, trying to take all my memories again. He wanted us subjugated, within his power, doing what we were told like good little dogs.

"You had no right." My voice shook with rage.

He stood and turned to face the grey plastered wall. I couldn't see his face.

"You messed with my memory. Do you have any idea what that did to me?"

Still, he said nothing. He didn't turn. He stood there like a statue, breathing deeply, evenly. Could he even hear what I was saying? Did he care?

"I grew up fractured from the strain of not knowing your face. I was teased because I didn't understand social norms, I was bullied, and raped—" My voice cracked as I said that word.

His eyes flashed as he turned. "Don't put all of that on me. I didn't want you to remember me at all. It's not my fault you reacted badly."

"You're my father, and you don't want me to remember you?" I bit the words off. The ring of truth inside them made me flinch.

"I gave you the best chance I could. If the Agency had found out that you were my daughter, they'd have imprisoned you the moment they got their hands on you."

"So you put me on the kill lists, instead?"

He'd tried to have me killed, he'd messed with my head, even when I couldn't remember him, he'd managed to have a hand in every single moment of my life!

He winced. "That wasn't my idea—"

I held up my hand. Lies. I could feel the untruth wafting from him like the stench from a long dead cat. Pressure started to build behind my eyes.

"It was your idea. You've never thought of me as a daughter! I've been nothing more than an experiment. Hmmm, let's see how long she can survive with both the Organization and the Institute on her trail as a seventeen-year old girl who just had to sever ties with her mother!" I was screaming now, but I didn't really care.

He squared his shoulders, and drew himself up to his full height. "You have no right to judge me, Agent." The anger coming from him almost knocked me off my feet, but I held my ground.

I cocked my head. "Really? 'Cause I think I have every right. You violated my mind—not once, but twice. You left your wife and child grieving, alone, and if that wasn't enough, you tried to have me killed."

His face turned into a snarl, and he lunged, faster than even I could track. The back of his hand smashed me against the wall at the other end of the room. My head hit the brick with a snap.

The pressure behind my eyes vanished, and the colors sharpened the same way they had sharpened during my encounter with the Instructor. There was a faint sizzle in my ears, and the smell of burning hair. I reached up and pulled the smashed neural damper from my head. Then flicked the wall between my logic and emotions into place. The blue lines didn't come with it—but they didn't need to.

My mind flicked through data, taking inventory of my mental and physical faculties. Numbers, images, equations, they were all a part of me again. I was whole.

The same thing that had happened during my fight with Ms. King had occured when the neural damper broke, and now I didn't need my blue lines any more. My thoughts flicked faster than I'd ever felt them.

I spun around my mind, checking things, taking snapshots just in case I was ever fractured again. This feeling right here. This was the way I was supposed to be. The tour of my mind took a fraction of a second. The processing relays were pristine. The shunts and bypasses were empty. My mind was beautiful and white like Mom's after I'd extinguished the fires. More importantly, I could revert back to this mental state in an emergency. I stored the pictures in a module I'd built in an instant, called RESET, then locked it against outside access and set it to vibrating up and down mental frequencies so quickly that no one but me would ever be able to enter that place. It was mine. No one would ever take my mind away from me ever again.

I picked myself off the floor, using the wall to pull myself up as fire reignited in my side. "You really shouldn't have done that."

The broken neural damper was in my hand, still smoking. I tossed it to the floor. I didn't need it anymore.

Director Carlisle's eyebrows narrowed. "I warned you. Now, get out of here before I have you taken into custody."

He hadn't seen the change yet. How could he? He had

no idea who I was. He hadn't been there when I faced Ms. King. He thought he was the most powerful teleprojector in the Organization. He wouldn't know just how wrong he was until it was too late.

"Leave." His mental finger reached towards me, and I reacted. Numbers flew in my mind, efficient, clean, and fast. A moment later, I was inside him. I didn't bother to match frequencies with his thoughts to slip inside. I smashed his shields and watched him flinch. ::Don't you ever try that again.:: My thoughts bled venom into his mind like green flames, licking everything they found. ::Make so much as an attempt, and I will show you exactly how it feels to have your mind violated. Director or not, you don't get to push me around.::

I brushed past the more heavily shielded area that protected the control center for his gift, and contemplated ripping it out of him. I could do it—and he would deserve it, too. Anger propelled my fingers forward. I grasped the connections in his mind.

Memories of Tolden's words stopped me. Destroying Director Carlisle's ability would unravel the Organization. Revenge would only hurt everything I'd worked to accomplish and prove that I was the monster they feared I was. I had the power. I could destroy my father the way he'd destroyed me as a child. But at what cost? Whether I liked it or not, he was still Director of the Organization. I needed him if I was going to stop the Institute. Leaving his abilities intact meant that he was still a threat.

One moment of inattention—one moment of lowered shields—and he could cripple my mind. He didn't like the fact that one of his underlings had enough power to rival his own, so he would incapacitate me just to insure he kept his place at the head of the Organization. The fact that I was his daughter meant absolutely nothing to him.

I weighed my options carefully, then reached deeper into his mind, into the very lining of his brain. I left a seed of debilitating fear—every nightmare he'd ever had—that would grow every time he contemplated hurting me.

I withdrew from his mind, and watched as he stumbled away. His face was suddenly pale. His muscles trembled as he raised his head to look at me.

"What are you?" I could see the awareness of his mortality shining in his eyes.

I arched an eyebrow. "I'm your daughter—whether you seem to want to acknowledge that fact or not."

"Crystal?" Mom was awake and blinking uncertainly in the harsh electric light. She looked at me with clouded emerald eyes.

I rushed to her side, leaving Director Carlisle still reeling. "I'm here, Mom," I whispered, clutching her ice cold hand in mine.

Mom's relief rolled off her in waves. Her other hand, pale and thin, clutched at the blankets. "Where did you go? I thought—" her voice choked off, but I could hear the rest of the sentence in her mind.

I thought I'd never see you again.

Tears welled up in Mom's eyes. The fog in her eyes grew. She watched me, desperately, like I was her only lifeline. "How did you find me? Who were those people?"

Her voice trembled. I wanted to squeeze her tight, but I was afraid she'd break if I hugged her. She was so very fragile. I mustered every fragment of kindness I still had and gave her a smile. "You don't need to worry about that, Mom. You're safe, now."

Something in Mom's mind changed. The fog deepened,

and her eyes began to wander. She didn't hear the words I spoke. Instead she stared past me and screamed. "No, no!" She jerked as if struck. Her fingers spasmed, curled into fists. She jerked away, and I let her. "Get away from me!"

A sob wrenched its way from her throat. Her eyes were fixed on an invisible monster somewhere in her mind. Her head snapped to the side, like someone had slapped her face. She moaned; a quiet sound that made my heart tear in two.

"Please don't do this," she pleaded in that barely audible, desperate whisper of hers. "Please—"

I stroked her hair, now soft and free of the blood that had matted it before. "It's alright, Mom. They're all gone. You're safe."

But Mom couldn't hear me.

I looked up to meet Director Carlisle's eyes. He was standing there, frozen, staring at Mom with something ugly in his eyes. I'd never seen such hate before. It made me shiver.

"She's reliving it," I told him—although I got the feeling he already knew.

He pursed his lips. The anger faded from view, waiting for a better time to show itself. "There are deep wounds in her mind. She never should have been taken by the Institute."

That much was obvious.

"Please! Please, no!" Mom threw her bandage-coated arms up to protect her face.

I grit my teeth. No one should have to live through that. What would it do to the Mom I knew? She would never be the same, kind, loving parent. This would haunt her dreams, and her waking moments. The Institute had done more than take her from her home. They had done more than beat her. They'd stolen her future and her peace of mind.

I looked at her again—indecision warring with love. Mom didn't have anything to do with this war. She didn't deserve what they'd done to her. I had the power to take those memories away. I didn't have to blur the faces. I could just remove everything and it would be like it had never happened. The pain and fear would just be gone. We could drop her back at home, and it would be like the past few days had never happened. A few extra guards around the house would mean she would never be in danger again.

I could give her future back. I could save her.

I reached toward her mind, then stopped as I remembered the betrayal and anguish my father had caused when he took my memories. His actions hadn't kept me out of the conflict with the Institute, it had dragged me farther in.

I stopped just a few inches from my mom's mind, hovering there, indecisive. Even if it gave her a few moments peace, wouldn't that be worth it? Maybe I couldn't heal her completely, but I could buy her some time. I had to do something.

Another mind grabbed me as I debated with myself and drew me inside Mom's mind. Fire coated my vision, obscuring everything but the overriding anguish that coated every thought. Was this what I had mistaken for fog in Mom's eyes?

I cordoned off Mom's pain from my own and started to sort out the smoke from the other images. Slowly, my vision began to clear.

Mom's mind was a battlefield between red fire lit by the Instructors who were tearing out fistfuls of thoughts and devouring them, and an image of Director Carlisle, using his green flame to try and destroy the Instructors. Everywhere the fire touched—green or red—left swaths of charcoal. The battle was doing more harm than the Instructors.

I looked around for the mind that had grabbed me to

find my mother, younger, and as insubstantial as a ghost standing at the edge of the battle just watching. Tears leaked from her despair-filled eyes. It was almost too late.

I willed myself toward her, and suddenly I was standing beside her. She looked up at me, blinking away tears.

::Do you understand yet?:: Her voice was pure, wondering, and deeply sad—like she knew I wouldn't make it in time.

"What are you doing?" Director Carlisle asked from outside my head.

I ignored him and focused on my mother's childhood ghost.

She wore a blue silk dress and clutched a burned piece of paper in her fist. It was the letter I'd seen in her room two years ago, signed by Porthos. There was a yellow flower, long wilted, in her hair. She closed her eyes and concentrated. Crystal walls grew from an undamaged spot in Mom's mind to encase an Instructor, trapping it until it snarled and beat at the walls with its fists. The ghost beside me jerked in pain as the crystal walls shattered.

::I can't hold them off any more.::

I grabbed her hand, but my mental fingers couldn't hold her. She was fading into the smoke around us. "I won't let them hurt her."

::How? Crystal, you still have so much to learn.::

I knew that. I also knew that I'd done this before. I pulled the memory from the last time I'd met this woman. She was surely the Instance Ms. King had told me about, and she was trying in vain to protect my mother's mind. The last time we had met, she had pleaded for my help. She had used my mind—my gift—to heal the crystal walls she could use to confine the Instructors. I wondered why she didn't just use my mind again, then stopped. Her form was fading. She was so translucent I almost couldn't see her any more. She had no strength to wield my gift even if she wanted to.

::Hurry…:: her voice faded into the chaos of my mother's mind.

I watched the memory of that first time, two years ago, and scanned my own mind to find what she'd done. She'd created an interface between my mother's mind and mine. She'd fed my mother's latent gift, then used it to mend what the Instructors had nearly destroyed.

I reopened that connection, and gasped as the fire started to burn my thoughts, destroying everything it touched. I couldn't shield myself from the pain this time. It was happening deep in my own mind. Thin metallic chains sprang from the darkness and wrapped around the centers that controlled my telepathic gift. For one terrifying moment, I was trapped. My thoughts wouldn't respond to the commands I gave them. I gave a tremendous jerk, and the chains snapped.

I ventured farther into Mom's mind, to the center that controlled her gift. When I found it, I gasped. The place that controlled her peleprojection wasn't full of modules and subroutines like mine, and it wasn't wiry and dark the way Director Carlisle's was. Mom's gift was a palace of art built of proud archways and decorated with delicate flower petals stained in yellows, blues, greens, and pinks. Once, it had floated freely in my mother's mind as a tranquil garden. Now, some of the arches had crumbled—destroyed by thick iron links that speared through the center of this masterpiece. The chains had toppled walls and shattered beautiful flowers carved of pink marble. They had dragged the palace down into a black tar pit of despair.

Black veins of living iron threaded through the building, pulsing with every labored breath Mom took. They turned archways to dust, subjugating her particle by particle. They had transformed the strongest, most magnificent stronghold my mother had built into something that would destroy her.

I had to shatter those chains and scrape those black veins away from the walls of her palace. I took a deep breath, marshalling every gift I had, and flooded Mom's mind with power. The distinction between Me and Mom blurred as I opened connection after connection, allowing the blue lines of my mind to permeate the layers of Mom's thoughts. The gateways went both ways, though, and the Instructors flooded through into my mind. They jabbed their syringes into the unprotected lining of my mind. I fought through the onslaught of pain. If they were focused on me, they weren't in Mom's mind. It bought time.

But time wasn't going to be enough. The Instance was right. I didn't know how to do this. I couldn't deal with the Instructors and shatter the chains that held Mom's gift. I needed an ally.

I used the connections I'd forged to search for the Instance who had since faded. She existed as a separate entity in my mother's mind. Surely, the core of her being had to be around here somewhere—

There!

A dozen Instructors converged on a tiny dome in the charred landscape of my mother's mind. It was the size of a tent, and shielded the only white spot left in the charcoaled chaos of my mother's mind. An Instructor with a shovel smashed the dome as I watched. The woman in the blue silk dress screamed as her last defense shattered around her.

::Crystal, run! This isn't your job. Save yourself!::

I watched the memory of how she had used my abilities to heal those shards of crystal, then subverted it. She used my lines to pry some of the chains away from Mom's palace and used that tiny freed portion of Mom's gift to heal her mind.

I focused on my gift. New blue lines climbed the flower palace in Mom's mind as I directed the machinery in my mind to help her. They replaced black iron veins, linking me even closer into her gift. Her power limped slowly, but I urged it faster. This was her mind, and only she could truly fix it. I could support her, but anything I built would ultimately fade. I willed my blue lines to merge farther into Mom's palace.

Almost there. Mom's power and mine merged. I grasped the first crystal shard and put it back in place, around the Instance's sanctuary, then the next, and the next. The Instance's eyes widened as she saw what I was doing. Hope lit in her eyes. Another gift, like Mom's but smaller, joined mine. A moment later, the dome was intact again. The Instance retreated from the battlefield, most of her strength spent.

::Break the chains, but beware. The one who set them is near. If he discovers your intent, he will bind you too. I will defend what little is left of her mind.::

It only took a thought to move back to the centers that controlled Mom's gift. I studied the chains. The ones that had bound me upon entering Mom's mind had been thin and easily broken. They'd been a warning, not a threat. The chains that crisscrossed Mom's gift were thicker than my body and blacker than midnight. They protruded from the fabric of Mom's mind like they were made here, but there was a different signature stamped into the metal. They rooted Mom's gift to the ground, where the black veins could subjugate her power.

I stored that image in my mind and gathered myself. The palace shifted, lifted away from the abyssal black, and stopped as the chains grew taut. There was a dull thunk as the chains tightened. A flower near the top of the palace, a white rose, fell to the parapet beneath it and shattered to dust.

"Crystal, no. She doesn't belong in this war!" Director Carlisle's words reached me, and I recognized the stamp in the metal chains poisoning my mother. I'd seen this same signature in Director Carlisle's mind.

Suddenly, I was back in my own mind. I whirled on him.

"What did you do?"

His eyes were dark with barely restrained fury. "How dare you question me? You have no idea what we've been through—what she's seen. I did her a favor! Now you threaten to undo everything I've worked for? I won't allow it."

The door opened to admit a dozen tactical agents with energy weapons in their hands. I looked at them with scorn.

"You haven't looked into her mind recently, have you?"

His lips thinned. My blue lines, still merged with Mom's gift, shifted. New data filtered into my mind through Mom's. An image. Her eyes flashed as he held her face in his hands. Raw will—he would not take her memories from her again. She would fight him with every cell in her body. She shut him out—too late.

I banished the image and looked into Director Carlisle's eyes. He was remembering the exact same scene. That was the day he lost his love. "You can't get into her mind. She set up filters to keep you out!" I could see them, now that I was looking. "You bound her gift, but not before she set up defenses."

I turned back to Mom. The Instance was starting to hold her own again against the Instructors, but the road to recovery would be long. Mom's gift still strained against the chains my father had set. He could see none of it. He had no idea the damage his meddling had caused. He hadn't healed her. He'd crippled her ability to defend herself.

I retrieved my blue lines and pushed them into the background of my mind again, where I could use them as effort-lessly as breathing. I gathered all my power into the smallest point I could. Merely pulling at those chains would do noth-ing. My only hope was to shatter them in one blow.

"Don't," Director Carlisle warned. He couldn't see what I was doing, but he guessed.

I looked back at him. "Or what? You'll kill me? Go ahead and try. I'm going to save Mom."

His eyes widened, and he motioned to the agents around me, who readied their weapons. I ignored them all. I pushed down the anger steadily rising inside my chest and discarded the half-baked plans I had to take them all out.

Tolden was right. Anger didn't help here. I had a plan—a real plan that could save Mom—and I would see it through no matter the consequences. I'd been selfish this last year. I'd abandoned Mom without question because someone had sewn an imperative into the lining of my mind and I had be-lieved it. I left her alone, and let my father hurt her. I couldn't turn back time, but I could protect her now. My will hard-ened into an iron bar harder than the chains that bound my mother. No one could keep me from helping her. Not even the Organization.

I swept my gaze along the line of tactical agents, think-ing critically. Even with this newfound power, I couldn't con-trol all of them and break my father's chains at the same time. I grit my teeth as the calculations flashed. Those weapons would drive enough electricity through my system to disrupt my gift, even with what defenses I could erect. The painkiller in my system was running out. I had lost a lot of blood—and I was still bleeding. My gift was healed, but it was still near the edge of its limits. If those tactical agents fired, they could kill me. Even if I didn't die, the consequences would be se-vere.

But if Director Carlisle couldn't see into Mom's mind—

That was my opportunity, and I refused to let it pass. I set what defenses I could. Energy was just another frequency, and my thoughts could go higher than most. I wouldn't let anything stop me from saving Mom. If I died, then I died, but Mom would be free from this living prison she'd been twisted into.

I dove into Mom's mind and jammed a spear of power into the nearest chain. It shattered. The arch in Mom's palace that the chain had wrecked drifted back together. A set of beautiful blue irises glowed at the top of the arch, encouraging me.

"So, Agent? I warn you, do not test me. You have your orders." Director Carlisle asked.

I made my lips work, even as my attention was focused elsewhere. "Don't make this about the Organization. It never was. This is about Adalind and what you did to her."

I smashed the second chain. Another archway repaired itself—white lilies, clean and pure glowed in candlelight that lit along one corridor, now free of Director Carlisle's influence. The soothing sound of violins drifted from that hallway. The seat of Mom's power was healing.

"You have no idea what you're messing with," he said.

I smashed the third chain. Metal littered the bottom of Mom's mind. It fused into an obsidian snake that started searching for me. I could feel its intent to restrain whatever attacker was undoing its master's work. It tried to call out to him, but the Instance destroyed the message before it could leave. I grit my teeth and smashed the next chain. The fragments fused with the snake, making it larger; more powerful; faster. I couldn't both hide from it and free my mother at the same time. I ignored the snake and focused on gathering my power for the next strike.

The snake wrapped around my thoughts, holding me. It was like a rope had wrapped around my neck. I could barely breathe. My heartbeat tripped in my ears. I could feel the blood pulsing through my veins like lava against my ice cold skin.

"I know you destroyed my mother's mind and then left us. That's enough." My words were shorter. It was getting harder to keep my attention split while I was inside Mom's mind, but I had to keep talking. Even if I couldn't get a full breath, I had to keep talking. When I stopped, he would know I was inside Mom's mind. She would never leave her prison. I couldn't let that happen.

I thinned my thoughts and slipped out of the snake's grasp. It hissed at me. Sweat trickled down my back, jerking my attention back to my body. I was panting, and the walls inside my mind started to slip. Director Carlisle was trying to tear them down, and I wasn't home enough to stop him. I couldn't split my attention three ways!

There was only one more chain. I took a deep breath to gather everything I had left and dove entirely back into Mom's mind. My body crumpled to the floor, spasming as Director Carlisle finally realized what I'd been doing and electricity coursed through every cell in my body. The pain was every bit as exquisite as the moment my mind had fragmented.

The last chain shattered. Golden crystals, beautiful, shining like stars, engraved themselves on the last archway. Mom was free. The tenuous connection I had with my body snapped. The pain died.

Suddenly, the Instance was in front of me. She grinned. The yellow flower in her hair was fresh and vibrant again. The paper she had clutched in her fist was gone. She clasped her hands in front of her light blue skirt and leaned forward with a girlish laugh. ::Thank you, Crystal. I need to go now, to help Adalind. Tell Carlisle—:: her eyes darkened for just a moment. ::Tell him he doesn't have to worry about me anymore.::

She sent me spinning from my mother's mind and I hovered there in the air, trying to process everything. Mom was free. The Instance could finish what I could not.

CHAPTER EIGHTEEN

I directed my thoughts, guarded by flawless shields as clear as crystal, downward to where Director Carlisle stood over my still spasming body. He held his head in his hands, fingers digging into his own hair, haunted by the nightmares I'd implanted into the lining of his mind. He'd harmed me, and now he was paying the price.

I reached into his mind and played the Instance's message into the storm of emotions—guilt, anger, terror, self-righteous fury—that whirled in his mind like a hurricane. The Instance's voice was in his head. Her ghost lit on the back of his eyeballs. He stopped holding his head and reached out, as if he could touch her. Then she was gone.

He jerked up straight and looked around, his hand fisted.

"Lin?" The clouds in his mind started to shift. I couldn't tell if it was for better or worse.

The heartbeat thumping beneath my thoughts was starting to slow. Soon, it would stop. There was nothing else left to do except go home, but I didn't want to go. Drifting outside my body was incomparably peaceful. There was no pain here;

only peace. If I returned to the body still writhing mindlessly on the floor, I would have to go back to the pain of living.

If I had possessed a head, I would have shaken it. My thoughts were illogical at best—suicidal was probably the better term. The last time I had detached myself from my body, I had almost died. The only reason I hadn't was because another mind, impossibly dark, like the black iron chains that had held my mother, had saved me. This time, I needed to go back before my thoughts unravelled. I craved this peace, but not the death that would follow. Living was pain, and it was a pain worth bearing. I wanted to see my mother's smile once she was free of the burning in her mind. I had friends waiting for me, and people to save. There was so much to live for that I would endure. I had to.

I prepared my mind for the shock of returning to my body when a thought hit me and confusion-tinged recognition propelled me halfway across the room. That dark mind that had saved me last time—I'd seen it again lining the storm in my father's mind. Was he the one who had saved me?

I dove back into his mind, searching for answers inside the storm of emotions. I found them in a memory sealed in the back of his mind. Kill lists aside, he didn't want me dead. If he had, there were plenty of opportunities to see to my termination while I was running around the city playing hero. The kill lists had been motivation for me to keep going, keep fighting, and keep stretching my mind. So when I had been at death's door and he had felt me fading, he'd reached out. He'd gathered me inside his mind and gently guided me back to the land of the living. Now, he was too far caught in his own personal hurricane to sense that I was near the end. My thoughts were unraveling. My common sense was going with it.

My heartbeat slowed. My body cooled. My muscles

twitched from the shock of the electricity, but the intensity had faded. I needed to go now or I wouldn't make it.

My mind fused with my body and I groaned as the pain hit. Muscles contracted as stray electrical signals gave them erroneous information. It was like every inch of my skin was simultaneously burning and my muscles were working to break my bones.

A quick evaluation showed that my defenses hadn't completely failed. I could still feel pain, which meant my nerves hadn't been completely burnt out. There was quite a bit of damage, though. I catalogued it as quickly as I could, and tried to remember that it could be worse. I could be dead.

The electric pulse had torn through my nervous system like a hurricane. Most of the damage was concentrated in my limbs, where my defenses had been the lightest, but my brain hadn't escaped unscathed. I wouldn't be able to stand, and my walls, all except the inner filters that had protected my mind while I was separated from my body, were in tatters. But Mom would recover. That made it worth it—no matter what happened now. Mom was safe.

The agents hauled me up by the elbows and turned me so I could see Director Carlisle, whose lips were pursed. "What did you do?" The anger in his voice was fading, replaced by wonder.

I tried to speak, but my voice wouldn't work. I could barely get a full breath.

"Crystal, what—"

He stopped as Mom shifted. Her eyes fluttered open. I could see the memories filtering into place as the Instance finished healing her mind.

"Adalind?" Director Carlisle—Dad—rushed to Mom's bedside. He gathered one of her hands in his.

Mom smiled and, in that moment, she looked exactly like the Instance. Young, full of life and hope. The crinkles around her emerald eyes were worn by joy. "Jerome Carlisle, you silly. What do you think you're doing?"

My father's face was pale. "It's really you?"

She sat up and pushed the blankets away. Her smile faded, and she shook her head. "You never did stop long enough to listen, did you?"

"Crystal freed all the memories. How are you—" his voice broke, but he pressed on. "How are you alright?"

She looked up at him through long lashes. "I've been adjusting to what happened for twenty years, now. The Instructors burned my mind, but I'm stronger than you think. Gentle doesn't mean weak."

His eyes were full of tears as he blinked at her. "Of course, love."

I stared at them. How could Mom not be furious with him? He'd sealed her memories away and set her mind on fire.

Mom looked at me, as if she could hear my thoughts—and maybe she could. My walls were in tatters, and her gift was healed. "The past is done, Crystal. There are more important things than anger."

Director Carlisle motioned to his agents, who were still holding me. "Take her to Interrogation. I'll deal with her later."

Mom squeezed his hand. "Jerome." The warning in her voice was unmistakable. "She's not one of your security people, she's your daughter. Look at her."

Director Carlisle dropped his gaze.

My mother's voice firmed. "Look at her."

He lifted his head, and then his eyes widened as he saw me being supported by his agents. My muscles still spasmed, and I still struggled to pull up the wall between me and my pain. My arm was bleeding freely, my side burned from where the Instructor had scored me with its claws. My gift was in tatters from fighting the monsters he'd let roam in Mom's mind.

He took a step toward me as he realized what he'd done. Then he looked at his agents. His eyes softened. "Leave her. You are dismissed."

The agents looked at each other. One holstered his gun and grabbed a chair to support me. I tried to nod at him in thanks, but my muscles wouldn't obey. When they finally released me, I fell into the chair, unable to stand. They left as quickly as they'd come.

Mom arched an eyebrow at my father.

"I'm sorry, Crystal. I went too far," he said.

Too far? He'd nearly killed me. Again. The fact that I'd expected it didn't make it hurt any less.

"But I did have the agents turn down the discharge on their weapons. You should be fine in a few hours."

Mom gave him a hard look, and he shrugged.

"I might be a complete failure of a father, but I wasn't trying to kill you."

"Y-you would have," I managed.

He shrugged again. "I was trying to protect Adalind."

"You made me leave her."

"You were a threat to her safety."

"I'm her daughter!"

Mom got caught in the echo of my desperation—projected at my father—and flinched away. I needed to make him understand what he'd done to me, but he just stood here, impassive and unrepentant. He'd forced me from my home by implanting an imperative in the lining of my thoughts. He hadn't just broken my mind and removed himself from my life, he'd left Mom defenseless and then wired my brain so that I couldn't stay with her. He'd managed to methodically take away every single thing that was important to me, and he still didn't see it. He didn't understand how close he'd come to ruining my life.

My father shook his head slowly. "The Institute was hunting you. When you diffused the bomb that hotel, they detected genetic components suitable for creating Alpha Superiors or, worse, Instructors, in your blood and they deactivated the device to avoid destroying the most valuable asset they'd found in a long time. They started following you. Sooner or later, you would have led them back to Adalind. I couldn't allow that."

"You had no idea about the bomb when you planted that imperative, so stop lying to me." He was blaming his actions from years ago on things that had happened relatively recently—justifying his actions. Somehow that fit with the image I was gaining of him in my mind. He was powerful, and he used that power to force everyone into their place, whatever he thought that place should be. For me, I was born to be the dutiful Agent 32. I didn't need a family to do my job, so he'd taken Mom away from me.

"I needed to protect her, and nothing you say will change that. I did what I had to," Director Calisle maintained.

He wanted to keep her as that weak, broken person who had just been trying her best to remember how to live. I loved Mom. I loved the way she'd always cared about me, and the way she'd tried to protect me. But this person sitting in the bed now was just as loving. She was happy, and I could already see the strength behind her skin. This was the Mom who had raised me, and who had started to waste away after Dad left.

I clenched my jaw against more accusations as Mom looked at Dad. She should have been furious, but she wasn't. She saw the deep part of him that was hurting and pitied it. I could see the emotion in her eyes, and how it quickly turned to love. In spite of everything that had happened, she wanted to heal his soul.

Somehow, I could feel my anger fade, too. Something about being in the same room with her sapped all the will I had to fight. I wouldn't ever trust Director Carlisle, but I would try to get along with him. Mom still loved him— though I couldn't fathom why.

How could she still love him after everything he'd put her through?

The muscle spasms died, leaving my limbs weak and trembly as the pain retreated. I finally caught a full breath.

Messages were flying between Mom and Dad at a dizzying rate. I could barely decipher a word they sent. It gave me a moment to process all my questions.

First and foremost was why had my father confined Mom's gift? Why had he really erased himself from our memories? She was powerful—more powerful than my father and maybe even more powerful than me—if my emotional state was any measure. Being in the same room as her was enough to suppress anger I'd built up over a year.

Second was about the Instance. Ms. King said it was supposed to protect people who had seen things they shouldn't have, but that hardly seemed true. I remembered her face as she'd asked me where I'd heard that word. She had been concerned—and not about me. The fact that my mother had an

Instance had been concerning to the Institute. Even though I'd been blind to it in the moment, it was glaringly obvious now.

I frowned as there was a break in Mom and Dad's conversation. They looked at me.

"You need to get to a doctor," Dad said.

Mom nodded. "Thank you for saving me, Crystal. You deserve a rest, and time in a Healing Pod."

I managed to get off the chair, but another stray twitch hit my legs, and I started to fall. Strong, warm hands grabbed my shoulder, catching me before I could hit the ground. Director Carlisle wasn't smiling—not really—but his frown wasn't worn as deeply into his face as he supported me to the door and passed me to one of the agents outside who was almost certainly one of the ones he'd brought with him when he'd come to rescue Mom.

"Help her to a doctor," he said.

The agent started to reach toward a pair of cuffs on her belt, but Carlisle shook his head. "She isn't under arrest, she's just injured. If there aren't any emergency cases, make sure she gets time in a pod. She went up against an Instructor today and survived."

I could feel the agent's shock in the way her grip changed. She nodded. "Yes, Director, right away."

A few minutes later, we were in the, admittedly small, hallway that housed Emergency MedDep. Tolden was sitting in one of the hard plastic chairs in the hallway, deep in conversation with Joseph Medina, who had worry lines I'd never seen before carved into his face. He looked up as we approached, and nearly leapt to his feet.

Tolden joined him a beat after. "Crystal, what happened? Your mom, is she alright?"

I nodded.

"Are the Instructors deploying electric weapons now?" Medina asked as he evaluated my condition. His eyes were dark, like he already knew the answer.

"No. That was Director Carlisle," I said. Now that I was outside of my mother's medical room, the anger was starting to resurge.

Medina's lips tightened. "Adalind. Is she—"

"She's better than she's been in years."

Medina froze, shot half a glance at Tolden, then relaxed again. "Well, I won't keep you from getting to—where was Director Calisle sending you, again?"

The agent supporting me spoke up. "The Pod, if it isn't in use."

Medina relaxed again. "Good." He nodded at the agent supporting me. "I'll take it from here. And you, Agent Tolden, should be getting some rest. I have a feeling you're going to be needed soon." He pulled my arm over his shoulder as Tolden hesitated and the other agent fled.

"Director Carlisle did all that?" Tolden asked, gesturing toward me.

I would have shrugged, if I had been able to manage it, but my limbs were starting to get heavy. "An Instructor did some, and Director Carlisle handled the rest. I did something he didn't like. It's becoming a bit of a pattern with him." I didn't mention that he was my father, or that I had been trying to save my mother when he ordered his agents to shoot me. Tolden wouldn't understand. I wasn't sure it had even completely sunk in with me, yet and, frankly, I hurt too much to go through the effort of explaining it all.

Tolden took a step toward me, concerned, and suddenly

suspicious of Medina, who was holding me. I shook my head, then regretted it as my headache—forgotten among the pain of everything else in my body—slammed back into my brain full force. I groaned. "Tolden, just go. Director Carlisle is not going to murder me in my sleep. My mother would glare at him, and he would never recover."

Medina laughed out loud, which was the first time I had heard any sort of positive emotion in his voice. Tolden blinked. "Are you sure?"

"Go!" I didn't have enough energy to restrain my exasperation. Tolden flashed a grin, then jogged off.

Medina helped me into a closet of a room with a bed in the center that looked like a coffin, with hinges on the far side, and a lid with one clear window that would close above the white pillow at the head of the bed. When the door clicked shut behind us, Medina helped me sit on the bed, then opened a panel in the wall beside the door. His back was to me so I couldn't see his face when he asked, "Adalind is really alright? Does she remember what happened to her? The Institute? Is she in pain?" The worry in Medina's voice was real.

"She is still a little bruised from her ordeal, but she seems happy enough—happier than I was when I found out that my father had been messing with my brain."

Medina looked up from what he was doing. "You know."

"That Director Carlisle is my dad? Yeah. It took a while, but I managed to undo whatever he did to me in that meeting. Thanks for the help there, by the way." I didn't even bother to blunt the sarcasm in my voice. I could see the whole scene now, in my mind. Medina had been worried, and had even stood up to try and stop Director Carlisle from reworking my brain. When the Director Carlisle told him to sit down, he had sat silent for the rest of the time. Sure, he had prompted me to follow the trail of things that didn't quite make sense, but he hadn't protected me when it had mattered the most.

Medina didn't react—he hardly breathed. "Adalind. How does she seem?"

I sighed. "The Instance fully restored her memories. She's happy, whole, and probably the most powerful person in this building right now."

"Instance?" Medina whirled. "She made herself an Instance before Carlisle—"

His mouth stopped working, but I could see his thoughts running a mile a minute. Self-hatred surged in one overpowering wave, then crashed against a synthetic wall. His eyes started to tear. "She was there this whole time," he whispered to himself, "and I didn't see it."

"What do you mean, 'there,'" I asked. "What exactly is an Instance?"

Medina's eyes flicked to my face. The tears were gone as quickly as they'd come, replaced by a quiet desperation. "When Carlisle sealed away Adalind's memories, it wasn't the first time. She knew it was coming. Part of her welcomed it. I wasn't sure. It helped, for a time, before the walls broke down and she—" He shook his head. "He didn't warn any of us. One day, Adalind was Adalind, and the next she was a walking zombie. He didn't just seal away memories of her time in the Institute. He destroyed every mention of Neurodivergence. Her family, her gifts, her kindness, her happiness—everything that made Adalind the person we loved—was gone in a flash. He didn't just seal the memories away, he destroyed them. I tried to find even a fragment, but there was nothing. Adalind was gone. She must have known it was going to happen, though, to make an Instance. She knew him better than we did. She cloned her mind and hid it away where he couldn't find it. She stored herself, or a snapshot of herself, in her own mind so that when Carlisle destroyed her memories, she wouldn't go with them. She protected herself better than any of us could have imagined."

I shook my head, sorting through the story for the answer I needed. "The Instance was a copy of her mind, then? How did she know about everything else that had happened to her after she made the copy?"

Medina's frown deepened. "Adalind must have let it watch through her eyes when none of us were around, or watch the new memories she was making. She trapped herself in her own mind and only came out when it was safe."

"But Director Carlisle left additional programs in her mind," I said. "They hunted down memories of the Institute and destroyed them retroactively."

Medina nodded. "So when the Instance tried to reassert control, it couldn't take root fast enough to recover. She was trapped, and I couldn't see it. And you," he lifted a finger, almost accusingly, and then dropped it. "You saved her."

He turned back to the panel and hit another button. Something beneath the bed began to whir. "I always knew that she would have to protect herself. I never imagined that her daughter would have to protect her, too."

Another button, and he turned back to me. "Lay flat and close your eyes. I'm setting it for thirty minutes. The beginning sequence can feel strange, but you'll be perfectly safe. Someone will be out here when you wake up."

I followed his instructions and watched with mental eyes as the lid closed over my body. A moment before it latched, I could hear Medina's whisper. "Thank you, Crystal. You did what I could not."

The hatch disengaged with a thunderous click. Light flooded in like the sun, and I blinked up at familiar faces. Medina, Carlisle, Tolden. Where was Mom?

I tilted my head to the side, expecting pain, but none came. My body was pleasantly warm from my nose, down to the tip of my toes. Mom sat in a chair by the door that hadn't been there when I arrived.

"Welcome back, Crystal," Tolden said, and extended a hand. I took it and let him help me sit up. I inspected my arm and side—completely healed. My mind had repaired itself, too. I stretched gently, yawning as a sudden bout of exhaustion crashed over me. Tolden nodded. "Last time I came out of a Pod, I felt like I could sleep for days. All that healing comes at a cost."

"Unfortunately, we don't have time to let you sleep it off. The Institute is moving," Medina said.

My eyes widened. "Another round of abductions?"

Director Carlisle shook his head, but it was Mom who answered. She was sitting in the only chair in the room, a tiny plastic thing. An agent probably would have dwarfed the thing, but the chair was sized just right for her. She sat there, calm, dressed in the same shade of blue her Instance had worn. "They have what they need, now." Her voice was infinitely sad.

"Have you ever wondered what they were using all these abductees for?" Medina asked. He was leaning against the wall, next to the panel that controlled the Pod.

"To create Superiors," Tolden answered.

Medina snapped his fingers. "Wrong."

I shook my head. "That's why they took Briggs. Trust me, I know." Even now, it was hard to think his name without being transported back to that terrible day when Tabitha Smith and I had been forced to kill him.

"That was Ms. King grabbing anyone she could get her claws on. These abductions are different. They're planned, and every single person they've targeted has been Neurodivergent and non-psionic."

I inserted that little tidbit into my analysis, thinking quickly. Zeta Superiors like the ones the Institute had been deploying since I'd joined this fight were stupid. The transformation burned out pieces of the brain that controlled things like empathy and critical thinking, while it boosted adrenaline and re-wired the reward centers. All those modifications together turned them into supreme predators whose only source of joy was the hunt and kill.

Zeta-Superiors weren't the Institute's end goal. According to D—the non-psionic Instructor who had revealed Ms. King's involvement with the Institute—Zeta Superiors were a convenient accident. They were easily controllable and almost impossible to stop without psionic resources. Their real goal was a breed of Superior human that mimicked the Instructor's cunning and psionic strength.

My blood ran cold.

"They're using these people to make Alpha-Superiors?"

Mom shook her head. "Not yet, but they're close." There was a kernel of fear in her eyes, although her voice was serene.

"Our working theory is that they've been taking Neurodivergents because they need the extra brainpower to get over that last threshold. The JoNA System has to be running at near full capacity by now."

Carlisle closed his eyes. "I wish I knew, but Earl was the only one of us with a hope of understanding that thing."

The room lapsed into silence.

Earl West had tried to save me from Ms. King, but she

lured Doug Houston into killing him with promises of rebirth as a Superior the night I got my biocard. I hadn't known him well, but his death had hit hard.

Looking around the room, I could tell that Medina and my parents had known him far better than I had. I remembered the letter burned on my mother's bedside table almost two years ago. It had talked about the fact that they had lost someone, and it had upset Mom so badly that she'd tried to set it on fire, then changed her mind and turned the fire-extinguisher on it. Analysis in my mind whirred, and I finally understood it. Athos was Earl West, Porthos was Director Carlisle. Medina? I wasn't sure where he fit. He obviously knew my mother from before her memories were sealed away, and he obviously cared for her. He'd looked after me when I joined the Agency, and tried to keep Ms. King from finding my mother—which was why he'd handled my background check instead of letting Ms. King do it. He, like Director Carlisle, had known who I was the entire time.

"I'm going to miss him," Mom whispered softly to herself. Director Carlisle nodded.

"He was a good kid."

"Even without him, we have to find a way to incapacitate the JoNA system. We've let it ride for too long." Medina looked at Director Carlisle meaningfully.

"You say that like destroying JoNA is going to be easy. We don't have the resources for that kind of strike," Director Carlisle said, but Medina ignored him. He was looking at my mother.

Mom nodded slowly. "You're right. The Instructors cannot be allowed to use it to hurt any more innocent people. It wasn't designed for this kind of destruction."

Tolden folded his arms, looking between Medina and my mom. "What, exactly, is this system?"

Medina's eyes were dark. "The Joint Neurodivergent Analysis system is a way of daisy-chaining neurodivergent minds together and making them play nice—like a giant technologically facilitated think-tank. More than that, I don't think anyone except the Institute understands."

"Oh, no. We understand a little bit more," Carlisle said. There was venom in his voice. "Going after it is suicide. The Institute guards that machine more closely than it guards their Administrators. I refuse to allow anyone back there."

Medina's lips thinned. This was obviously an old argument between them. "We have more knowledge this time. If we can find a way to circumvent the Master Instructor, we can get in and out without them ever knowing we were there."

"Master Ins—" I started to ask for clarification, and then stopped as images began to flow into my head. Mom smiled at me from across the room.

In front of me was an Instructor wearing a crystal the size of his fist on a black chain around his neck. On his head was an equally black crown with ports for wires to plug in. He stepped up to a wall covered in wires and jacked them into the crown. His eyes widened and, for an instant, I could see the way his mind fragmented, covering miles of distance in a moment. His mouth opened in a silent scream, and he fell to his knees, supported a moment later by two more Instructors, who helped him to a chair. His eyes were barely alight—his mind was still tethered there, but only barely. He was watching everything around him. He could feel every single mind, watch every movement. He became the space.

Across the facility, mind-controlled missiles whirred to life, moving as they received targeting information from the Master Instructor.

A moment later, one of the other Instructors unplugged the crown and removed it from the first—the Master—Instructor's head. The Master Instructor's eyes were still vacant. He was still spread over unnameable miles.

I blinked, and the memory faded. Only moments had passed. Mom winked at me.

"That's the problem with the Master Instructor, isn't it, though?" Director Carlisle was saying. "You can't avoid him. If you enter Grafton, he will know you're there. Even in a Neural Shield, he will notice that there are places he could sense before that he can no longer feel and send Superiors to investigate. Once one of them sees you, he can track your position with missiles and destroy you any time he wishes. In that compound, the Master Instructor reigns supreme."

Mom stiffened in her chair suddenly. "They're calling."

Director Carlisle crouched by her side. He held her hand, worried. "Who is?"

She looked down at him, and I could see the shadow of infinite horrors in her eyes. "The Administrators are recalling the Instructors back to Grafton."

She stood and turned, heading for the door, but Director Carlisle held her hand fast.

"Where are you going?" he asked.

"To Grafton."

"No." Medina and Director Carlisle said it almost at the same time.

Mom turned around, a wistful smile on her face as she took Director Carlisle's other hand in hers and stared deep into his eyes. "You know I can't let them finish this. They are my mistake, and I have to fix it."

"They're *our* mistake, and I refuse to let you go into that compound."

She shook her head. "You're afraid, but you shouldn't be. They can't do anything to me they haven't already done, and I won't get caught."

"No." Director Carlisle's answer was immediate. "If that thing really needs to be destroyed, then I'll do it myself."

"And leave the Organization without a Director when you get caught?" I snorted. The puzzle pieces were finally falling into place. He'd ignored the compound so far because he was terrified of the place. Promises aside, he would never set foot in there. "We all know you're too much in love with your position here to risk it falling into the wrong hands."

Out of the corner of my eye, I could see Medina nod. He knew where I was going, and he agreed with me—but what else was new? This was what he always did. He stood on the sidelines pointing vaguely at a problem he either couldn't or wouldn't solve for himself and then watched others—people like me, Briggs, and Tabitha Smith—get hurt trying to do the impossible.

Plans began to form inside my newly healed brain as my resolve stiffened. I had the information and abilities that had been kept from me for far too long, and I was done passively following his trail of breadcrumbs. This time was going to be different. I was whole, and I wouldn't be surrendering to anyone like I had last time. I was finished trusting the Organization. There was nothing holding me back.

Director Carlisle gave me a suspicious look. "So what? You'll storm Grafton by yourself? Do you have any idea what it's like in there? Don't let the psionic net broadcasting 'I'm a small innocent town with 500 people' fool you. The Institute has turned it into a base with a factory in the center. The streets are crawling with Superiors. If any of them see you, their thoughts are picked up by the Master Instructor, who can activate an automated arsenal of neurodivergent weapons."

Images from Mom's mind flowed into my own, underscoring the point. I could see the missiles already tucked into their launchers and the Superiors patrolling cement grey streets. Through it all, I could still hear Director Carlisle's voice. "If the missiles or Superiors don't get you, there are fourteen more Instructors who have been recalled. If half of them aren't there already, I'll resign as Director. You may have destroyed Ms. King, but even you can't take on nine Instructors while dodging missiles and a town full of Superiors."

I grit my teeth and started running calculations in the back of my mind. He was right. I couldn't do it by myself. "I have one thing you don't," I finally said.

His eyebrows raised. "A cocky attitude?"

I bared my teeth. "No. A team."

Black was whole again, after spending a few hours in a Pod while I was off saving Mom. Tolden had passed all the medical checks MedDep could think up to make sure the Superiors hadn't slipped some sort of poison into the concoction they'd stuck him with earlier. Hunt and Steele were still mostly untouched from the mission earlier. The backup I'd made of my mind had cycled through, restoring my shields, and the Pod had done the rest. I was tired, but exhaustion was the least of my worries.

I explained the situation to the team.

Hunt whistled. "Your mom was one of us the whole time?"

I bit my lip. "I'm not really sure how involved she was with the Company, but she's definitely a teleprojector. My dad sealed away her abilities and entire swaths of her memories."

Hunt rubbed the bridge of her nose. I could see her trying to figure out how this new, complicated family relationship would impact the mission—and the Organization as a whole. "I can't believe Directory Carlisle would do that to his own wife. Not to mention you. He put you on the kill lists, Farina. How are you alright with this?"

I bared my teeth. "I'm not. But that discussion can wait until the Alpha Superior serum and JoNA System are destroyed."

Tolden nodded. "I've got the Organization's file on Grafton, but it doesn't say much. It's designated as a no-fly zone, and we are prohibited from operations in the area."

Black leaned forward. "That's where the Superiors are being made, and we aren't allowed to go blow them up?" The disgust was evident in his face.

I shook my head. "That sounds reasonable, actually, given what the Director said. The entire place is covered in some sort of psionic net. Even if we go in with neural shields on, the first Superior that sees us will give our position away. They've got an Instructor standing in the middle of it all with a targeting system that will blow us up before we manage to set enough explosives to make a difference."

Steele tapped a few things on his tablet, then looked up with a gleam in his eye. "What kind of psionic net is it?"

I shrugged. "The Director didn't say." I quashed a surge of bitterness. Director—Dr. Carlisle—Dad. Everything he'd ever told me was on a need-to-know basis. When I didn't need to know anymore, he ripped the memories out of my head.

I wondered, for a moment, if that consistent treatment was one of the reasons why I was such a powerful teleprojector. The only way to defend my mind from the people who would violate it was to build walls so high that even an Instructor wouldn't be able to tear them down.

Steele was tapping his tablet again. "I'll see what information I can convince our archives to release. If there's a way to hijack that net, being on the other side of it would give us an enormous advantage."

Tolden nodded. "While you're at it, try to dig up some sort of plans for the town. Odds are, they have ways of keeping the reality off satellite images, but it's better than going in blind."

I nodded. "Once you get the images, I'll try to see if I can build us something more accurate."

Tolden turned to Black. "Weaponry options?"

He smirked. "Century Mark III missiles might do the job. Just sit back and watch it explode."

Tolden was already shaking his head, as was Hunt.

"Why not?" Steele asked. "I've seen the specs on those things, and it'll only take one to level the compound. There won't be any civilian casualties—the abductees are all souped by now. Mrs. Farina said the system works at a higher efficiency if the Institute plugs their brains directly in, which they can't do if the brain's still attached to a body, so they're dead either way. Using the missiles means we don't have to infiltrate it, and we can be sure all the Instructors are dead. No more Institute."

"You forget that we aren't operating in a vacuum here," Tolden said. "If we launch those missiles, there's a chance a government will pick it up. If they think they're being attacked—which, remember that they think Grafton's a nice, innocent little town—they're going to retaliate."

"But they won't be able to pinpoint the origin of the missile. Or if they do, they won't believe it," Hunt said. "That means they're going to assume a world power attacked them, and welcome to World War III."

"Alternatively," Tolden said, "We go to them and confess our capabilities, and now it's open season on Neurodivergents. You thought the Institute was bad. Once the world at large knows something like Superiors and Instructors are possible—forget them torturing psionics to try and understand our powers. Plenty of that will be going on, but there are also going to be those who believe they can succeed where the Administrators failed. That's a lot worse than World War III or Mutually Assured Destruction. We are barely holding our own against one Institute. Imagine if there were a dozen, all working independently."

I shuddered at the picture Tolden painted. "So no missiles."

He nodded and turned back to Black. "Any other ideas?"

"There's a new tank I've been wanting to try out."

"We're trying to be inconspicuous," Hunt said.

Black only grinned and leaned back in his chair.

"The JoNA System isn't some delicate little thing we can hit with a wrench," I said. "The plans Director Carlisle gave me include entire rooms. The technology is going to be built into the walls. Destroying an entire compound isn't going to be quiet. Stealth in this mission is only going to go so far."

"I don't understand why we aren't sending half the Organization in here. This isn't a small mission," Hunt said. "Just because we can't blow it up with missiles or drive a tank through its streets doesn't mean we can't requisition more support."

"The Institute has two retraining facilities in the vicinity we don't want to tip off. The only thing worse than a five hundred Superiors and a dozen Instructors is a thousand Superiors and a dozen Instructors who know exactly where we are." I shook my head. "We go in quietly or not at all. Every person we add to the mission increases the chance that we get caught." That was one point, at least, where I could agree with my father.

Steele jumped to his feet. "I found the Organization's mockup of Grafton's psionic net, and you're not going to believe this." He pushed the image to the holoprojector, and we all blinked at it. The thing was a grid of blinking colored lights around the faint outlines of a double handful of buildings. If I had passed in the hall, I would have thought it was a data-motivated art piece.

Tolden gestured at Steele. "Explain, please?"

"Oh, right." He gave us a sheepish grin. "Do you see the conduits right there? In the substations stationed around the outside of the town?"

I noted the six blinking red lights that appeared in the tall buildings that formed a hexagonal border around the town. "There isn't a single building outside that shape," I said.

"Exactly." A hexagonal grid presented itself above the holographic town. "Now look at what happens to the field when one of the substations goes down."

One of the red dots blinked out, and the field faded. A moment later, it rebounded full force, although the field itself was smaller and pentagonal. The glow from the red dots brightened as the strain on each substation increased.

"It's not a long window. Maybe six seconds, but it might be long enough to sneak in if we're all wearing neural shields. Well, everyone but Farina. Her shields are high enough that she should be fine. The rest of us are going to end up mind-blind for most of this."

I nodded. The problem with a psionic net was that, much like I could tell when someone was there even if I couldn't pick up their thoughts, the Instructor would be able to tell the moment something inside the net changed—even if the new person was wearing a neural shield. That would draw Superiors down on us. If we all entered during the time the field faded, the Instructor would have a hard time telling between fluctuations from the field reestablishing itself and fluctuations from neural shields crossing the boundary. As long as we stayed quietly out of sight, we would seem like part of the scenery.

"That's the simplest of our problems solved, but there are still hundreds of Superiors in that facility. We can't avoid them all, and killing them would leave a trail just as strong. The Master Instructor will be able to see it when a Superior goes down."

Steele shook his head. "That's just it. Taking down one of the towers makes the whole system go back to the next towers, average the data, and re-establish the field from the most recent copy—what the other five towers were recording. Taking down all the towers, though, makes it go back to the central amplifier and re-compile. This means we can use one of two opportunities. We can take down the entire system for something on the order of fifteen minutes by taking out all the towers—if we're precise about the timing. The other option is hijacking the system, which will only work for as long we can keep the Instructor in the center from jacking back into the primary amplifier. The second option will let us work without our neural shields, but it's a bigger risk. If we don't get to the central tower fast enough, the Master Instructor will know exactly where we are. The moment the Instructor gets kicked out, they will know they're being attacked."

Tolden nodded. "Here's the question. Where's our primary target?"

Steele flipped the holograph to the satellite photos he'd

found, and I scanned them. I pointed at a flaw in the pho-to where the color matching was—different. "That building doesn't end right there."

Tolden arched an eyebrow. "I take it you can get us a more accurate map?"

I nodded. After a few minutes of adjustments, I pointed to a large grey building in the center next to the central tower. "What do you think? Could that be what we're looking for?"

Tolden frowned and shook his head. "It's too big."

I squinted at the picture. "Yeah, big enough to be the JoNA System."

"But it's too obvious," Tolden said. "This isn't some little base manned by Superiors. The Instructors are de-vious. They installed Ms. King in the Agency to watch us, and they've been using telepathy to keep us away from this place. No." He frowned at the board.

Hunt reached past us and put her hand through the ho-logram. It fizzled out, then resolved. "There."

Tolden nodded. "I agree."

I frowned. "Where?" Hunt hadn't pointed to somewhere, she'd put her hand in the middle of hologram.

She winked at me as Tolden nodded to himself and pointed to a smaller tower, adjacent to the big one. "Verify that for me. Would the architecture accommodate the JoNA System?"

I nodded. "I can't be sure without the building plans, but it's certainly big enough. Close, but sufficient."

Black licked his lips. "So that's the one we're blowing up?"

I looked at Hunt with furrowed eyebrows. ::Did I miss something?::

Hunt grinned. *Tolden's a great social thinker. That's why they put him in charge of this team. He second guesses himself during tactical application, though, or Medina would have snapped him up. I just made him think I agreed with him. Gave him a little push.*

Which was why she was our infiltration specialist. I nodded at her.

"If we can find another way, I'd rather not blow it up. This tech is valuable," Tolden said.

I straightened. "We can't exactly transport it, the tech's built into the building. Even frying all the electrical leaves the Institute with most of it intact. The last thing we need is for them to rebuild it."

Tolden frowned. "Fine. Black, I need destruction options. No tanks."

Black folded his arms and leaned back in his chair, thinking. "C-4 isn't going to cut it, but I think I can get what we need."

"And that building is close enough to the center to make taking out the Master Instructor an option," I said.

Steele's eyes widened. "You're kidding, right? Have you forgotten what the last Instructor did to you?"

I tapped my head. "Yeah. He hit me hard enough to reboot my brain. Taking down the Instructor won't be easy, but it isn't suicide. It'll be camping out in the central building, probably wired into the psionic net, right?"

Steele nodded.

"And Tolden, correct me if I'm wrong, but the Master Instructor will be guarding the serum we need to destroy, right?"

Black lifted a finger. "If stealth is what we need, there's a rumor of some new camo tech based on some sort of a shield down in R&D."

Steele nodded excitedly. "I heard about that. 32, we might be able to tailor your shield to make us more-or-less invisible. Put that together with the new tactical suit that's got a smell damper on it, and we might really be able to pull this off."

Tolden nodded. "Looks like we've got a plan, people. We lift as soon as we've got everything together. The faster we crash this party, the fewer Instructors we'll have to deal with."

CHAPTER NINETEEN

I stared at the outskirts of town. It all looked so normal. The houses were squat little things in shades of blue, brown, and grey. Kids played in unfenced backyards, and dogs barked at stray squirrels. Precisely what I would expect on the other side of the corn fields. The buildings were almost identical to what we'd seen on satellite—except slightly different. I could pick out the discrepancies. I waved away the psionic net's influence, and pursed my lips as the mirage faded.

The barking dogs were replaced by Superiors patrolling grey cement streets too narrow for standard vehicles. Good thing Tolden had vetoed the tank, because it wouldn't have fit—which was part of the point.

What areas weren't being surveyed by Superiors had technological security that made the Organization's electronic locks look like toys. The JoNA System was busy designing little presents to make my life harder.

The compound itself was massive. I could see glimpses of a barbed wire fence between grey cement buildings that ringed the outside.

Hunt got on the com. "You going to be able to deal with that fence without tipping them off?"

I grit my teeth. We were going with the stealth option until the building blew, which meant I couldn't go in guns blazing. The shielding unit on my belt had been modified to serve passively as a sort of obfuscator. It wasn't anything close to true invisibility—although I had a few ideas on how to improve its abilities—but it was better than nothing. "I'll figure it out."

"Shields going up in sixty seconds," Steele said. "Stay off coms unless it's an emergency. Their equipment is advanced, so all it takes is one wrong word to blow the entire operation."

In other words, I was on my own until I got that serum. "Copy that."

"Good luck, Farina. Watch your six," Black said. "I'm not dragging your corpse back from another mission."

I smiled in spite of myself. "You too."

I could feel their neural shields snap up, and I slapped my com off. Twenty seconds later, I was on the other side of the wall. I kept my thoughts running at the highest frequency I could, which left little room for the rumble of fear in my mind. If I kept my thoughts above the frequencies the psionic net could scan, I would be completely invisible.

I pressed myself against a wall as a Superior walked past, praying that the new tech worked in the field as well as it had worked in testing. We hadn't had much time to put this all together, after all. I slipped past her mind, grabbed all the information I could, then got out without disturbing her thoughts. She continued on, completely unaware that I had stolen the routes and locations of every Superior on this side of the compound.

The Master Instructor didn't alert, either. I released a breath and continued farther into the facility. I had three more minutes before the rest of the team began their breach. It wasn't a lot of time, but I was fast.

I spotted the JoNA System building as I found my way into the center of the compound. It was shaped like an obelisk and plated with solar panels, all operating at ninety-six percent efficiency. That was plenty of energy to power the device—and the rest of the compound. I moved past it as the psionic net flickered once, then crashed.

There was a Superior in front of the door I needed to get inside the central building—the big one I had originally pegged as the JoNA System that we now knew probably held the Master Instructor. If I moved out of the shadows, the Superior would see me. The obfuscator wasn't quite that good. It needed to move, and it needed to look like an accident.

I grabbed the Superior's mind, and poured violent thoughts in. It snarled and looked around. When it saw the Superior patrolling the premises, it dashed across the cement street and raked its claws across the patroller's stomach. I watched as the second Superior tried to fight back. It gored the first one, but surprise had given the frenzied Superior too much of an advantage. It slit the patroller's throat and buried its mouth in its guts. I pushed down nausea at the sight of such a humanoid creature chewing on its compatriot's intestines. It froze as motion drew its attention, and sprinted toward the next Superior, trailing blood in its wake.

I slipped inside the central building as the psionic net went back up and the Master Instructor noted the rogue Superior. That was just part of working with these monsters. A momentary lapse of control—perhaps caused by the psionic net's crash—was enough to make these half trained Superiors attack each other. Hopefully, the Master Instructor wouldn't look too closely at what had caused the Superior to frenzy until they'd managed to catch the rogue for retraining. I'd been careful, but even the most careful teleprojector wasn't infallible.

A sound alerted me that I was about to have company as I strode down the hall. I jerked open a closet and stepped inside. The shadows of a dozen Superiors passed me, and I wiped sweat from my forehead. Keeping my thoughts at such a high frequency was more tiring than running the WATCH and PREP modules at the same time.

I took a deep breath and looked around as another round of Superiors barreled down the hall. This closet wasn't for brooms. There was a camera feed in the corner of the room, running with minimal sound. I bent to study it.

It showed a man tied to a table, halfway through the transition from human to Superior. An Instructor with that thin telltale sheen of the new armor stood above him, holding a syringe in clawless, humanoid fingers. Her chin jutted out of her face, and so did her nose—giving her the look of a Halloween witch, except with skin that had never seen acne. I'd seen this face before, in the files I'd stolen from the Superior base I'd blown up earlier. This was Phrenolia, the Instructor's version of a mad scientist. I watched her lips as they moved.

"Test six-thousand, nine hundred, fifty-six. He's a feisty one. Gave the guards no end of trouble." Her clawless fingers grabbed his chin and waved the syringe in front of his eyes.

His lips parted and bent into a grin, even though his eyes screamed with terror. I could see the thin coat of perspiration that covered his bare chest.

"Do your worst," he muttered. He didn't even react as Phrenolia's claws slid out of her fingers and plunged into his cheeks.

The increased pain tolerance Superiors displayed had already started to take hold.

I bit the inside of my lip. I really should go. I was wasting precious seconds.

The Instructor ripped her hand away from his chin, leaving him bleeding freely. She grinned as she inserted the tip of the two inch needle just below his sternum. He clenched his teeth and jerked against the restraints as she depressed the back with medical precision. When it was done, she removed the needle.

He lay there, panting as he watched her. "This isn't so bad."

"Give it a moment," Phrenolia said. "We'll see if you survive the third stage."

His eyes dilated as the muscles started to shift beneath his skin. An inhuman moan ripped its way from his throat. His fists were clenched, and he beat the table he was tied to, but it didn't stop the sick crunching as bones snapped.

I looked away as his ribcage flexed. A moment later, he was dead on the table. His tears had turned to blood, and there were streams of red down his cheeks. The Instructor stepped closer. "You were so very close." She snapped her fingers. "No matter. Bring in the next subject, and update the drug library."

I backed out of the room, fighting the images of that neurodivergent dead on the table. I swallowed and checked the time. I was behind. The others would be reaching their objectives, and I still hadn't found the serum. Still, if what that Instructor had said was true, I was looking for an entire drug library, not a simple vial of mystery drug. If I didn't destroy the list of chemicals they were using as blueprints for synthesizing this serum, they would just start over. It would maybe set them back a few months. If I wanted to keep them from making an Alpha-Superior, I needed to get all of it.

CHAPTER TWENTY

I found a server rack in the basement behind a massive amount of heat shielding, and hurried to set the charges Black had given me. Without Steele, there was no way to know if this was actually the right set of computers, but blowing it up couldn't hurt.

The charges were linked to my phone as well as all of Steele's electronics. We could detonate them just as soon as they didn't compromise our cover.

I scanned the room one last time, then turned to leave—only to freeze. The sound of footsteps complemented a shadow under the door sweep. There was someone out there, and they were coming this way. By the shape of the shadow, it was a superior. A glance around the room revealed nowhere to hide—except there was just enough room at the very bottom of the server racks where heat was being vented out for a slim person to wriggle under. I slid under the server racks feet first as the door swung open, then shut again. A moment later, there was an energy pistol in my face with clawed Superior fingers around the grip.

"Agent Farina. What a coincidence seeing you here again."

I knew that voice. I racked my memory, then stiffened as I found a match. "D?"

The energy pistol was joined by a face just a moment later. The Superior grinned at me, displaying long fangs on either side of her face, then jerked the pistol to the side. "Can't talk like this, can we?" She clicked her tongue. "Come on out. Touch a weapon, and you die."

I rolled out from under the racks and splayed my hands to the side. "The Master Instructor will know you're here, D. What are you doing?"

The last time I'd seen this Instructor, she'd been handcuffed to a table inside the Agency. She'd explained all about the Institute and the Instructors and how they'd planted Ms. King inside the Agency to keep us pointed where they wanted us. Apparently, she was trained with the greater physical abilities of the Instructors, but without their psionic abilities. When she'd broken her training to warn the Agency about Ms. King, the Institute had started hunting her. Apparently she broke out of InDep just after the Agency took my Biocard. I had warned Medina to leave her to her own devices, and then she'd dropped off the map.

D clicked her tongue. "I could say the same thing about you, but I guess we both have tricks, now don't we?"

I checked the time and sighed. "Really running late, D. What do you want?"

D waved the gun in her hand. "Oh, you know. Little vengeance, dash of blood, and just a tinsey bit of fire. Knives wouldn't go amiss, but I'm not picky."

I shuddered. "I was asking what you wanted with me."

D's eyes widened. "Oh, right. Nothing, really. Just wanted to let you know that the serum's actually two floors up. Psycho keeps it with him while he's on duty in a little data crystal around his neck."

I bit the inside of my lip. Psycho must be the Master Instructor. "Why are you telling me this?"

D holstered her gun. "We're even. Now get out of here. Phrenolia should be in the lab for a while longer, and the others are in the JoNA System."

I watched her pull a match out of her pocket.

"Wait," I said. The explosives I'd planted weren't heat triggered, but I wasn't about to count on that. If she lit the room on fire, any element of surprise we had would be ruined.

She turned, her expression bored. "What do you want, now?"

"Just give me about an hour before you try to light this room up. It's laced with explosives."

She pocketed the match with a grin. "Why didn't you just say so? Can I watch the fireworks?"

"Fine. But I have a question. Where is the rest of the information about the serum kept?"

She flicked her fingernails at the server racks. "Why else would I be here?"

"Because you're a pyromaniac?"

She bared her teeth. "Fine. The primary storage site is in the JoNA System. Secondary copies get sent here, and the Master Instructor keeps a copy in the data crystal. If they have any more backups, they were too busy torturing me to say." She spat on the floor.

"Then where's Psycho?"

D paled. "I'm not going to show you, if that's what you think. No way. I'm getting out of here. You have no idea what they'll do if they find me." She turned and made for the door.

"I thought you wanted to watch them burn."

She stopped and looked at me over her shoulder. "I can do that from the outskirts. I was just here to slow them down again, not to solve all your problems, brain girl." She bit her lip. "One tip. If you're crazy enough to stay here, don't let Phrenolia get ahold of you. She seems the most reasonable, but she's mad-whacko-insane. If she finds out who your parents are, you'll wish they'd only flayed you alive."

I suppressed another shudder as she left, then checked the charges one last time—just to make sure D hadn't touched them. Her intel had checked out last time, but she was seriously deranged. Even Tolden would have a hard time figuring out what she was thinking. I'd been inside her head twice, and it was studded with so many layers completely disconnected from each other that I was amazed she could even function. Maybe that was how she'd slipped in here without the Master Instructor noticing. He was keeping track of so much that he'd never see an extra Superior. So long as the outside layers thought like one of them, she could move unnoticed.

I started toward the floor D had mentioned as my thoughts shifted to a new problem. Why would Phrenolia care about my parents so much? In fact, why had the Institute wanted my mother so badly? The Instructor from before had mentioned that we were both wanted by the Administrators while he was monologuing, and he hadn't seemed to make the connection that she was my mother so he couldn't have just been using her as bait.

I came up with a dozen reasons as I started really thinking about it, but they ranged from past actions, to genetics, to the history with the JoNA System, There was no way to confirm or discard any of them without knowing more of my parents' pasts. I pushed my questions to the back of my mind. Right now, I needed to focus on finding this Psycho quickly, before someone inevitably slipped up and caught me or any of the other members of Tac 47.

The floor D had indicated was littered with laboratories. Some were set up as testing facilities for new mechanical inventions, while others resembled organic chemistry labs. Whenever I saw a good hiding spot, I stuck a charge there and moved on. There was no way to know what kind of information they had in these labs, and I didn't have the time—or the weight in explosives—to rig them all. I would just have to hope the explosions knocked out all the essential information.

With this spacing and the shape of the hallway, the blast was guaranteed to take out at least the front half of any labs. I smiled as I thought of another thing. With all this shaking and uncontrolled heat that came with the blast, it would be a miracle if some of the chemicals in the chemistry labs didn't do part of my work for me. The blast would almost certainly knock out the fume hood's air evacuation system, which meant the building's wreckage would fill with poisonous fumes.

No. Every single hint of this serum's existence was going to go up in flames. After this mission, it was over. The Institute was never going to recover.

At the end of the hallway with all the labs was a thick steel door. I tried the handle. It was unlocked.

I cracked the door open and listened, but there wasn't any sound. I pressed my face to the crack. It was another set of hallways. I closed the door behind me as softly as I could. This was going to be the section where the Master Instructor spent all his time while he was on duty, right here. The door would serve as extra security in case the compound was attacked, so that the Instructor could coordinate defense without worrying about his personal security. The fact that it wasn't locked meant that no one had found the rest of my team. The feral Superior distraction had served its purpose, and Psycho had attributed any disturbances to the chase that was going on.

I took another deep breath as a sudden bout of light-headedness washed over me. I wiped the sweat from my forehead and waited it out. A moment later, everything was back to normal. Holding my thoughts at such a high frequency was taking its toll, though. I wasn't going to be able to do it much longer.

I spotted a likely room and pulled a plasma handgun from its holster. Black had issued everyone plasma weaponry for this mission because there were no civilians in play. We didn't need to worry about collateral damage. For once, I agreed with him. This mission was dangerous enough without having to worry about self-imposed handicaps.

Hopefully when it was done, the Institute would no longer be a threat, and we could destroy all the plasma weaponry we'd built in favor of a line of toned down electric weapons designed to stun. When these monsters were gone, things could go back to being morally black and white. The war would be over. My family would be safe.

I would have to fully process the fact that Director Carlisle was my father and my mother was a neurodivergent.

I took another breath and slipped inside the room.

My eyes went wide as I saw the Instructor sitting with his back to the door. He held a cigarette between two fingers as he looked out at the compound through bulletproof glass.

The door clicked shut behind me, and I checked the charge on my weapon. In a few moments, this would be done.

"You are devilishly difficult to find, you know," the Instructor said without turning. I grit my teeth. He shouldn't have known I was here. "I haven't seen a projector as power-ful since—well, me." He waved the cigarette in the air, then it disappeared from my vision—blocked by the back of the large black chair. A moment later, a stream of smoke began to diffuse into the air.

"It's going to be interesting to see what calamity created you. Things like us," he waved the cigarette again, then swiv-eled the chair to face me. His skin was pale, with deep set jewel green eyes framed by black hair that shimmered in the evening sun streaming through the windows. "Well, we don't happen naturally."

There was just a bit of stubble on his upper lip, and a scar, thin enough I couldn't see it until the sunlight caught his face, that ran from the bottom of his eyes down to his cheek-bone like permanent tears. This was the same face I'd seen in the file I'd stolen from the Superior base I'd blown up. Psycho.

He lifted the cigarette to his mouth again and puffed. The smoke rearranged in the air until I could see, quite clear-ly, a knife still dripping with blood. That image was joined by a fist, and then a scalpel.

"No. I think your tortures were mental," he said, tilting his head to consider me. "The people you thought you could trust betrayed you. A boyfriend," he grinned as I thought of Zachary, "a teacher, a father who you only wanted to love you. Instead, he ripped thoughts from your mind again, and again, and again. When that no longer satisfied him, he sent people to kill you just to watch if you could survive." He clicked his tongue. "Now here you are. A freak, but powerful." He set the cigarette aside and leaned his temple against the side of his chair. "The best operatives are the ones with horrendous childhoods, and yours certainly was no picnic."

I clenched my jaw. "Cut the crap. You know what I'm here for."

He closed his eyes and took a long, deep breath. I sighted the plasma gun on his forehead. As I started to feather the trigger, he sighed.

"You're in such a hurry. I'm just starting to get to know you."

I pulled the trigger, but the discharge hit the window to his side. I checked my aim. It should have hit.

Even with half his gift tied up in the psionic net, this Instructor was powerful enough to bend a plasma charge with telekinesis?

Psycho lifted his other hand. "I haven't even started to dig into how it felt as the people you trusted betrayed you, one by one. What about Director Carlisle? He watched as a man you knew would kill you forced you to the ground. He watched you laying there, but what did he say?"

My lips tightened. There was only one way for him to know these things. He was in my head. I checked my thought frequencies, but they were still above the psionic net. How could he read my mind?

Psycho's eyes snapped open. "He said nothing, Crystal. How about that? This is the man you're serving under? If the man with his knee in your spine had put the muzzle of his gun to the back of your head and pulled the trigger, what would your director have done?"

I clenched my fists and focused on keeping my thoughts moving as quickly as possible. He was trying to elicit an emotional response, but there was only one reason for him to do that. Emotions, by definition, were low frequency thoughts. If I got angry, he wouldn't just be able to read my surface thoughts. He would take full control of my mind, the same way I'd taken control of Ms. King.

I reviewed what he'd said. Was there anything he could have gotten from shielded thoughts? He'd started with the general—things Houston could have told them before the Agency confined him. What he'd said after that came directly from my surface thoughts.

Psycho stood and smoothed down his black dress shirt. "Very good, Agent Farina. You're smarter than I gave you credit for. Unfortunately, brains won't save you." He arched an eyebrow. "Distrust might have, but you've started shedding old habits. Oh, Crystal, when will you learn that everyone you know will betray you?"

Something shimmered, then D flipped down from the ceiling. Psycho must have been using his gift to hide her. I grit my teeth as she plucked a little black dot from her skin, then held it up to the light. She flicked it off her finger, then pulled another one from her collar bone. They looked like little electrodes. "Sorry, Crystal. I tried to warn you, but verbal subtleties never were your things, were they?" She shrugged and turned to Psycho. "You leave me alone now. I promised you someone else to chew on, and now you've got her. I won't bother you, and you won't bother me."

Psycho grinned. "Of course."

D waltzed past me, toward the door and flung it open. Phrenolia stood on the other side in a white lab coat. "Go have some fun, dear. Be back in time for your tests," she said

D scoffed. "I've brought you someone else to torment, Phren. If I never see you again, it will be too soon for me."

Phrenolia pouted, but there was a gleam in her eye. "Pity." She turned to Psycho. "What is this new creature you've brought me, brother?"

He looked at his fingernails. "Just a little something that was trying to sneak into our facility. I'd say it's a PS13. Can't lift a penny, though."

"Pity," Phrenolia said again. Perhaps that was her favorite word. "I wonder what kind of genetics it takes to make a natural PS13—besides ours, I mean."

One Instructor was going to be difficult. Two was going to be impossible—but I didn't have a choice. Surviving Houston was impossible, and so was defeating Ms. King, and rescuing Mom. My life was built of impossible things, and this was no different. I cycled the electropulser and prepared to fight.

Lightning ran up my spine, and suddenly my muscles weren't my own as electric shock coursed through my body. A voice came over the room's hidden speakers.

"You owe me one." It was D.

I convulsed on the ground as I remembered D pulling that dot off her collar bone. She must have stuck it on me when she passed by to get to the door.

Hands hauled me up, and then Psycho's feral grin was in my face. "Well wasn't that nice of her? Maybe I'll give her another few years before I go track her down. We have all the time in the world. Immortals, you know."

I tried to stop my twitching muscles, but nothing I could do could keep muscles from contracting when hit by an external electrical charge, so I just hung there in Psycho's grip as they brought me to a dark room and strapped my hands and feet to a cold, metal chair. I started calculating any possibility of escape or—lacking that—any way to get to the silver crystal hanging from Psycho's neck. If I could destroy it, I could still blow the building. I'd seen how Mom looked when I rescued her from the

Instructor earlier, and I wasn't going to let them do that to me.

Psycho's form, barely distinguishable from the inky blackness of the room, grabbed something, and my vision went white. Minor pain started in my head as I tried to process the sudden change in lighting. A moment later, my eyes were adjusted. I could still see Psycho sitting on the other side of the light pole that focused a beam of light on me. Ordinarily, it would mean that I was blinded, and he could see every little thing that crossed my face.

I was anything but ordinary. After a few moments, I could make out the broad features on his face. I started refining the data.

CHAPTER TWENTY-ONE

Psycho chuckled. "You really are an interesting specimen, aren't you? I haven't seen anyone with eyes so keen for a very long time. They exist, you know, but they're hardly common. And someone with eyes like yours—well, there must be a story behind it."

I barely spared him a thought. I was too busy cataloguing my restraints and the room I was in. The convulsions were slowing, so I was almost back in control of my own limbs. Besides that, I had an absolute ceiling on how long I could spend here. I could only keep my thoughts at this high a frequency for a few more minutes before some thoughts started to slip. After that, Psycho would force his way inside, and I would be finished. Right now, I still had the high ground.

"Oh, but a few minutes is hardly enough time to free yourself," Psycho said.

I grit my teeth. He was right. Keeping my core thoughts at such a high frequency meant fewer of them were behind my shields. That wouldn't matter so much, because—surface thoughts or not—the only ones who could read them were telepaths with as high a rating as mine was. Ms. King wouldn't have been a problem—but this Instructor was far more powerful than Ms. King had ever been.

"Well, not all siblings are alike," he said. "Ms. King was the best actor out of all of us. She was, quite possibly, the least deranged. She could understand how to make people do what she wanted—and that included the Administrators. They changed her physical form to disguise what she was, then sent her off to control the Agency. The fact that you managed to restrain her is impressive, but she was, mentally, one of the weakest siblings—well, except the Defect, that is."

"You all have specialties?"

He laughed. "Oh, yes. We're no less neurodivergent than you are. I have the greatest psionic abilities, Phren is our greatest analyst and," he leaned into the light with a gleam of anticipation in his eye. "Between us, we've never failed to break our victims."

I matched his grin as best I could. "You've got great technique, but you can't get inside my walls."

He spread his hands. "Not now, perhaps, but you're straining your mind—you know it as well as I do. That you've managed to pour that amount of energy into your thoughts without burning up your own mind is impressive."

I scanned his face closely. He was telling the truth, but if he only matched my projection strength, how was he staying abreast of my thoughts? My grin widened as I found the answer. He was straining his mind just as much as I was.

"It's a race, then."

Psycho was good at hiding the symptoms. There was only a slight sheen of sweat on his face from the effort of pushing his mind so quickly—slight enough I had attributed it to the invisible armor he wore like a second skin.

He leaned back out of the light. His eyes were speculative as he watched me. "You would have made a fine Instructor," he mused. "Here's the thing about an endurance competition. You have been sustaining a high burn for what, an hour now? I've been doing it for a few minutes. No, my dear Crystal, this is hardly a race. This is merely a prolonged execution—and your director won't be disappointed. He wanted to see what would happen when adversity elevated your mind, and we are in the perfect place to show him."

Someone—Phren—grabbed my chin and yanked my head back. She stood behind me with pain in her eyes and a scalpel in her hand.

"I bet you were wondering where Psycho got his tears from, is that right?"

My throat constricted. "No, I think that's fairly obvious." My voice was level even as my heart pounded in my chest. I forced my breathing down.

She set the scalpel just below my eye, and I prepared my-self for the pain. The scalpel was sharp; it wouldn't hurt any more than the gunshots Houston had put in my abdomen almost a year and a half ago.

Psycho flicked a hand at his sister. "Really, Phren?"

She pouted. "I need a blood sample to run. I need to know how closely she's related to the other Farina."

Mom?

Psycho's eyes narrowed. "You know she only took the name Farina to try and throw us off her trail, but fine. Take your blood sample. Just don't get in my way."

"Fine," she snarled. There was a needle-like pain in my shoulder, and then it faded. "I'll be back when the match program's through."

She released my head, and then I heard the door close.

I grit my teeth. The other Farina they mentioned had to be Mom, and match programs didn't take very long. This was about to get a lot more complicated. Currently, Psycho seemed to be under the impression that the Director and my Dad, the guy who kept ripping memories out of my mind, were two separate people. The moment Phren got back, all of their delusions would be gone, and I was going to be in a world of hurt.

At least I had a timeframe.

Part of me wondered just how much they could tell me if I let my parentage slip. Mom and Dad certainly hadn't seemed to want to explain anything, but Psycho was being rather talkative. Sure, his version of events was likely to be shifted, but it would be first-hand information.

Psycho was looking at me again with the eyes of someone watching an ant he'd just cut in half to see what it would do before the inevitable.

"You're quite a lot calmer than I thought you'd be," he finally said. "But, then, I don't think you quite understand where you are."

A package presented itself outside my mental walls. I looked at it, indecisive.

"Go on," he said. "Open it. You're the one who wanted information. You want to know what happened to me, and this is the answer."

It was also a Trojan horse.

His eyes were amused. "Of course it is. But you'll berate yourself forever if you get back to the Organization and realize that all the answers were within your grasp and you refused them for fear of—what? Things that are going to happen whether you open that or not? At least this way you'll know."

I slipped my walls around the package, my face slick with sweat. When it was inside, I opened the box.

The room around me faded, and I was strapped to a table. No. Not me. There was a mirror in the ceiling that let me see everything. There was so much blood. People in masks. A surgical slit where my—her—belly should have been. They were lifting something out. She turned her head, mumbling something sleepily. My eyes widened. I knew this person who was on the table.

"Mom?"

The memory exploded in my head, and Psycho was in my face. His breath smelled like the cigarette he'd been smoking earlier.

"What did you say?"

There was fire in his eyes. His claws dug into my arms. He shook me, and I clenched my jaw against a sudden wave of pain. Just because it wasn't the worst pain I'd felt didn't keep it from making me want to gag.

He grabbed my chin and dragged my head forward. For a moment, I thought he was going to twist it off, but he only stared into my eyes. The pressure outside my walls built as he tried to tear them down.

"That monster is your mother, that vile traitor of a woman?" He threw my head against the back of the chair, and I blinked away stars.

Psycho started to pace. He turned and leveled a claw at me. "You—" he bit the word off, and fisted his hand. The claws in his fingers dug into his palm, but it was like he couldn't feel pain. He smashed his fist into my side, angling back toward my spine. I heard the ribs crack and groaned as he smashed into my kidneys. My vision died. I couldn't breathe. His absolute rage surrounded me, pounding at my mind from every side. He would tear down my walls and inject every nightmare he could think of into my mind. He would make me watch as they took Mom apart over and over again, and then he would dismember me himself.

I braced my mental walls as they started to crumble, but there was only so much I could do under this onslaught.

"What is going on here?" Phren asked.

The assault stopped. Her clawless fingers peeled my eyes open. She looked back at her brother.

"Careful, Psycho. It's breakable." She held up a reflective sheet, and I could see Mom's face on one side. The match program was through, and it had told them exactly what I knew it would. "It's also valuable."

I took half a breath, then groaned as all the air whooshed out again.

"See what you did?" Phren's voice oozed disapproval.

Psycho bared his teeth. "It's the spawn of that woman. It deserves to die slowly, like they killed us."

Phren shook her head. "Such disloyal words, Psycho. I might have to report you to the Administrators."

His lips tightened, but he backed off. Phren looked back at me with evaluation in her eyes. There was a hard core of fury cordoned off by logic. A slow smile spread from one side of her face to the other.

"Of course, she's not really the valuable one." Phen stabbed a finger at my abdomen. "Those are. We can extract them, and then exact whatever revenge we'd like. The Administrators will be happy, and we—" she clicked her tongue. "Well, there's no point in scaring the poor thing now, is there?"

Psycho crossed his arms. "I don't know, there is a certain entertainment in watching them gag when they learn what is going to happen to them. This one deserves all the fear we can give it."

I balled my fists. "Why do you hate my mother so much?"

Psycho cocked his head. "Perhaps I'll let you know, memory by memory. You deserve to know what that monster left us to endure. You should know what her betrayal caused."

Phren put a hand on his shoulder. "Careful. If we break her now, with memories, we will hardly be able to have as much fun."

They would never be able to break me. I'd lived though too much pain and gained too much strength.

There was a sound at the very edge of my hearing, and I redoubled my calculation efforts. It was going to be a little more difficult now, with shattered ribs, but possible. Psycho had made mistakes when he'd gotten angry, and D wasn't the only one who could split her thoughts.

I retreated into my safe space—sealing my mind behind shields as impenetrable as diamond—and began to set filters to wake me. I would make the most of this time to heal inside the walls Mom had helped me build. If I knew Black—and by now, I was starting to—this was going to be an interesting rescue. I started running the RESET module to mend my shields. The pressure wave against my skin from the explosion woke me from my safe space. Psycho had been in front of me, and there were new shallow slits in my skin. They'd been too focused on trying to drag me from my own mind to wonder what could possibly make me retreat when I was finally starting to learn something useful. The pain was minor, and I evaluated the rest of my surroundings in an instant as the two Instructors started to stir. The blast had thrown the chair to the ground, so I lay sideways, but I'd come off far better than Phrenolia, who had been standing between me and the wall and was now a heap of broken skin and bones underneath the rubble. She started to shift as I watched.

There was blood trailing from my forehead—either from the impact, or from the Instructors. I didn't waste time trying to figure out which. Psycho was below me, pinned to the ground by the chair. His eyes widened as he saw me, and deployed his claws. I grinned at him. "Thanks for the help."

My fingers grabbed his hand, and I used his claws to cut the bonds around my wrist. He snarled and brought his other hand to bear. I caught the strike on my forearm. His claws shredded my skin, but I was still alive.

"Brace yourself, kid," Black warned.

Psycho jerked with electricity, and I bit my tongue as the shock ran through me, too. When it stopped, I grabbed his other hand and used his claws to finish freeing myself. Hunt ripped the chair away from my back and helped me up.

"You look great," she said.

I tried to wipe the blood from my eyes, but all that accomplished was smearing it all over.

"Is the building rigged?" I asked.

She nodded. "Tolden and Steele are babysitting the rest of the charges. Thanks for keeping the Master Instructor busy."

I leaned on Hunt until my legs stopped twitching, then reached for my med kit. A few sealing patches took care of the places where I was bleeding freely. Black secured the two Instructors with a new restraint R&D had thought up. They would keep even someone with Instructor level strength from getting free.

"Give the male two neural dampers, then crank them like you were trying to keep me down. The data crystal is around his neck."

Black arched an eyebrow. "Got that big a brain, huh?"

He cranked the second neural damper up, and I felt the psionic net disconnect. I let my thoughts return to their natural frequency, and nearly fell as the world started to spin. The pain and fear I'd been holding back flushed through my system. I grabbed for the little white pill in my upper pocket and crushed it under my tongue.

The Superiors' thoughts—once held in check by Psycho's psionic net—spiked. I grabbed Hunt's arm.

"There are still a bunch of Instructors here. None of them are nearly as strong as Psycho, but they'll notice if the psionic net is down for long. The Superiors are going to go insane, too. They'll pounce on you if they see you." Just like the one I'd helped frenzy earlier.

Hunt nodded. "Do what you have to, 32. I'll get you out of here."

Black handed me a mess of wires, and I stared at them blankly. My RESET module could handle a lot, but it still took a certain amount of time to bring my brain back up to speed—especially after that much damage. "What are—"

He arched his eyebrows. "You sure you're up for this, kid? You're running at half speed after that blast."

I nodded as I finally recognized the thing Black had handed me. It was the interface device Steele and I had worked up. It would let me hijack the psionic net. I held the thing up to my temple while Black attached the wires.

"Keep those Instructors off our tail, Farina. You can do it."

He pressed the last one to my head, and suddenly I was spread over eight square miles. Voices battered my mind, fighting for attention. I could feel the hunger for blood. They wanted me to free them—a thousand Superiors at once.

I gasped and grabbed at Hunt.

"It's too much. Too loud."

My other hand started to tear at the wires, but someone grabbed me.

Black. "If you don't do this, 32, we're all dead."

They wanted to sink their claws into something, tear its insides out, gorge on the flesh, and then watch as the creature screamed. All of them, all at once, inside my head. Their claws were sharp. They watched each other, waiting for a moment of weakness. All it would take was a moment. They were fast. The Superior predator. One swipe, and they could watch the other creature's blood lust turn to fear as they scrambled to put their innards back inside.

I screamed. I didn't want to hear this. Didn't want to be inside their minds. I couldn't do it!

Black and Hunt kept going, step by step, impassive to my pleas to make it stop.

"Push their minds back. You're the most powerful Projector I've ever seen, Crystal. You can do it. Hold them back."

I clawed at their monstrous heads, tearing thought after thought from their mind. They calmed. They watched two inferior creatures—good for entertainment and not much else—carry a third through the compound. They wanted to pounce. They longed to feel hot blood turn cold as they ripped the humans hearts from their chests. I smothered those thoughts. I forced every one of them motionless. They would not hurt my friends. They would not hurt anyone ever again.

Hunt and Black shoved me through the hole they'd made in the fence.

My connection to the net strained. It was everything I could do to stop the Superiors guarding the edges from launching themselves at the three creatures climbing into the black armored van.

But where were the others? Tolden, Steele? Where were they?

I found them at the other side of the compound, two shielded blobs nearly gone.

"Go," I said.

I held onto the connection as long as I could.

"Get clear, Farina," Black said. An explosion wiped my mind from existence.

EPILOGUE

I didn't wake up in a hospital bed, but my surroundings were familiar. The walls were a calm beige, interrupted here and there by a framed design for a device I'd once thought would be impossible but had since built. Home. This was the room I'd had as a child, inside the house I'd lived in until the Agency had taken my biocard.

I closed my eyes against tears. It was over. The serum was gone, and so was every bit of information about it. There might still be some Instructors on the loose, but the core of the Institute had been obliterated in the explosion. We hadn't just destroyed their capacity to invent an Alpha-Superior, we'd taken away everything they needed to create Zeta-Superiors as well.

I was safe. My mind was whole. Mom was healed, and Dad—

My eyes caught on his form. He sat on a chair against the wall next to my desk. His legs were crossed, and he looked at something streaming across a tablet.

Well, he hadn't tried to kill me in my sleep. That was a good sign.

He deliberately met my eyes. "You did well, Crystal, holding that psionic net for as long as you did. I read the mission report. I guess you met Psycho."

I looked up at my ceiling, away from his prying eyes. "He was aptly named."

"He left a little gift packet in your mind that warned the other Instructors to get out the moment you joined with the net."

I winced. I had known at the time that accepting that package was a bad idea, but it had kept him occupied enough that he hadn't noticed Hunt and Black.

I checked my ribs. Whole. That meant time in a Pod, or time with that new nano technology I'd gotten at the research base earlier.

"So you've spent some time in my mind. Satisfied they didn't plant any more Trojan horses?" I tried to put an edge in my voice, but it just came out tired.

He shrugged. "For now."

"Good. Because that's the last time you get inside my walls."

His eyebrows drew together. "Come on, Crystal. I was trying to help."

"If I need *help* again, Mom can do it. Her genes gave me these abilities, right?"

Dad sighed. "No one is entirely sure. There's certainly a genetic component, or the Instructors would have been impossible."

"The Instructors?" My interest sharpened, and I started probing his walls to see if he would let any thoughts bleed. There was nothing.

There was a rustle of fabric on fabric, and then Mom stood in the doorway wearing a silk dress the color of the summer sky. Layers of the silk drifted around her ethereally, which lent itself to the fragility I saw when I looked at her. Deeper, though, she had a core of undeniable strength. This was the mother I remembered from my childhood. She was finally free.

Mom smiled as she saw me, but her smile quickly turned sad. "You want to know what happened with the Institute, don't you? Why I was trapped inside an Instance, and why your father left?"

Dad stood. "Lin, no. That story is far too long."

"And painful," she said, holding his gaze steadily. "But Crystal is no stranger to pain. Better to suffer for truth than the lies that have been spun around her in this neurodivergent world of ours."

"I said what I had to in order to protect her," he said.

Mom's smile turned sad. "I know that you believe it, but Jerome—" she caught her breath, a flash of pain in her eyes that was quickly subsumed, "belief isn't truth. You can't twist reality the way you twist words. In trying to protect me, you hurt our daughter, and nothing will change that."

He opened his mouth to refute her, but a shake of Mom's head made him close his mouth again.

"I still love you, and I understand why you did this to us. Understanding is not the same as forgiveness, and forgiveness is not the same as forgetfulness. There are some things that a tea tin at Christmas won't fix; some things an apology won't heal."

I felt the brush of Mom's mind against mine, felt the pond of tranquility that lived deep inside her soul start to waver. My father's mind was hidden behind a wall of dread. His eyes darkened. His fingers curled into fists.

"Don't do this, Lin."

Her smile stayed constant, but I saw it for what it really was—a shield. "Goodbye, darling. I wish you a long, joyful life, but I cannot share it with you anymore." She stepped aside so he could make use of the doorway. His face was rigid.

"You know I didn't mean to hurt you."

She shook her head softly. "It was never about me. But you ignored the one light in my life, and you hurt her so that she would be forced to fix our mistakes. I found a family again, and you tore it apart."

"But I am your family," he protested.

Mom shook her head again. "Not in the same way. Crystal and I each need to decide for ourselves what that relationship is going to look like. For now, you need to go."

A general feeling of unwelcome filled the room, and I shuddered. This was the opposite of how home usually felt. There were tears in my father's eyes, but he left without another word.

A long moment later, I could hear the front door shut. Mom's projection faded, but she couldn't get rid of my unease. She sat on the edge of my bed, her smile more genuine than before but no less sad. "I wish I'd been here to raise you," she said. "I watched, when I could. I did my best through the fog, but I was gone when you needed me most."

I couldn't stop the tears in my eyes from flowing down my cheeks. Mom wiped them away.

She was right. The mother I knew had been a shade of the woman she was now. I'd spent so much time trying to remember my father that I hadn't realized my mother was fading before my eyes. Now I'd found my father, and he turned out to be a royal jerk.

I gripped Mom's hand. "You're here, now."

Her smile brightened. "That's right. And I'll never leave again."

There was a long moment of silence, and then Mom reached out to me, mind-to-mind.

::Are you ready to learn the rest? About what happened to your father and I, about the Instructors, the Institute, and D?::

I nodded. Whether I liked it or not, my parents had shaped the world I lived in. It was time to hear their story.

THANK YOU

Dear Reader,

Thank you for taking the time to read Crystal Truth. I hope you enjoyed learning about Crystal and her family. Stay tuned to learn even more about them in the next book!

Before you go, please take a moment to leave a review of my book. Tell me what you liked, what you loved, and even what you hated—I just want to hear what you think. Reviews aren't easy to come by, which means that you—the reader—have the power to help Crystal's story reach the people who most need to hear it. Here's a link to my author page, which includes all my books on Amazon:

amazon.com/author/kaexcell

Thank you again for spending time with Crystal. I hope to meet you again between the pages of another book!

Sincerely,

K. A. Excell

LOOKING FOR MORE?

Join the mailing list at KAExcell.com to learn more about new releases. Exclusive short stories, deals, and more, delivered right to your inbox!

9 781952 856068